كاباني تنت ميمبر
فياميل پاپ سينغر
غوفرنور

THE
ASSASSIN'S
LIST

كونغريرسمان
موفي ستارلت
نهين انكور
فدارا ل جوج
اإنافإل كوارتارباك
مايور

Scott Matthews

THE ASSASSIN'S LIST by Scott Matthews

First Edition, August 2012

Author Services by Pedernales Publishing, LLC.
www.pedernalespublishing.com

ISBN: 978-0-615-68285-3

Printed in the United States of America

Acknowledgment

Writing is a solitary endeavor, but it's not accomplished alone. I am indebted to many, but need to acknowledge a few who contributed most recently to this novel.

For Ric, Debbie, Dorothy, Margo and Paul, thank you for reading and helping me with the final draft. Your feedback was invaluable.

For Barbara at Pedernales Publishing, thank you for guiding me through the process of editing and publishing. You knew what needed polishing and made sure I kept working on it until it shined.

For Becky, your skill with a camera made me like a photo of myself—a first. If anyone needs a great photographer, visit Becky@thirdwishstudio.com.

For my family, thank you all. You never stopped believing.

And for my wife, who shared my dream and sacrificed our time together while I wrote. You are my inspiration.

For Diana

Your encouragement and support made this happen.

THE
ASSASSIN'S
LIST

Chapter 1

Being in the wrong place at the wrong time happened to other people, not Janice Lewellyn. Not until the last night of her life, anyway.

Just before twelve o'clock that night, she was speeding back to her office on the sprawling campus of Martin Research in a yellow Volkswagen Beetle. A memo her boss needed before a field test of their new chemical weapon detection system wasn't complete. The itinerary for next week's visit by the Secretary of Homeland Security had been left out. She had time to get that done. Everything was packed, a couple of hours at the office, and she'd still have time to get the kids up and family to the airport. She'd sleep on the plane, and rest in Maui.

The vacation, ordered by her doctor, was supposed to provide a rest before starting an aggressive chemotherapy treatment for ovarian cancer. The vacation couldn't have come at a worse time. Cancer scared the hell out of her, no question, but she was prepared to fight it with or without a vacation. She wasn't prepared, however, to let her boss down. Properly hosting the head of Homeland Security when he visited was her responsibility.

A rich perfume of roses carried on the summer breeze as she stepped from her car in the executive parking lot. Some savvy landscaper had placed a small rose garden nearby. Deep red rhododendrons and azaleas lined the walkway, and two acres of lush green lawn surrounded the four-story glass and stainless steel office building. A reflecting pool ringed the building on three sides, bathing it in a soft blue light. It was the most beautiful place in the world to work, she thought for the hundredth time.

~~~

At the back of the executive office building, Kaamil Sayf waited in the shadows outside an emergency fire door. At midnight, the security system his company installed and maintained would crash and go offline for five minutes. In those five minutes, he needed to run up four flights of stairs to the CEO's office, retrieve a keylogger device he'd placed on the CEO's computer a month ago, and get back out before the security system rebooted.

On the outside, after his prison conversion to Islam, he led a covert cadre of assassins working as employees of the International Security and Information Services, or ISIS. The mission he trained for, and was selected to lead, aimed to assassinate powerful American leaders. Mighty America killed its enemies with cowardly high-flying drones, but the world would soon know how jihadists killed enemies, up close and personal.

Before the first strike next week, he had to ensure encrypted passwords for the security plan at the chemical weapons depot had not changed. The only way to know was to retrieve the keylogger that recorded every keystroke on the CEO's computer.

When his watch flashed 12:00 a.m., Kaamil used a key to open the steel fire door and ran up the stairs. He knew the old security guard posted at his station at the main entrance wouldn't hear him, just as he knew the security cameras wouldn't record his visit for the next five minutes. No one was expected in the building.

He raced down a long hallway to the middle of the top floor. Through Janice Lewellyn's office, he entered the CEO's inner sanctum. Kaamil was under the large rosewood desk when the elevator doors chimed. Somebody besides the security guard was in the building. Kaamil pocketed the device, getting up as the office lights came on, and froze.

Sweat formed on his forehead when he heard someone walking into the office.

"What are you doing in here?" Janice Lewellyn demanded. "Why are you hiding in Mr. Martin's office?"

"Take it easy, Mrs. Lewellyn, you know me. I didn't mean to frighten you. I'm just checking to make sure the upgrade for the security system is working."

"Since when do you do middle-of-the-night upgrades without my clearance? I think you better stay here while I call security. You shouldn't be in Mr. Martin's office."

"Call security. They know all about it. I'm just doing my job, Mrs. Lewellyn." Kaamil feigned a smile, hoping she didn't notice the beads of sweat on his forehead.

As Janice Lewellyn turned toward the phone on her desk, Kaamil took an Emerson combat folding knife from his pocket. Moving quickly, he caught her from behind and pulled the razor-sharp blade across her throat.

Lowering her body to the floor, he cursed his rotten luck. He would keep on the surgical gloves he was wearing until he left the building. And pray to Allah nothing was left behind to identify him, because his five minutes were almost up.

He would have enough trouble explaining the collateral damage to his leader without worrying about the police.

3

Chapter 2

Adam Drake stared at the ocean from a window seat in their favorite restaurant. Kay had been gone a year, but the memory of her laughing, sitting across the table from him was as vivid as a beautiful hologram. If only they had found a cure, or her chemo had worked, he would still be holding her hand. Still be looking forward to every minute he got to spend with her.

That kind of magical thinking didn't help. The reality was, she was in pain and now she wasn't. The pain was now his. She was dead. He wasn't. The Bible might say there's no greater love than laying down your life for a friend, but what it doesn't say is the greatest pain comes when you can't. Especially when the friend is your wife.

He could not believe it had been a year. Every day of it had been a miserable, aching, lonely waste and drinking too much hadn't numbed the pain. It just left him with sleepless nights, thinking of their three short years together. All he had was one whirlwind year courting the most beautiful girl in Oregon, one happy year still in shock she said yes, then one long year watching her succumb to cancer.

"Mr. Drake, you have a phone call, sir," said Joyce, the Tidal Rave's dining room manager, touching him lightly on the shoulder. "I'm sorry for intruding, but he said it was an emergency."

Drake got up and followed her past the window tables and booths to the front desk. How had someone found him? He hadn't known where he was going when he took the day off.

"Drake here."

"Adam, I'm sorry to bother you," his father-in-law said, "but I need your help."

Senator Hazelton, a four-term United States Senator from Oregon, rarely needed anyone's help and had never asked for his. Coming on the anniversary of his daughter's death, Drake suspected the Senator, or more likely his wife Meredith, was making sure he was all right.

"How'd you find me?"

"As chairman of the Senate Intelligence Committee, there are some perks. I tracked you by satellite," Senator Hazelton said dryly.

Some perks, Drake thought.

"I know you don't want to think about business right now, but I need a favor. A friend of mine could use some legal help. I can't think of anyone better than you to help him."

Drake was now certain his mother-in-law's concern had prompted the call. The Senator knew top lawyers in Portland, Washington D.C., and the country, for that matter. He didn't need Drake's legal talents to help a friend, even when he was at the top of his game, which he hadn't been for the last year.

"My friend's company is handling some important research for us," the Senator continued. "His secretary was killed in his office last night and aside from the tragedy of it all, it couldn't have happened at a worse time. You've prosecuted complicated cases like this where corporate theft may be involved. Would you give him a hand, act as a consultant, and guide him through this?"

So that was it. A supporter was in a mess at an unfortunate time, and the Senator owed him a favor. True, Drake had handled some big trade secret cases in the D.A.'s office as the lead felony prosecutor.

"Senator, I don't think I can help you. I'm just not ready to take on a case like this right now," Drake said.

Senator Hazelton hadn't seen him in six or seven months. If he had, there was no way in the world he would ask him for help. Dark bags under his eyes, a puffy face, he looked haggard and felt like a fighter too tired to come out of his corner for the next round.

"Adam, I need you on this one. There are reasons I can't discuss over the phone. I need someone I can trust."

There was more to this than just walking a constituent through some crisis, Drake thought.

"All right, Sir. Tell your friend I'll call him tomorrow when I get back to town."

"Actually, I invited him to come over tonight. Could you be here by seven? We'll have dinner. Meredith has been asking when we'll see you."

"Okay, I'll try to be there by seven," Drake said and ended the call.

He knew he couldn't put off seeing Kay's parents forever. Tonight was as good a night as any to get the meeting behind him. They lost a daughter, he recognized that, but hugs and kisses weren't going to help him sleep through the night, or make anything matter again.

Drake walked back to his table to finish his coffee. His father-in-law was used to getting his way, in politics and life in general, but he never interfered in his life. He appreciated that. If the Senator wanted his help now, he'd get it, whether it was politics or his mother-in-law asking to see him. Either way, it didn't matter. They were all that was left of his family, and he'd do what he could.

Drake's father died in Vietnam on his second tour, wearing a green beret. Aside from the legend that went with his Distinguished Service Cross, Drake only knew his father from his mother's stories. She raised him as a single mom, working as an emergency room nurse, until she died in a car accident caused by a drunken teenager. He'd been a sophomore in college then. There was no other family, and he'd been on his own after that, until Kay.

Chapter 3

Senator Hazelton's home was in Lake Oswego, an old money suburb of Portland. He and Meredith moved there shortly after he became the managing partner of the most powerful law firm in the city. He wasn't born rich, but the careful and graceful use of his legal skills soon made him one of the most respected and wealthy men in the city. Encouraged to enter politics, he served two terms in the state legislature before he was asked to run against the incumbent U.S. Senator, Willard Monroe. Despite the incumbent's five terms in the Senate, the younger attorney connected better with the citizens, won the election, and hadn't been seriously challenged since.

Two hours later, after driving his Porsche 993 as hard as the absence of detectable State Police would allow, Drake approached the exit for Lake Oswego. He thought about the night he met Kay. It was after law school, after his time in the army and after working in the District Attorney's office for five years. The athletic club he belonged to was hosting a dinner and dance for participants of a triathlon he had just finished. Kay had attended and asked him to dance.

"I've seen your picture in the paper. Are you as good a prosecutor as you are a triathlete?" she asked him.

"I'm a better prosecutor," he answered, as she led him to the dance floor. "I don't come in second as a prosecutor."

She introduced herself simply as Kay Hazelton, but he

knew who she was, just as she knew he knew. The papers called her the brightest flower on the Portland social scene. She didn't seem to care. She appeared in more newspaper photos working a soup kitchen line in jeans and a sweatshirt than at charity events in a fancy dress. She was attracted to people and causes that mattered, she told him later. What attracted Kay to him that night was still a mystery.

"Does that mean you're willing to send innocents to jail, just to win? Do young men, trying to survive by selling drugs, deserve a lifetime behind bars? Why not restorative justice instead?"

"Miss Hazelton, if you and your father want to restore felons, whatever that means, you're welcome to try. You'd be making a mistake, in my opinion. Drug dealers have a choice to make, just like the choice you made when you decided to become a teacher. They make bad decisions. Those decisions hurt people. Your decision to teach helps people. Both have consequences, and it's my job to deal with the ones that hurt people."

They danced for a moment before she asked, "If I made bad decisions in my life, would you still dance with me?"

"Miss Hazelton, I can't imagine any decision that would keep me from dancing with you. Of course, I might still have to put you in jail."

That had been the beginning of a courtship that lasted almost a year before he asked Kay Hazelton to marry him. Then, of course, he'd had to talk with her father.

"I've been expecting you," the Senator said, when he led Drake into his den. "Would you like something to drink?"

A couple of double whiskeys, Drake remembered thinking, would be nice.

"No, thank you, I'm fine, Sir. I'd like permission to marry your daughter," he blurted out. No use beating around the bush, the Senator was expecting him.

"I appreciate your good manners, son, but I'm afraid you're too late. I gave my daughter permission to marry you months ago," the Senator said with a smile. "Now, would you like that drink?"

That was four years ago. Now, driving to the house where he had that first drink with the Senator, his memory flashed scenes of their outdoor wedding. The manicured lawn sloping down to the lake from the brick Victorian Kay lived in most of her life, a reception with bridesmaids dancing barefoot in front of a bandstand after the guests had left, and finally, following the curving cedar-lined driveway when they left on their wedding night.

He hadn't been back to the Hazelton's home since Kay's funeral. He had talked with her mother on the phone, of course, and had lunched with the Senator once, but he'd declined invitations for dinner.

The house looked the same as he turned in. Lit by the soft glow of wooden luminaries, he saw Kay's old upper bedroom window between the tall western red cedars that lined the drive. It was the very best of the six bedrooms, she had proclaimed. On the northeast corner of the house, it offered a view of the lake and of Mount Hood's snowy peak in the distance. She didn't mind that it was the smallest of the six bedrooms, it was the room she picked when she first walked through her new home.

As he neared the turnaround in front of the house, Meredith Hazelton stood at the open front door. She hadn't changed a whit, but her vigilance told him that they must have added security cameras since his last visit. His mother-in-law was, in his opinion, the best looking seventy-year-old woman he had ever seen. With light brown hair and sparkling eyes, she was a vision of what Kay would have looked like in another thirty-three years.

Rolling to a stop, he got out and waved over the roof of his car. Drake stretched to get rid of the tightness in his shoulders, and gave himself a moment to compose his emotions.

"Adam, I hoped I would see you today," Meredith said, as she hurried to greet him with a kiss, wrapping her slender arms around him. She didn't let go, and Drake felt her sadness as she rested her head on his chest.

A year of loneliness swept through him.

"I shouldn't have stayed away so long, I've missed you. I'm sorry."

"We knew," she said, taking his hand and leading him up the front stairs. "You're here now. Come say hello to your father-in-law. He's missed seeing you."

He found the Senator in his study standing at the window, looking at the lake with a cell phone held to his ear. Walnut paneling above a caramel Berber carpet gave the room a serious, solid sense in contrast with the framed black and white political cartoons adorning the walls. The desk was red oak topped with glass, a legal pad, and a flat-screen monitor.

The Senator waved to Drake and ended his conversation. Even in jeans and a V-neck sweater, the sleeves pushed up over tanned and still well-muscled forearms, the man looked like a senator. His silver hair framed a face that made you think of Cary Grant, with a smile that said everything was going to be all right. Tonight, the smile was familiar, but the eyes were different. They attempted to match the smile, but didn't make it.

"Adam, thanks for coming," he said, giving Drake a quick hug. "How are you?"

"I've had better days."

The Senator nodded and put his hand on Drake's shoulder. "Let's go outside and talk before my friend gets here. We have time for a drink while Meredith finishes the dinner."

The terrace at the rear of the house was red brick, with a waist-high wall lined with flowering planters. Sweet smells of flowers mixed with the scent of freshly mown grass. Sadly, it was all just as he remembered.

"Here, hope you're still drinking bourbon," the Senator said behind him.

Not just bourbon, Drake recognized with the first sip, but Jim Beam Black, his favorite. The Senator preferred single malt Scotch, but this was the first time he'd served him bourbon.

The Senator looked out over the lake, and finally said, "I met Richard Martin twenty-five years ago when I first ran for the state legislature. He'd just started his company here and was promoting Oregon for high-tech industry. We became friends, and he's been one of my most loyal supporters. His company's doing research for Homeland Security. I helped him get the contract, and I'd like you to help him."

"Does his secretary's murder have anything to do with his work for the government, or you for that matter?" Drake asked.

The Senator turned and seemed to be surprised by the question. "No, no, this has nothing to do with me. He's developing monitoring systems for chemical and biological weapons we don't want smuggled into the country."

So this was something more than just helping an old friend whose secretary had been murdered.

"We think the work Rich is doing will be a real breakthrough, but he says they've been having security problems. He brought in a new firm to tighten up security, and now this. He's worried the death of his secretary and the security problems could mean the end of top secret projects he's been awarded. I'm worried about the loss of the technology he's capable of developing for us."

What did the Senator think he could do about his friend's problem, Drake wondered.

"Why do you think Martin can't trust the police to handle this? They've done good work on cases like this. They'll find out who killed his secretary."

The Senator turned and leaned against the terrace half wall. He appeared to have expected the question, but also appeared to be undecided about how to answer it.

"Adam, Homeland Security would like to keep this matter out of the news as much as possible if this turns out to have something to do with national security. We also don't want to blow the whistle too early and call in the FBI. The Secretary of Homeland Security is a friend. I chair his oversight committee. I suggested that you take a look first. You have the background to know if there's more to this than a homicide."

Drake knew the Senator wasn't referring to his experience as a prosecutor.

"You've seen my military records?"

"When I saw Kay was serious about you, I checked out your background. There were missing years after you graduated law school. You passed the bar exam two days after 9/11, so I thought you might have enlisted. The Army said there was no record of you ever being in the service. So I pulled a few strings. When I saw your file, I understood why it wasn't initially provided to me. Delta Force personnel records don't officially exist."

At least it had taken a senior U.S. Senator to get his records, Drake thought. His training, his missions, were not for public consumption. America didn't want to know how it was able to sleep soundly in a troubled world. Its warriors knew, but they were forbidden to tell.

"Does your friend know my background?" Drake asked.

"No, it's not something he needs to know. If you're concerned, it's not something Meredith or I share with anyone. We're proud of the way you served and the sacrifices you made. But there are things some people will never understand, and don't ever need to know."

"Did you share my file with Kay?"

"No, we didn't. We felt that was something you would do, if you felt it was necessary."

Drake nodded his thanks and looked out over the lake and the lights beginning to twinkle across the way. Kay had known there were secret places in his soul that he hadn't shared. She'd never pushed, waiting for him to open up. He had wanted to tell her about the army, how he idolized his father, memorized "Fighting soldiers from the sky, fearless men who jump and die" from the lyrics of "The Ballad of the Green Beret" as a young boy, and hated that his father wouldn't be around to pin silver wings on his chest. How proud he was when he was invited to selection and survived to become a member of Delta Force. He'd wanted to tell her all of it, but had never found the right time before she died.

"All right. I'll talk to your friend and help him if I can. If this involves more than theft and murder, I want your promise you'll call in the troops. I'm not going to play Lone Ranger on this."

He didn't resent the Senator asking for his help, but if the reason centered more on his military training than his legal skills, the two of them were headed for trouble. Politicians had a habit of getting soldiers into trouble, eager to stick their noses in someone's mess and then not being around when things got rough.

Chapter 4

"Let's walk down to the boathouse before Martin gets here," the Senator said, changing the subject as he led them off the rear deck.

Drake knew what the Senator had in mind. Before she'd left them alone, Meredith warned him her husband would try to slip off and have a cigar.

"If he starts inhaling, you tell him to stop. He's stopped smoking cigarettes behind my back, but he hasn't gotten over his love of cigars. The doctor and I will put an end to this if he doesn't," Meredith said.

When they reached the dock beside the boathouse, the Senator took a Hemingway Short Story from his pocket, clipped off the tip, and lit it with a silver lighter. When it burned evenly, he smiled at Drake.

"I imagine Meredith warned you to keep an eye on my smoking. She pretends she doesn't know what I'm doing, and I pretend I never inhale. She's better off not knowing everything. Like, how you've been doing lately. How's your practice?"

Several boats were out on the lake, and Drake smelled steaks being grilled somewhere. He was drinking too much and letting his work slide, but he thought no one had noticed. His marvelous secretary was skilled at covering for him.

"If you phrase the question that way, you probably know."

"I practiced law for fifteen years before I entered politics. I still know lawyers here. No one blames you for losing your focus after Kay died, but your friends don't want you to get in trouble because of it. I don't either."

Drake focused on a boat passing by. Its wake slapped against the side of the dock, like the nightly memories that pummeled his mind.

"Senator, I'm okay. A little depressed at times but Margo, my secretary, keeps things running. I won't let my clients down, don't worry."

"Son, I'm not worried about your clients, I worry about you. You let me know if there's something you need help with. I mean that. This thing with Rich Martin is important, don't get me wrong, but you're more important. I just need to know if I can count on you bringing your A game.

"I'll let Richard Martin tell you what he's working on when he gets here. You've probably guessed my interests are a little broader than his. The Secretary of Homeland Security is visiting next week to dedicate the chemical weapons disposal facility at the Umatilla Depot. He will also pay Martin Research a visit. I want to make sure Martin's project hasn't been compromised and the Secretary's visit isn't upstaged by this murder."

So that was it. A little worry about his son-in-law, but a bigger worry about a defense project and a Cabinet member's visit being upstaged. He had been mildly flattered for a moment, being asked to help the Senator's friend. Now he was mildly angered.

"Concern noted. Keep the Secretary's visit on the front page and Martin's dead secretary off, for the good of the country. Your friend must be here, we're being summoned," Drake said, breaking the beginning of an awkward silence when his mother-in-law waved from the terrace.

Standing on the terrace next to Meredith was a man perhaps ten years younger than the Senator, and better tanned. A little less than six feet tall, he looked like tennis was probably his game. Trim, in gray slacks, a light blue button-down shirt and a yellow tie loose at his neck, the man looked like someone in shock, unfamiliar with violence and death.

"Richard," the Senator called out, as they stepped onto the terrace, "this is my son-in-law, Adam Drake. He's the attorney I wanted you to meet. Let me get you a drink while I walk Meredith inside."

Left alone, Richard Martin shook hands with Drake without speaking. His eyes were bloodshot, his shoulders slumped.

"Your father-in-law thinks highly of you, but I don't need an attorney," Martin said.

"You've dealt with murder investigations and security problems that threaten your company?"

When Martin answered him with a silent stare, Drake continued.

"I've prosecuted cases like this, dealt with the police and managed the press. I know what you're in for. You could use someone to help manage the situation. I can help if you want. Or, you can do it and run your company at the same time. The Senator is trying to help, but I don't particularly care, one way or the other."

Martin shoved his hands in his pockets and dropped his chin to his chest.

"Janice Lewellyn was the nicest person I've ever known. She worked for me from the start-up of the company and never asked for anything. Everyone loved her. I can't begin to explain this to her husband and children. We had the best security we could afford, and she's still dead."

Drake stepped beside him and looked across the lake, following Martin's unfocused gaze.

"I lost my wife a year ago today. Things get turned upside down when you lose someone. The Senator wants to make sure you have someone to help you through this, that's all. Any idea why this happened?"

"No idea," Martin answered. "Looking for something in my office, I guess. But there's nothing missing. All of our research is on the main computer, completely secure."

"Anything in your office that might be of value to anyone?"

"Not a thing. The police think this was a burglary, but other than computers and stuff, there's nothing anyone could quickly sell."

"You said you had the best security you could afford. How did someone break in?" Drake asked.

"We don't know. We've had vandalism a couple of times. After we landed the DHS contract, we had to upgrade our security. I hired a new company. They're supposed to be the best in the business, certainly the most expensive. They revamped our whole system. Even they don't know how the killer got in."

"If you want my help, I'm willing to step in, as your attorney. I'll deal with the police. They'll want to take up a lot of your time, and I'll deal with that. I could visit tomorrow, if you want."

Martin continued to look out over the lake, then nodded his agreement as the Senator walked out and put an arm around Martin's shoulders.

"Richard, you could use a decent night's sleep. Why don't you head home? Let us help you with this tomorrow. You have a tough week ahead of you."

Martin didn't argue and said goodbye, with a little wave of his hand, before he allowed the Senator to walk him to his car.

The dinner was subdued, despite their best efforts to talk about everything except the empty chair across the table.

Drake thanked Meredith for preparing his favorite *paella,* told the Senator he'd call him after he visited Martin Research, and headed home.

Kay had fallen in love with a run-down vineyard and an old stone farmhouse in Dundee, the heart of Oregon's wine country, and had convinced him to make it their first home. A retired orthodontist from New Jersey had grown tired of farming grapes and sold the vineyard. The farmhouse needed a lot of work, but it was home.

In twenty minutes, he drove beyond the suburbs of Portland into wine country and the wineries dotting the gentle western slopes of the Willamette Valley. The region was magical to him. Its rows of grape vines, undulating over rolling hills of red earth, and the year-round white peak of Mount Hood in the distance surpassed anything Napa Valley had to offer.

Tomorrow, he'd go for a long run with his dog, then try to help the struggling CEO.

Chapter 5

Twenty miles to the north, in an upscale condo in the Pearl District of Portland, Kaamil paced, looking out onto a small terrace. He had a call he did not want to make. Jazz playing on his Continuum Audio turntable system didn't help to calm his nerves. Expensive things and good music only helped when you weren't afraid.

The keylogger he retrieved last night from Richard Martin's computer did provide next week's password. He confirmed that no changes had been made to the security system at the chemical depot. He did what he was asked to do, but killing Martin's secretary would still be counted against him.

The man he was about to call gave him nightmares. He had seen men killed before, shot several himself, but the images of men beheaded by this man still haunted his mind. Two or three strikes with a sword and the screaming stopped. Sawing with a knife to finish the job was bloody, but the victim was quiet by then. It was what followed that scared him. The man's eyes turned red, blood red, as the capillaries in his eyes exploded with the pleasure of killing.

The man was older now, and looked like any other successful western CEO, but Kaamil knew a raging fire of hatred burned in the man's heart. He was, without a doubt, the West's worst nightmare.

It was nine o'clock, and the call had to be made before nine thirty. The leader lived in Las Vegas and, despite all its distractions, still followed a rigid prayer discipline which included *Eshaa,* the evening prayer.

Kaamil wasn't as disciplined and poured himself a second tumbler of Scotch before walking to his study. He entered the number for the day, on a disposable cell phone, and tried to slow his heart rate. Any sign of weakness, any sign of hurried speech or unclear thinking would be noticed. The man was uncanny in his ability to detect deception.

When the connection was made, he sat forward in his chair and prepared to report on last night's event.

"Kaamil, my brother, I am worried. I thought I would hear from you last night."

"I'm sorry, Malik. I wanted to make sure of something before I called," Kaamil explained.

"Like how close the police are to finding out who killed that woman? Is that what you wanted to make sure of before you called me? Or were you hoping I wouldn't hear of your failure before you worked out your excuses?"

"Malik, please, killing the woman was a mistake, but it couldn't be avoided. I had no way of knowing she'd return that evening."

"Did you consider having someone outside, to warn you? Of course not, or you wouldn't have been surprised. Is there any evidence you were there?"

"No. I wore surgical gloves, and the surveillance system was turned off. There's nothing that could identify me. I took precautions."

"Except for posting a lookout. Were you able to verify the current password?"

"Yes, nothing has changed in the security system at the depot. We're okay."

"Make sure that we are. Also, make sure the investigation of the woman's murder doesn't get close to you. A third mistake would be your last," Malik said, ending the call.

Kaamil wiped off his fingerprints and dropped the cell phone in his briefcase to be thrown away. If Malik counted two mistakes against him already, he couldn't afford another. His old football coach used to say, "Son, if you can't carry the ball without losing it, I'll find someone who can." In the game he was playing now, benching would be more permanent than the old coach ever contemplated.

Chapter 6

Drake opened his eyes at five o'clock with Lancer, his five-year-old German shepherd, licking his face. It was time for their morning run. He threw his arm around the neck of his companion. Time to get back to their old routine. He had to meet Richard Martin, and a good run would get his blood flowing for the day.

"Lancer, old buddy, I know you think I'm going to be an easy mark this morning, but I might surprise you. If I do, you get dried dog food and I get breakfast out. How about that?" he asked his tail-wagging dog.

He pulled on his running gear, laced up his Nikes, and followed his dog. Lancer had been trained for protection dog competition since he was six months old, and was the best in Oregon. One-hundred-ten pounds of obedient aggression, Lancer was a perfect companion. Except on early mornings when Lancer was ready to run and he wasn't.

"All right you masochist, let's get it on," Drake said, opening the laundry room door onto the back porch.

Stepping off the porch, Drake stretched his hamstrings, breathed deeply, and began jogging along the brick walkway to the unfinished winery parking area behind his house. Tall fir trees stood behind the winery building that now served as a shop and garage for Drake's Porsche and Kay's Range Rover LR3. The surrounding vineyards filled the air with the scent of green lushness. Early in the morning, you could even smell summer lavender.

From the paved parking area, he followed Lancer down the long gravel driveway that ran along the southern border of the farm, down to Worden Road. At the bottom of the driveway, they turned north for two miles of steady uphill climbing before heading east toward the small city of Newberg. Then they ran downhill, past farmland not yet planted and young vineyards still maturing, until they reached Worden Road again and headed back to the farm.

Drake ran sluggishly after his dog, a tan reminder of better morning runs. It looked like breakfast was on him again, he thought, as they turned back up the driveway of his farm. Time to get back in shape.

Fixing breakfast for Lancer was easy. The dog enjoyed anything Drake fed him. His own breakfast was more of a problem. Nothing he fixed lately had any taste. The usual scrambled eggs with bacon, marmalade and toast tasted like sawdust. Maybe it was time to pay a visit to his friend at the Black Walnut Inn to see if their gourmet breakfast offerings would taste better.

After a quick protein drink, shower, and shave, Drake left for Martin Research, driving north. The sound of the Porsche's restrained whine begged him to unleash the car's power, but he didn't need another speeding ticket to distract him before meeting his new client.

The thought of a new client reminded him to call his secretary. Punching the speed dial on his dash-mounted cell phone, he waited to see what mood she was in this morning.

"Law office. Wondered when you'd call. Kind of got used to you keeping in touch and all. When I didn't hear from you yesterday, I assumed you were dead. So, I accepted a job with your enemy, that guy from the Public Defender's office. He wants to pay me big money to learn the secret of your past wins. Back when you were an attorney that gave a damn, and had some wins. How are you this morning, boss?"

Drake resigned himself to her mood. She was the person closest to him, next to his wife, and he hadn't told her where he was going yesterday.

"Good morning, Margo. Thought I called the wrong number and got someone's secretary dealing with a bad case of PMS. Until I recognized your voice, and realized you must be upset because there weren't any billable hours yesterday."

Drake heard her swallow her anger, almost.

"That wasn't my concern, and you know it. I was worried about you. You're not the only one who knew what yesterday was. I'm mad that you didn't call and say you needed time away. You think I had a party here myself?" Margo asked.

"Sorry, I wasn't thinking right yesterday. I just called to say I'm headed to Hillsboro to meet with a new client. Thought that would make you happy. I should be back shortly after lunch. I'll explain things then, okay?"

"Sure, new clients are good, right? Means maybe we'll be able to pay the bills this month."

She wasn't mad. They'd been through too much together over the years for either of them to misread the other's mood. Drake knew Margo was just worried about him. Hell, he had to admit he was worried too.

"Margo, before you hang up, do me one favor and call your husband. Find out what he's heard about the murder of the secretary at Martin Research in Hillsboro. That's where I'm headed, that's our new client. I know it's out of his jurisdiction, but senior detectives hear things. Anything I can learn about this will be helpful. Could you also check into the security company Martin Research uses? It's ISIS, or something like that. Call me right away if Paul knows anything, and tell him lunch is on me."

"Do I get to come along, or is this a guy thing?"

"Depends on how well he comes through, so I guess it's up to you. Call me."

The city of Hillsboro, where Drake headed, was west of Portland on the Sunset Highway. The city grew, along with Oregon's metropolis, when the high-tech boom exploded. Intel and other Silicon Valley firms expanded there, and the area was dubbed the Silicon Forest. But with the tech bust in the nineties, satellite offices downsized, leaving a lot of Porsches and BMWs on the dealer's pre-owned lots. The tough survived, and Martin Research had been one of the survivors.

Twenty minutes after talking with his secretary, Drake pulled off the freeway. He followed 185th Ave. for a block or two, then turned west onto a parkway lined with sweeping lawns and modern sculptures. He was driving past these modern monuments to art, when his cell phone buzzed.

"Paul talked with the head of detectives in Hillsboro. They're sort of friends. They don't think much of the burglary motive. The surveillance system was turned off, and they can't find fingerprints or any physical evidence. Burglars aren't that careful. That's all they know at this point," Margo relayed.

"Tell Paul I owe him lunch. I'm going to meet with the head of security after I take a look at Martin's office. I'll call when I'm finished, and yes, you can join us for lunch."

Martin Research occupied two modern buildings at the end of a cul-de-sac. The buildings were surrounded by lawn, with a small lake that had a fountain in the center. An amphitheater with rows of cement benches sat to the south. Drake doubted that lectures took place there, but the scene suggested learned discussions taking place in a park-like setting. Investors would be impressed.

A crime lab van was parked in front of a glass and steel building that had to be Martin's headquarters. Drake parked his car behind the van and entered the fashionable reception area that opened all the way to the top floor. The whole area was illuminated by a giant skylight above.

The receptionist sat behind a raised teak surround, with two security guards standing at each of the two doors leading from the reception room.

"May I help you?"

"I'm here to see Mr. Martin."

"He's not seeing anyone today, sorry."

"Just let him know I'm here. I'm his lawyer."

"Oh Mr. Drake, I'm glad you're here. The police are here, they're going through everything. It's awful what happened to Mrs. Lewellyn."

Drake looked down at her identification plaque.

"Kimberly, I need you to reach Mr. Martin immediately, can you do that for me? He doesn't need to speak to the police without me there."

With tears beginning in her eyes, Kimberly entered the numbers for Martin's office and waited for someone to answer.

"Mr. Martin's attorney is here, would you please let him know?"

After a moment, she looked up at Drake.

"The policeman said they're busy right now."

"Kimberly, I need to get up there. Tell security to show me the way. Now, please."

The security guard on Drake's left had been listening, and motioned for Drake to follow him. He held his door open and led Drake to the bank of elevators beyond the reception area.

"Mr. Martin shouldn't have to put up with the crap the police are giving him. We run a tight ship here, it isn't his fault Mrs. Lewellyn was killed," the man said. Beefy, in his sixties, the man looked like a former cop.

"You know any of these guys he's talking to?"

"Only the detective, and just by reputation. Name's Carson, and he's a mean son of a bitch. He had Kimberly crying because she wouldn't let him up to see Mr. Martin without calling ahead. Kimberly was just doing her job."

Mean son of a bitch was an understatement where Detective Steve Carson was concerned. Drake knew him well. Carson had been prepared to perjure himself in one of Drake's drug cases. The felon had agreed to accept a favorable plea deal in the middle of the trial, which prevented the perjury from occurring. When Drake was forced to explain the plea arrangement, he'd refused to cover for Carson. Carson was demoted and later terminated from the Portland P.D. Rehired in Hillsboro, Carson had apparently worked his way back to detective rank.

When the elevator door opened on the fourth floor, Detective Carson was waiting for Drake.

"I heard they kicked you out of the D.A.'s office. You doing criminal defense work now?"

Carson had changed. He'd been a tough cop, crew-cut hair, five nine with a barrel chest and thick shoulders. He was still five nine but now just thick all over, with a shaved head and droopy mustache. The man looked like a heavy G. Gordon Liddy, President Nixon's break-in "plumber," famous for putting cigarettes out in the palm of his hand. Drake doubted Carson had ever done anything as painful, though he probably wanted people to think he had.

"Where's Martin? I want to see him, now."

"No problem, counselor, no problem. We're just doing our crime scene investigation and asking questions. Why does Mr. Martin think he needs an attorney? They're the victims here, right, or do innocent people need attorneys now?"

"You'd know that better than me, right? Take me to my client."

Drake saw a flicker of understanding that quickly flamed to anger before Carson turned and walked down the hall.

The hallway to the right took them past two offices before they reached Richard Martin's executive suite. Two plain-clothes detectives stood in the outer office where Martin's secretary had worked. In his office, Richard Martin stood beside his desk, talking with a young detective taking notes. When she saw Drake enter with Detective Carson, she quickly asked another question before Drake reached them.

"Richard," Drake called ahead, "before you continue, may I speak with you for a moment?" He motioned to Martin to follow, and walked to the back of his office.

"Have they been here long?" Drake asked.

"For an hour or so. They're asking, 'Was I having an affair with Janice? Who could have turned off the security system? Did I suspect any of my employees?' This is a nightmare. This is the stuff you see winding up in the tabloids."

"Relax, that's why I'm here. Go tell your people everything's under control, this is routine, and you'll brief them before the end of the day. I'll talk with the police for a while."

Martin left, and Drake walked up to Detective Carson.

"Steve, I want you to listen carefully. There's important work going on here, and we'll cooperate fully with your investigation. You need to minimize the disruption, though. You're scaring these people."

"Well, I'm sorry all to hell, Drake. There was a murder here. It's my job to find the lady's killer. If that disrupts some new video game this company is working on, then the consumers will just have to suffer a while."

"As usual, you haven't done your homework. Martin Research is a defense contractor for the government. The consumers are us, and no, we can't wait for you to plod your way through this investigation. Now, why don't you tell me what you need. I'll make sure you get it, as quickly as possible."

Detective Carson looked like he wanted to settle old scores with one punch.

"Drake, I don't like you. I'll never forget what you did to me. This is my investigation. What I need to know is how this buttoned-up, high-tech place allowed some killer to get in and kill this lady. Was this an inside job? Does someone know something he's not telling me? If you can help me with that, great. If not, get out of my way or I'll arrest your ass for obstruction of justice."

Drake smiled and gently put a finger on the detective's chest.

"Steve, as much as we both don't like it, we're on the same side here. But don't ever threaten me again. I kept you out of jail once. I won't do it again. Do your job and remember, I know the rules better than you do. If you need to talk with Richard Martin again, call me."

With that, Drake left, in search of the CEO, and some answers.

Chapter 7

The United Airlines flight from Las Vegas to Aruba via Charlotte, North Carolina took nearly thirteen hours on the same day Drake was meeting with the police at Martin Research. The man sitting in the rear window seat of first class, however, didn't mind.

He wore the casual dress of a business traveler, comfortable with the anonymity it provided. Of course, he also had a false passport and altered appearance. Most observers would remember dyed-gray hair, stylish wire-rimmed glasses, and the cane he used when he moved, if they remembered anything at all.

His private jet would have been faster and more comfortable, but it could be tracked. At this stage, he didn't want anyone to know where he was going or who he was meeting. Especially not the man he was meeting.

David Barak was known as Malik, or the Leader, to his followers. They knew him by no other name. He was traveling to meet the man coordinating the war against the West from the Tri-Border Area of South America. Of the three-quarters of a million residents there, more than twenty-five thousand were Arabs. In that number, a significant number of jihadists and international terrorist organizations were represented.

Western intelligence hadn't been able to identify all the players in the TBA because it was a wild frontier, for the most part lawless. The various agencies knew the cartel and jihadist organizations were getting along, or at least cooperating with each other in unusual ways. The reason, Barak knew, was that one entity, known as the "Alliance," coordinated the efforts of the cartels and the worldwide Islamist jihad for their mutual benefit. It also took a healthy profit for doing so, but it was deserved.

Barak took a glass of champagne from the first-class attendant and considered what little he knew about the upcoming meeting. The encrypted message from his sponsors simply directed him to the island of Aruba and a villa on the eastern shore. There, he was to meet a man who would identify himself only as Ryan. He was instructed to brief the man on plans he'd been putting in place for twenty-five years. Actually, longer than that if you counted all the years since he'd decided to become a warrior. That was two days after his eleventh birthday, when his father had been hunted down and assassinated. The Jews had learned of his father's close relationship with the Grand Mufti of Jerusalem, the head of Hitler's SS Muslim Panzar Division in World War II, and had sent a team of young Israelis to kill him. Barak had vowed his revenge on the Jews.

His father had fled to Egypt after WWII. He lived under the protection of Gamal Abdul Nasser, until the Jews tracked him down. He had worked with the Mufti to plan the liquidation of the Jewish population in the Middle East after Hitler won the war. Those participants the Jews found, they killed, often in front of their families. Barak remembered. He had watched his father, on his knees in the street in front of their home, still cursing the Jews when he was executed. He would never forget. It was a memory he kept alive each night, as part of his evening prayers.

With the help of the Muslim Brotherhood, his mother fled to France and opened a small village bakery. A lot of

Arabs were in France after the war, and Barak assimilated easily and did well in school. After de Gaulle rose to power, France reached out to the Middle East to assist it in limiting the powers of Russia and America. Barak was soon courted by the military for service in its special operation forces. His ethnicity and physical prowess were factors, of course, as well as his reputation for a fierce determination to win at any cost. While still in secondary school, his red flags playing soccer were legendary.

After the selection process and recruit training, he was given specialized training to work with foreign local forces that France wanted to support militarily, especially in the Middle East. Colonialism was a thing of the past, but providing the assistance of its Quiet Professionals, as its special forces were known, often reaped some of the same benefits.

While he was in Iran working with the Shah to assist the Sultan of Oman to put down a rebellion, he came to the attention of the movement. When the Shah fled Iran in 1979 and the *Savak*, Iran's secret police, was dissolved, Barak and other foreign sympathizers were imprisoned. When his true sympathies were discovered, albeit under torture, he was asked to join the Islamic fundamentalist movement. He hadn't hesitated.

In the end, a farsighted plan was approved with his unique gifts in mind. It required him to assume a new identity and move to America, to establish a base for training fifth column forces capable of striking deep into the heart of the Jews' ally.

With a nest egg of twenty-five million dollars and twenty-five years, he had accomplished everything that had been asked of him. Now he was directed to discuss it all with someone he'd never met and had little reason to trust.

When his United Airlines flight landed at Aeropuerto Internacional Reina Beatrix in Oranjestad, Aruba, Barak collected his Hartmann carry-on and deplaned. After passing through customs, he made his way directly to the taxi area in front of the island airport. Waiting beside a white Mercedes S600 sedan he saw a driver wearing the dark green cap he'd been told to look for. He nodded to the man and glanced around. Several men seemed to be interested in the Mercedes, but no one seemed to be overly interested in its passenger. Aruba was only twenty miles long, and six miles wide at its widest point, so the five hundred ten horsepower of the S600 Mercedes was transportation overkill on the small island.

The chauffeur opened the rear door without offering to take his carry-on. They drove east and then southeast on a road to Boca Daimari, a beach area on the rugged east coast of the island. The terrain was mostly flat, with few hills and only scattered vegetation. It offered little in the way of scenery to enjoy.

As they neared the sea, however, the view of the Caribbean along the highway south was breathtaking. The ocean stretched to the east as far as the eye could see, and small beaches carved from the black rock of the island's crust passed by on the left. Occasionally, he saw a villa or small resort perched on a rocky outcropping, isolated and private. At least Ryan understood their need for privacy.

Beyond a desolate stretch of shoreline, a white villa came into view atop a rocky finger reaching out into the sea. Its outline suggested Moorish architecture, with square lines, a scalloped roof, and arched windows. The white-graveled drive leading to it from the highway was lined with palms. The villa itself was surrounded with beds of bougainvillea, hibiscus, and frangipani.

When the chauffeur pulled to a stop in front of the villa, a tall blond man stood in the shadows of the arched portico spanning the front of the villa. He wore white linen slacks and a long-sleeved white shirt with rolled-up sleeves. Large aviator sunglasses hid the color of his eyes, but Barak knew they would be blue. The man was a poster boy for the Aryan race, military bearing and all.

Barak got out of the Mercedes and walked to greet the man in the shadows. As he approached, the man turned and led him into the interior of the villa before turning and extending his hand.

"I never know which of our enemies might be watching. I'm Ryan. Did you have a pleasant flight?" he asked.

"I usually don't fly commercial. It was a long flight."

"Quite. Sorry it was necessary. Travel here is carefully monitored, thanks to the antics of Venezuela's El Presidente. The Americans were used to watching Cuba, but when Chavez invited the Cubans to run his intelligence apparatus, you don't fly down here without caution. That's why we're here instead of Isla Margarita. Hamas and Hezbollah are almost as numerous there as they are in the Middle East. Come, sit by the pool and we'll talk."

With that, Barak's host turned and led him through the villa. Dark-tiled floors and heavy, dark wood furniture contrasted with the alabaster walls and drapery. Bright floral paintings, however, gave the place vibrancy and spirit. If the villa wasn't someone's permanent residence, it certainly was a beautiful safe house.

White tiles outside the villa surrounded a large zero-horizon pool. Ryan, or the Aryan, as Barak was beginning to think of him, signaled a servant and a tray of beverages and appetizers was brought to their umbrella table. He saw his host knew he drank Glenmorangie Scotch, but he didn't recognize the small potato *tapas* that filled the serving platter.

"I thought you might be hungry and, perhaps, thirsty. *Salud,*" Ryan said.

"*Salud.* Do you come here often?"

"Shall I call you David or Barak?" Ryan asked.

"Barak will do."

"I know you have many questions. I will answer the ones I can. It isn't important how often I come here, who owns this villa, or who I am. You trust the people who told you to come here, just as I trust the people who told me to meet with you. I was told to find out if there are services you might provide us, in exchange for financing your cause."

"My company provides security services and sometimes business intelligence for our international clientele. What services are you interested in?"

"Barak, let's not play games. Your company, ISIS, was started with a twenty-five million dollar stake from the Muslim Brotherhood. You were sent to gain a foothold, to develop a front capable of carrying out strikes against America. You have done that remarkably well. But, plans change. I'm here to see if you are flexible enough to take on more than you were originally asked to do."

Barak had assumed as much. What he didn't know was whether he could trust this man, or the men he was fronting for.

"And why would you want to do that? You seem to know a lot about me, but I don't know a thing about you. What do you care about my cause?"

The man calling himself Ryan smiled and helped himself to a *relleno*.

"You should try one of these, mushroom stuffed with *chorizo*, excellent. To answer your question, we need someone to provide the services you have trained your elite recruits for, assassinations. Some of our clients have a clumsy way of dealing with adversaries. Their methods need to be more sophisticated, if you will. As for your cause, your enemy has been our enemy for a very long time. We failed before, and now we may have another chance."

Barak picked up his crystal tumbler and swirled the scotch around the ice that remained. The tropical climate had many attractions, but ice lasting more than a couple of minutes wasn't one of them. From what he was told, Ryan's organization was powerful in Europe, North Africa, and Latin America. Its specialty was money laundering for major crime syndicates, and it owned or controlled banks around the world, originally financed with stolen Jewish money and gold from World War II. After the war, it had developed a relationship with the Brotherhood. What he didn't know was what the Alliance was doing these days, and what their ultimate goal was.

"Ryan, you are quite the diplomat. If I hadn't lived in America for nearly half my life, I would enjoy continuing to beat around the bush, as we say. So let's speak plainly. You want me to provide assassins for your drug cartel clients, in exchange for money you'll funnel to me. Why?"

His blond host took off his sunglasses and smiled.

"I have lived in South America as long as you have lived in America. Perhaps I am used to speaking obliquely. The answer is, since 9/11 the terrorist finance tracking program the Americans put together is causing both of us problems. You have legitimately earned money you wish to put to illegal use, and we have illegal funds we want to place in the international financial system. We propose a bartering arrangement. You provide the assassinations our clients want, without a trail back to them, and we provide untraceable funds to you.

"Personally, my grandfather was branded a war criminal by the Jews, but he wasn't brought to trial. They killed him in Brazil where they found him. My father organized our current efforts, and I work to see those efforts succeed. We share a common goal, Barak. You want to avenge your father, just as I want to avenge my grandfather. We can do that by working together."

The hatred burning in the eyes of the Aryan warmed Barak's soul. There were many details to discuss, but he felt a kinship he was willing to trust.

"Ryan, I'm willing to work with you, but you only. My true identity is not to be revealed to any of your clients. I will only communicate with you, face to face. Our meetings will be arranged by hand-delivered correspondence. If that's acceptable to you, then let us begin."

Both men stood, touched their glasses, and drank more of Barak's favorite Scotch to toast the destruction of their enemies.

Chapter 8

After Drake brushed aside Detective Carson's blustering interference in Richard Martin's office, he led the CEO outside.

"Is there some place we can talk privately? Carson will leave you alone for now, but I need to get a handle on this pretty quickly."

"There's a cafeteria in the basement. I'll treat you to an espresso."

"Don't tell me there's a Starbucks here," Drake moaned.

"Don't insult me. I like coffee, but I don't need it with a triple shot of caffeine. We buy and grind our own," Martin said, leading Drake to the elevator.

They rode down to the basement. Black and white photographs of the Oregon wilderness lined the light saffron walls of the cafeteria. A salad bar and small food service counter ran along the wall, advertising daily specials listed far below local market prices. Obviously, Martin Research took exceptional care of its employees.

Martin asked for an espresso and Drake asked for a cafe au lait. While they waited for their coffee, Drake asked about the cafeteria.

"Is there an outside service entrance?"

"No, everything comes down the service elevator from the first floor. Surveillance cameras monitor the place twenty-four seven."

Drake saw two cameras over the service counter and three more spaced around the large room.

When they were seated, Martin held his coffee in both hands and fixed his eyes on the nature scenes lining the walls.

"I have no idea how this happened, Drake. The detectives asked me every question they could think of, and I told them the same thing."

"Tell me what you told them."

"That I was not having an affair with Janice. My God, she was my secretary for almost twenty years. People can work together without having affairs. There's no way I would ever have crossed that line. I respected her too much. I'm married, and I'm not looking for anything else."

"Okay. She was married too. How were things on her side? Any chance she was seeing someone?"

"No way. She adored her husband. She lived for him and her kids. Her biggest thrill was when the two of them could get away for a long weekend."

"What was she doing here so late at night? She was murdered between ten o'clock and midnight, if the police are right."

"She was getting ready to leave for a vacation. She told me she wanted to make sure everything was covered for the two weeks she'd be away. I guess she was here working."

"Is there any reason someone would want to hurt her? Any problems her husband had that could have led to this?"

Martin shook his head and set his coffee down.

"You had to know Janice. There's no reason anyone in the world would want to hurt her. She could convince a mugger to turn himself in rather than take her purse."

"So that leaves us with someone stealing from your company, or something involving you, since they were in your office. Any ideas?"

"I haven't stopped thinking about this, that somehow I could have prevented this. I hired the top security firm in the country and installed everything they recommended. I still had problems. I don't know what else could have been done."

"I'm not suggesting there was anything, Richard. What about something business related?"

"I have competitors who fought me for the Homeland Security contract, but that's all that I know of."

"Okay, what about your competitors? Anyone who might be involved in something like this?"

"No, there was only one real competitor, and DHS wound up splitting the contract between us. We work on biological and chemical monitoring, and they work on nuclear monitoring. There's no way they'd do something like this for the rest of the research. They have enough work to keep them busy."

Martin finished his coffee and stood up.

"You need to talk to my head of security. He might have some ideas, because I sure as hell don't."

Chapter 9

With Martin's directions, Drake found his way to the first floor office of Risk Management & Corporate Security. The secretary in the small front office announced his presence, and soon a grim-faced man of fifty or so brushed past her and greeted Drake. Short and broad shouldered, the man had the piercing look of law enforcement in his eyes.

Sam Newman wore the uniform of corporate security, a blue blazer over gray slacks with a red tie set against his white shirt. He still looked like someone who could make an arrest in a biker's bar without interference.

"Mr. Martin called and said you needed to talk to me. Come on in," he said, holding open the door to his office.

Drake saw that he'd been right about Sam Newman's background. The wall behind Sam's cluttered desk was covered with pictures of citations received, plaques attesting to years of service and photos of his family and friends. The office was unpretentious, a place to work, not a monument to the man's ego.

"Where'd you serve?" Drake asked.

"Palo Alto, twenty-six years. I've been here in God's country for the last four. Thought I'd find a cushy security position for a few years, and slow down. Hasn't quite worked out that way. How can I help you, Drake?"

"Mr. Martin's told me some of it, but he's not a security expert. I understand the security system failed around the time his secretary was murdered. That doesn't sound like a coincidence to me."

"You here to find a scapegoat, or find out what happened?" Sam asked.

Drake recognized the response. He interviewed too many police witnesses who wanted to know he was on their side before they told him what really happened.

"Sam, I'm here to help the company get through this, with as little damage as possible. If you screwed up and you're responsible, then I guess you're the goat. I'll know sooner or later. If there's another explanation, I need to know what it is sooner rather than later."

Sam watched Drake's eyes for a good ten seconds before making up his mind.

"I'm trying to quit smoking, but this doesn't look like the week that's going to happen. Care to take a walk with me out of this no smoking zone?"

When he walked by his secretary's desk, Newman showed her his pack of Marlboros, eliciting a nod and a smile. Drake caught the smile and wondered if she covered for him for other things.

They walked out of the office and down the hall to an outside door with a security pad. Entering his security code, Newman led them out of the building and down an outside path to a bench beneath two white-flowering magnolia trees. He sat down, lit a cigarette, and looked out over the expanse of lawn.

"You ever work in the D.A.'s office?"

"Five years. Why?"

"How long did it take you before you could spot a felon on the street?"

"Not long."

"Well, I know an ex-con when I see one, and three of the new security guards assigned here have been in prison, I'm sure of it. I checked their records and couldn't find a thing. They all have adopted Muslim names, but suspiciously clean records. I know the look, I know the walk."

"What does that have to do with Martin's secretary?"

"Someone got into this building, and we're supposed to have the best security system money can buy. It had to be an inside job. Somehow, this involves these ex-cons, or the company they work for," Newman said.

"You're not buying the theory that this was a burglary that ended in murder?"

"No way. Janice Lewellyn was a careful person. She didn't like working at night and didn't work late often. We talked about it. When she walked to her car, she always had her mace in hand. She would fight like a hellion if someone tried to rape her. If someone tried to rob her, she would let the thief take what he wanted. This had to be something else."

"So how did the surveillance system get turned off? All the cameras, all the touch pads, everything went down at the same time. How'd that happen?" Drake asked.

"I don't know," Sam answered. "There are only two people who have the code to shut down the security system. I have it, in my safe. The guy from ISIS who installed the system has it."

"Could a security guard obtain the code somehow?"

"I don't think that's possible, but I guess we'll know soon enough. Detective Carson said they were going to polygraph all the ISIS security personnel assigned here. Hell, he's even got me scheduled for first thing tomorrow."

Newman didn't appear to be worried about tomorrow's polygraph.

"So if this is an inside job, you think somehow it involves one of these ISIS security guards? How did he know to turn off the security system, assuming he did, the night she was here? Did anyone know she was working that night?"

"According to Mr. Martin, the answer is no. She was leaving for Hawaii the next day. She probably was trying to make sure everything was done before she left. But no one would know she was coming back that night."

"You honestly think the security company you hired, or one of its employees, is responsible for this? Is that what you're telling me?"

"I don't know what to think," Sam said. "What I know is that ex-cons are working where they shouldn't be working, for a company that should know better than to hire them. You figure it out."

"So why do you use this company, if you suspect them?"

"I didn't hire them, Martin did. DHS pressured him to upgrade security. Martin thinks big is best. ISIS is the largest private security firm in the country, hell, maybe even in the world. Who am I to second guess his choice? Besides, I need this job. Everyone thinks twenty-five years and a pension earns you a cushy retirement. Don't believe them," Newman said.

Chapter 10

Drake left Sam Newman's office with more questions than answers. The police didn't have any leads, and Newman suspected the security firm hired to protect his company. Someone with the ability to shut down the company's security system had to be involved. What he didn't know was if you had to have the security codes to shut down the security system. If there were other ways to do it, then any number of players might be involved. All of which meant a visit to the ISIS office was in order.

After leaving a message for Martin with the receptionist that he was headed to the local ISIS office, Drake left the Martin Research campus and started back to Portland. Driving east on the Sunset Highway, he hit the number for his office on his dash-mounted cell phone and noticed his secretary had tried to reach him.

"Hi, boss, you headed this way?" Margo asked. "I have information on that security firm you might need. The ISIS office is located on Kruse Way, next to the State Farm Insurance building. The regional manager's name is Kaamil Sayf. Paul couldn't find anything about him."

"You're a mind reader. Tell me about ISIS."

"ISIS stands for the International Security and Information Services. It was started twenty-five years ago by a man named David Barak. Headquartered in Las Vegas, they have offices around the world and are rated as one of the top two or three firms providing corporate security, VIP protection services, and business intelligence. Their clients include a lot of celebrities, CEOs, and government types not protected by their governments. It's a huge company."

Drake absorbed the information. Why would a company like ISIS hire felons? They obviously had the resources to do background checks. Of course, Newman might be wrong, trying to create a scapegoat.

"I think I'll check out ISIS and then head your way. Before I get there, run a check on Sam Newman, the head of security at Martin Research. He's not a suspect, at least in my book, but see what you can find about him."

"No problem. Be neat to see you someday, maybe even get some work done."

When the connection ended, Drake had the fleeting thought it might be wise to take another day off. Margo didn't hide her feelings. When she mentioned getting work done, it usually meant that he forgot a deadline or appointment. Sizing up ISIS seemed like a piece of cake compared to what the rest of his day promised if he returned to his office.

Drake drove on, thinking about ISIS. He'd heard of ISIS, but that was like saying you had heard of Halliburton. Multinational corporations with more money than most third world countries were almost impossible to get answers from. The Portland ISIS office would say they needed to talk to corporate, and someone would get back to him. He'd be as lucky as he had been when he called about his coffee maker, and wound up talking to someone in India.

Take a deep breath and relax. Follow the thread. See if you can find a way to help your client. Big corporations are a part of the twenty-first century landscape. Drake shook his head, punched in XM 70 to listen to commercial-free jazz, and accelerated the 993 up to ninety before backing off when he ran out of open lane ahead.

He crossed over I-5 and continued east, entering the area where ISIS had its corporate office. Stands of oak groves surrounded the office buildings and restaurants, and beyond them, high-end residential developments. ISIS had chosen carefully and well. It was the kind of place where trusted businesses located.

The four-story brick building, with brass letters proclaiming it to be the regional office of International Security and Information Services, Inc. wasn't ostentatious. Except for the fact that ISIS was the only tenant. All of the surrounding office buildings housed multiple businesses.

Drake drove down the ramp into the parking garage and pulled in next to a black Suburban with darkened windows and an ISIS logo painted in gold on its door. When he got out of the Porsche, he stretched and studied the ISIS logo. The round logo had a hieroglyph of the Egyptian goddess Isis, representing the idea of eternal life and resurrection, of life and blood, over arched with the words International Security & Information Services, Inc. It wasn't the logo Drake expected from a company promising clients protection and security. Instead, it suggested life ever after, granted by an ancient Egyptian goddess. What had some advertising consultant been smoking when he came up with that one, Drake wondered.

He also noticed the Suburban had antennas on the roof and rear window, twenty-four-inch wheels and heavy-duty red shocks that made armor a strong possibility. At least the company had some of the right equipment to do its job.

When he walked to the parking garage elevator, Drake noticed direct access to the fourth floor via keypad. Visitors and employees had to enter on the first floor. With a glance and mental salute to the surveillance camera over the elevator,

Drake took it to the first floor and found a receptionist, who looked a lot like the NFL player they called the Refrigerator, waiting for him. The semi-circular redwood kiosk was four feet tall, but the giant sitting behind it made it look like furniture for a first grade classroom.

Drake had to announce himself before the man looked up from the paper he was reading.

"Hi there, I'm the attorney for a client of yours that had a security malfunction and wound up with someone dead. I'd like to see your manager."

The giant in the sharkskin suit squinted his eyes, as if to say you're not cute, or welcome. Nevertheless, in a soft voice he offered a non-standard business greeting.

"Mr. Sayf is busy at the moment, Mr. Drake. Step back and raise your arms to shoulder level. The security guard behind you will clear you for a meeting with Mr. Sayf."

Drake hadn't heard the security guard approach, but when he looked over his shoulder, the guard was standing right behind him. He had to smile as he raised his arms and allowed the scanner wand to trace the outline of his body. Ten years ago he would have sensed the man's approach. Good thing he wasn't back in the field. A loss of focus like that would get you killed.

He spotted a two-inch round lens, disguised to look like the ISIS logo, mounted in the center of the kiosk. The lens aimed at his midsection. He assumed it was an x-ray device, used to see if he carried a weapon. At least he'd noticed that, he thought.

When the security guard finished his search, the sumo at the kiosk nodded and spoke into his cordless headset.

"Drake is here. Shall I send him up?" He listened for a moment, then told Drake to take the elevator to the fourth floor. Someone would take him to Mr. Sayf. There was a smirk on the sumo's face when he turned back to his paper.

Three floors later, the elevator opened onto an executive suite that outdid most large corporations, and certainly the top law firms in the city. This time a pretty secretary sat behind an impressive desk. It was a slab of smoked glass on a black onyx pedestal with only a flat-screen monitor and a small black phone console on it. Drake noticed the long slender legs and model's body as he approached. Her black hair was cut short and her hazel green eyes challenged him to keep his eyes off her generous cleavage. He tried hard to comply.

- "Mr. Sayf will be with you in a moment, Mr. Drake. Is there anything I can get you while you wait?" she asked, in a voice that would seduce a vice cop.

"Not right now, thank you," Drake said, returning her offer with a smile that said you're beautiful, but your boss is the main attraction here.

Behind her, Drake saw open glass doors and a black man with a phone to his ear, sitting behind a beautiful rosewood desk. He was turned toward a wall-to-wall glass window that looked over a wooded area and a small stream. Off to the right of the wooded area was a helicopter pad with another black Suburban parked beside it.

The man who turned around in his chair had to be at least six foot seven or eight. He reminded Drake of a professional athlete, NBA or NFL. His creamed-mocha polo shirt barely contained a muscled upper body. When he put the phone down, the wafer-thin gold watch and thin gold chain around his neck reflected sunlight from outside.

The secretary told him he could go in, and Sayf turned to watch Drake enter his office.

"I have an appointment in a few minutes, I wasn't expecting anyone. I can give you a few minutes," he said.

The man was a poor liar.

"Oh, I think you were, or at least your staff was. My name's Drake. I'm here to find out how you screwed up so badly that my client's secretary was murdered. Why your expensive security system conveniently malfunctioned."

"Who are you?" Sayf said, rising from his chair.

"I'm the attorney Martin Research hired. What do I call you, Kaamil or Sayf?" Drake said, looking down at the nameplate on the desk. "I've never figured out which name you Muslims prefer to use."

For a moment, he thought the man was going to dive over the desk at him. Just as quickly, the anger in Sayf's eyes dimmed. Not as cool as he thinks he is, but he's controlled, Drake observed.

"I am Muslim, Mr. Drake. You may call me Kaamil. You can disrespect my religion, but be careful when you start blaming my company for that woman's death. Slander has a hefty price tag."

"Truth's a defense. We don't know what the truth is, do we Kaamil? Have you discovered how the security system went down? Was it turned off? According to Sam Newman at Martin Research, there are only two people with the access code to disable the system. He has the code and so do you."

Kaamil sat down and leaned back in his chair. His hands were still on the top of his desk, but his eyes were taunting.

"Why would anyone here want to turn off the system? We get paid to make sure it's functioning. Sometimes systems do fail. But you're asking the wrong person. Ask Mr. Newman. He has more reasons to disable that system than I do."

Drake noticed the personalization of the accusation, a subtle deflection from the company to Kaamil, and wondered why.

"If you have reason to think Sam Newman is involved, why haven't you told anyone? There's a murder investigation underway, and Martin Research is one of your clients. I'd think you would want to keep your company out of this."

"If I had something solid for the police, I would provide that information. All I have are rumors. Now, I've told you all I'm going to, Mr. Drake. I'm a busy man."

With that, Kaamil stood, dismissing Drake.

Walking by the secretary, he couldn't help wondering why Kaamil pointed him to Sam Newman. Had he missed something? And who was Kaamil? The security malfunction may have been just a malfunction, but he was certain there was more to Kaamil and ISIS than anyone knew. They were hiding something. He was sure of it.

When he got to the parking garage, the black Suburban next to his car was gone. One space over was a black Mercedes SLS AMG roadster in the only reserved spot. It had to be Kaamil's. Powered by the largest V8 Mercedes produced, with a price tag over one hundred eighty thousand dollars, the car fit the arrogance of the man. The salary he earned as a glorified security guard, however, shouldn't be enough to pay for the SLS.

There was a lot about Kaamil he was uncomfortable with. He also had questions about Sam Newman. It was time to take a closer look at both.

~~~

As soon as he saw Drake's Porsche leave the parking garage on the building's secure cam display, Kaamil swore loudly. The attorney didn't believe him, he could tell. Pointing at Sam Newman would buy a little time but probably wind up biting him in the butt. Newman lived alone, and drank too much. But he had no reason to disable the security system. This time, he'd let Malik make the call. Surely he would see they needed to deal with the attorney. If he didn't, Kaamil would take care of the problem himself.

He entered Malik's personal email address on the company's ultra-secure, encrypted email system, and briefed him on this latest development.

> The Martin Research attorney just visited me, asking about the security system I disabled there. He's suspicious. I told him to take a look at the head of security who had the other code key. Suggest we make it look like the head of security was behind the murder. Please advise. K

While he waited for directions, Kaamil googled Adam Drake. The attorneys he knew were arrogant bullies, little men hiding behind the law to make themselves feel important. Drake wasn't like that. He was in decent shape, and looked as if he could hold his own in a fight. It was his eyes that told you about the man. They were the eyes of a fighter, confident and unafraid. Eyes like Malik's.

According to the internet, Drake had been a prosecutor who left the District Attorney's office at the peak of his career. His wife, the only daughter of Oregon's senior U.S. senator, had died a year ago. He had a solo law practice in an office overlooking a marina on the Willamette River.

Kaamil didn't care that the man looked like he could defend himself. His men wouldn't have a problem with that. It was his connections that would make Malik nervous. If he were eliminated before he knew too much, however, his connections wouldn't matter. He might have to suggest that Drake be silenced, as well as Sam Newman.

His computer signaled his email had been answered.

> Give me Newman's bank account number. I'll have $100,000 deposited that will trace back to one of Martin's competitors. Leave a note on his computer saying how sorry he is the secretary

died, and make him drink a bottle of his favorite alcohol before he eats his gun. Let me know how the attorney responds. He might have to be next if you can't keep this contained. We're too close to our deadline next week for any interference. M

Kaamil deleted the message and made three calls. The first to the team leader at the ranch who would take care of Sam Newman, and the second to the head of his security clearance division with instructions to find out everything about Adam Drake there was to learn. The last was to his head of security to follow Drake.

Chapter 11

Drake left the ISIS building and headed to his office, thinking about Kaamil's SLS and whether his cherished 993 could keep pace. His car handled better and, with all the improvements he'd made, could reach a top speed of 180 mph. But the SLS AMG could go from zero to sixty-two miles per hour in three point two seconds, with a top speed of 197 mph. Money couldn't buy you love, but it sure could buy you more speed.

Drake was still thinking about Kaamil's choice of transportation when he noticed a black Suburban like the one at ISIS in his rear view mirror. Suburbans are popular in the Northwest, but Drake was wary of coincidences. He downshifted into second gear just before the exit to I-5 and accelerated down the entrance ramp.

The Suburban cut in front of a UPS truck and followed. Drake caught a flash of the gold lettering of the ISIS logo.

Traffic was congested, and Drake kept several cars ahead of the Suburban as he entered the Terwilliger curves at a sedate five miles per hour over the speed limit. When traffic slowed for the curves, he spotted an opening in the middle lane that gave him a path to the next exit. Downshifting again, he rocketed through the opening and raced ahead to Exit 298, speeding down the exit ramp at seventy-five miles per hour.

At the bottom of the ramp, Drake took full advantage of his car's braking power, slid to a stop, turned left, and accelerated to catch up with the traffic heading up Macadam. He glanced in his rear view mirror and saw the Suburban was nowhere in sight.

The rest of the way to his office he assessed the situation, as if he were an operator again. Kaamil had every reason to be curious. He would have been, if their roles were reversed. Why act like his visit had been a surprise? Why point him to Sam Newman so quickly? Kaamil should have been concerned their security system failed and said they were investigating. He didn't even voice a concern about that. Something was wrong, and it had something to do with Kaamil.

Drake's office was on the Riverplace, a quarter of a mile south of the Rose Garden Arena. The Riverplace ran along the Willamette River next to a marina. The wide promenade was lined with shops and restaurants, and ended at the north end with an upscale hotel.

Before he married Kay, Drake lived in a condominium above a small bookstore that specialized in rare books. When he left the D.A.'s office, the bookstore became available after its owner died. He bought the bookstore and converted it into a law office, with the office and the condo connected by a back flight of stairs. The deck of his condo looked out over the marina and the river beyond. If he needed a break, a walk along the boardwalk did the trick.

After Kay found the old vineyard in Dundee, Drake rented the condo to his secretary and her husband, Paul. He often thought about living in the condo again, but Margo and Paul were happy there. He couldn't ask them to move. There was also the promise he'd made to Kay before she died, to replant the vineyard and restore the old stone farmhouse.

Drake pulled into his building's parking garage, entered the security code and drove up to his second-floor parking space. At the door to his old condo, he buzzed his secretary to let her know he was entering from the back stairs.

When he walked into his office, Margo greeted him from her desk.

"Good morning, or should I say, good afternoon," she said, without looking up.

Margo was the first secretary assigned to work for him when he'd joined the D.A.'s office ten years ago. She was a senior secretary then, and only available because the man she'd worked for had recently died of a heart attack. She'd been bitter, depressed and difficult to work with at first, but they had gradually warmed to each other and become a great team.

She was fifty, black, and a woman you did not want to mess with when she was in one of her moods. Her short hair was graying, but her eyes were as dominant behind her silver wire-frame glasses as they had ever been. Her dress code was always law-office professional. Behind her I'm-in-charge-here attitude, however, she had a warm heart for anyone who earned her trust.

"All right, Margo, cut me a little slack here. I've been away for a day and a half, and this morning has all been work."

"I'd be the last to know, as your formerly trusted and relied-upon secretary. As I've been telling your clients, I'll let you know how and where he is when I see the whites of his eyes, if they are still white, that is."

"Enough. I should have called. You win. Bring two cups of coffee to my office and we'll talk," Drake surrendered.

He walked up the stairs to the loft and waited for Margo to follow. The space had been the upper level of the bookstore and also served as the store manager's and bookkeeper's office. Now it contained his desk, bookshelves and a leather couch he slept on when he worked late and didn't want to drive home to the farm. From the half wall of the loft, he could look down on Margo's work area and the waiting area.

Margo walked in and set his coffee on the desk blotter. She sat down carefully, with her own cup, in one of two chairs in front of his desk.

"So talk," she said.

"I met with the manager at ISIS. Not a nice guy. He said I should look at the head of security at Martin Research. He didn't seem concerned at all that their security system malfunctioned and someone was killed there. When I drove here, they tried to follow me. And to top it off, when I got here I found my beloved secretary had developed a severe case of insubordination."

"Actually your secretary isn't insubordinate. She's scared, and isn't skilled at hiding it. Turn on the video cam and take a look at our friend outside on the bench."

The old bookstore owner had been pistol whipped by a robber and had installed a security camera over the front door. There were two monitors for it, one next to Margo's desk and another on the wall next to his.

Drake switched on his monitor and stared, clenching his fists. A muscular black man, wearing a black Trail Blazer T-shirt, black jeans and black running shoes sat on the bench, glaring at the front door through wraparound sunglasses.

"Doesn't look like a potential client, does he? Maybe I should see what he wants."

"Be careful. I doubt he's here because of your legal acumen. If he is, please refer him to someone else."

Drake dashed down the stairs, through the waiting area and pushed through the front door. In less time than it took for the watcher to swivel his head from a pretty girl passing by, he covered the distance to the bench.

"You need an attorney? You've occupied this bench for more than twenty minutes, without feeding the parking meter over there."

Drake stood with the sun at his back, a six-foot-two shadow looming over the thug. He noticed a crescent moon tattoo on the man's forearm, and calloused knuckles on both hands. Possibly a Muslim, but definitely a martial arts devotee. Drake resisted the urge to step back when the man stood, all six-foot-eight of prison-yard muscle and meanness.

"You got a problem, me being here? This a public place, ain't it?"

"Sorry," Drake said, as their eyes locked in stare down, two feet between them. "I thought you were trying to get up your nerve to come in and see me. If all you want to do is sit and stare at my front door, be my guest. If you change your mind, come in. And tell your boss he's welcome too."

Back in his office, he studied the watcher on Margo's security monitor. The man pulled a cell phone off his belt, talked for a few moments then walked off.

"Wish our security system included audio. I'd like to know who our watcher reported to," Drake said. "You okay?"

"Sure. You want me to send Paul a picture of this guy and see what he comes up with?"

"Couldn't hurt, although I doubt we'll see him again. He was here to let us know they know where we work. But let's be careful. I'm not sure what's going on. Keep the front door locked unless you know who it is."

Drake asked Margo to get Sam Newman on the phone and returned to the loft. He liked Newman, but he'd only talked with him for thirty minutes or so. Still, as a prosecutor listening to felons and to their attorneys, he had developed a pretty decent internal polygraph. Sam Newman didn't make his needle quiver.

Before he was halfway through the phone messages on his desk, Margo buzzed and said Sam Newman wasn't available, that she'd left a message for him to call.

Chapter 12

Since he'd learned Janice Lewellyn had been murdered, Sam Newman had not been able to sleep. Nothing on any of the surveillance tapes showed anyone in the building. The tapes were not just blank, as in nothing there blank, but as in turned off and nothing recorded blank. That could only happen if someone deliberately turned the surveillance system off, or the system malfunctioned. He guessed some hacker could have shut the system down, but there was no reason for anyone to do that. Everything that had any industrial value like research data, product development information—the company's intellectual property—all of it was secure and safe.

There was something he was missing. He just couldn't grab hold of it. He left the office early to think, trying to get away from the emotion numbing everyone at Martin Research, and returned home to walk his golden retriever, Copper. The mile-and-a-half walk with his tail-wagging companion hadn't helped much though.

His small bungalow in the upscale Orenco Station community was warm and professionally decorated, but it was just a place to live. He had retired from the Palo Alto police force after twenty-five years with a ruined marriage. Then he had been hired by his brother-in-law to make sure Martin Research and its employees were safe. In that he had failed.

Newman gave his dog fresh water, poured himself a double Smirnoff on the rocks and settled into his leather chair to watch the recorded video of his San Francisco Giants playing the Arizona Diamondbacks. Four to nothing, top of the sixth. He needed to see someone winning, because he sure as hell didn't feel like a winner at the moment.

He kept going back to his conversation with Drake, the attorney Martin had hired for crisis management. It didn't make sense that ISIS employed felons, but that's what his experience told him they were doing. He'd run all the background checks and found nothing. The men he suspected had clean records, but he didn't believe any of it for a minute. Prison changes men, and these men had the look of hard-time criminals.

Newman had pushed himself up out of his chair to refill his drink when he heard Copper bark and then whimper. His subconscious mind replayed the moment, identified the sound of a silenced pistol, then signaled danger just as a hooded man stepped from the kitchen in front of him. The 9mm Glock aimed between his eyes didn't waver when the man motioned with his other hand to back up.

"Return to your chair, Mr. Newman, we need to talk."

"I don't think so. I'm not used to talking with someone wearing a hood and holding a gun on me."

"I apologize for the hood," the man said, pulling it off. "I'm afraid the gun stays."

When Newman looked into the man's eyes, he knew this was not going to be a friendly chat.

"Put your tumbler down on the table and sit back in your chair. I'll get your drink refreshed, and we'll talk. Mohammed, pour Mr. Newman another double."

Two men walked from his kitchen, one taking up station at his front door and the other picking up his tumbler and returning to the kitchen. Both men wore black masks, jeans and black T-shirts.

"What do you want?" Newman asked quietly.

"Tell me about the attorney, Drake. What'd ya tell him?"

"Are you the one who killed Martin's secretary? Is this what this is all about?"

"No man, this ain't what this about. This about you feeling sorry for killing that secretary, then killing yourself. We just want to know what you got that attorney thinking about first."

Knowledge isn't always power, but Newman felt better knowing he knew his killers were from ISIS.

"I got him thinking you ex-cons from ISIS were somehow involved. When you kill me, he'll know for sure."

"Maybe, maybe not. A suicide and a note on your computer may make him think you're just one drunk old pig that sold out and couldn't live with it. Time will tell. Make it easy on yourself, old man, finish your drink. We got to be going."

Newman set his drink down and breathed deeply. He wasn't going to get out of this. If he could force them to shoot him, it wouldn't look like suicide. He started to bolt from his chair when hands grabbed him and forced him back. His head was pulled back and the bottle of Smirnoff was forced between his lips. As he struggled and gagged on the vodka, he prayed Drake would figure out it wasn't suicide.

He felt the barrel of the pistol push against his right temple.

Chapter 13

Drake finished dictating responses to phone messages for Margo to return, and punched her number on his desk console.

"Margo, would you dial Sam Newman again? If he's not there, go ahead and get Richard Martin for me."

In the time it took Drake to pull out a legal pad and make some notes about what he had learned, Margo rang back. Newman was still not answering his home phone and Mr. Martin was on line two.

"Richard, I'm sorry to have kept you waiting. Have you seen Sam Newman recently? I tried to reach him at home, but he's not there."

"Sam left an email saying he was going home to get some sleep. Didn't you talk with him this morning?"

"I did, and then I paid a visit to your security firm. I was told to take a look at Sam Newman if I wanted to know who had a reason to turn off the security system. You know what that might mean?"

"It means someone's blowing smoke up your skirt, trying to impugn Sam Newman. I hired Sam personally. I know his background, his personal story and why he's here in Oregon. Sam has no reason to do anything that would hurt this company."

"Why are you so sure about Sam Newman?"

"Because he's my brother-in-law. I hired him after my sister got tired of the hours he worked and divorced him. I've known Sam Newman for twenty years. Money's not important to him, and he loved working here."

"So you think he's just sleeping and not answering his phone?"

"He might be sleeping, that's what he said he was going to do. It's not like him, not answering his phone. More likely, he couldn't sleep and is out trying to find out who killed my secretary."

"All right, I'll keep trying to find him. Thanks for the information."

Drake hung up and asked Margo to get Detective Carson on the phone.

"Carson here."

"Anything new your investigation has turned up?"

"Hell Drake, I thought you were going to solve this one for me. I took a long lunch and just been waiting for you to call."

"Sounds like your work habits haven't changed much. I'm following up on something and need to talk with Sam Newman. Have you seen him recently?"

"Not since this morning, but then I do have more than one case to work on and may have missed him. You remember how it is to be busy, don't you counselor?"

"What I remember is how busy I was cleaning up your messes. That's what I remember, but thanks for all your help anyway."

"Anytime. I have to ask Newman some questions myself. If I see him, I'll try to remember to have him call you."

When Drake broke the connection, Detective Carson shouted to the homicide division's one secretary to get Sam Newman from Martin Research on the phone, pronto. He didn't know what Drake was up to, but this was his investigation and there was no way he was going to let Drake get in his way.

"Sorry, sir. Martin Research says he's gone home to get some sleep."

"Well, then call him at home. Did I tell you to quit trying after just one call? Jesus, do I have to come out there and do your job for you?"

Detective Carson sat fuming about the quality of his support staff when his phone rang again. Sam Newman wasn't answering his home phone. He slammed down the phone, grabbed his coat and stormed out to find Sam Newman.

The drive to Orenco Station took less than ten minutes in the afternoon traffic. Newman's house was in the middle of the block on NE 64th Ave., a brown two-story bungalow with a Chevy Trail Blazer parked on the street. Carson was mildly impressed. Orenco Station was where his last wife had wanted to live.

Carson rang the doorbell twice without an answer, then banged on the door.

"Newman, police. Wake up, open the door!"

When there was no answer, Carson tried the door and found it was open.

"Newman, Detective Carson. We talked this morning. You in there? I'm coming in."

Carson walked into Sam Newman's home and knew he wasn't going to get an answer. The old cop was sitting in his leather recliner with a .45 on the floor below his right hand. An empty tumbler was on the floor below his left hand. He was dead, no question. Blood and brain matter was on the wall and sofa to his left.

In the kitchen, Carson found an empty bottle of Smirnoff vodka sitting on the granite-topped cooking island, next to an IBM ThinkPad. With a pen from his pocket, he depressed the on-button and read the note Sam Newman left behind.

> I didn't mean for Janice to die. I'm sorry. I needed the money but I didn't want it to end this way. Sorry.

Carson walked to his car and told his driver to call in the crime scene investigators. Nice to wrap it up this way, but it was way too easy. Drake mentions Newman and he finds Newman dead. Drake or someone was way ahead of both of us, Carson thought. He'd have to figure out which tomorrow.

~~~

When Kaamil was told the old cop was dead, he emailed Malik.

> Newman is dead. I'm watching the attorney. My contact in the police department will let me know if they don't buy Newman's suicide. If they don't, the attorney is next unless I hear otherwise. K

Kaamil sat back in his office chair and smiled. Allah, and therefore Malik, would be pleased their plan was moving forward. The necessary death of one *kafir* didn't bother him in the least. This was what he lived for, to kill all those who had made his life miserable.

Nothing else in life had provided him satisfaction. Playing football had been his early passion. He was the best wide receiver in Oregon, with two state-championship rings, when he graduated with a scholarship to UC Berkeley. He tried drugs, enjoyed the girls and wound up suspended for most of his freshman year.

By his sophomore year, he was a starter, and by the third game, a star. He ran the forty-yard dash in three point five seconds, and at six foot seven inches, two hundred forty pounds, he was hard to stop when he caught the ball. He found it was more fun running over cornerbacks and safeties than outrunning them. By the end of that year, sports writers were already projecting him as a first-round draft pick.

Then, a damn, dumb white lineman who wasn't even a starter fell on his leg in spring practice and put him out for the year. He had worked hard rehabbing his knee, and then been asked to take a drug test. No one told him who'd talked to the coaches, but his best guess had always been someone on the depth chart wanting his position. That ended his collegiate career, and his last attempt to make the American system work for him legally.

With the NFL out of reach, the next quickest way for a young black man without a stellar academic reputation to make it was by selling drugs. It hadn't take him long to build a sizeable market among former teammates and other athletes in the Bay area. An irate high school coach put the cops on him and he was in prison before what would have been his junior year.

His two years in Folsom, however, proved to be the best years of his life. He found a religion that promised him personal peace and a way to strike back at a nation of fools.

Less than a week and this phase of the operation would be over. Allah willing, his latest plan would be satisfyingly accomplished.

Chapter 14

Thursday morning held promise, a clear sky and not too warm for a workout and run with Lancer. Drake was enjoying a breakfast of hash browns, sausage, and eggs when Paul Benning, his secretary's husband, called.

"Margo said you wanted to know if I heard anything about the murder at Martin Research. Their head of security committed suicide yesterday afternoon. He left a suicide note. Seems he was selling inside information. They found a recent deposit in his bank account for a hundred thousand dollars. Detective Carson went to his home, found Newman had been drinking. There was a gun on the floor under his hand, and a note on his computer said he was sorry for the secretary's death."

"Any forensics evidence, except for Newman's, on anything?" Drake asked.

"Not that they've found."

"That doesn't sound like the Newman I talked with yesterday. He wasn't defensive about anything, but he was suspicious of their security firm. He thought they were employing a bunch of felons with new Muslim names."

"You think he was just pointing you in another direction?" Paul asked.

"No, I felt he was genuinely concerned that his company's security had been compromised."

"Have you talked to Carson yet?"

"No. We have a history. I'd be surprised if I ever hear from Carson about this."

"Margo said you had a visitor. If you need someone at your office for a while, I can work something out. This whole thing's starting to hang together in a way I don't like."

"Paul, if I think we're in the middle of something, you'll be the first to know."

"Well, be careful."

"I will. Tell Margo I'll call her, when I head in."

Drake finished breakfast and thought about his meeting with Sam Newman. Why would he turn on his brother-in-law's firm for money?

He needed to talk with Detective Carson, as much as he disliked the man. Carson could run checks on the ISIS guards. If there was something there, Carson could follow up. If it was a dead end, he'd be able to tell Richard Martin his brother-in-law was a bad apple. It wouldn't do much for the company's security clearance, but that was something Martin would have to handle.

Drake found the card Carson had given him the day before and called.

"Detective Carson."

"Adam Drake. I heard about Newman. You have time for coffee this morning? Thought I'd share what I've learned so far, stuff you might want for your report."

"Appreciate your concern for my report, Counselor, but I've got this one covered. Doubt there's much you can tell me. Newman's suicide note made it pretty clear."

"Did you know Newman was Richard Martin's brother-in-law, and owned enough of the company's stock to be financially comfortable if the company did well? Why would he betray his brother-in-law and do anything to hurt the company?"

Drake waited for Carson to answer. "I didn't think you knew. We need to meet. How about the Starbuck's at Tanasbourne? I can be there in thirty minutes."

"You buy and I'll listen, but I don't think it's going to change anything. Thirty minutes."

After a short drive in the 993 and a quick call to let Margo know where he was, Drake pulled into an open space in front of the ubiquitous green and white logo of the world's largest coffee chain. Through the front window, he saw Carson sitting at a small table reading the paper.

Drake ordered a light house blend, added some cream and walked over to Carson's table. The detective was working hard to look as if he hadn't noticed Drake.

"Drake, thought you weren't coming," Carson said, looking down at his empty cup.

"Let me get you a refill. What are you drinking?"

"Grande cappuccino. Thanks."

When Drake returned, he noticed Carson's empty cup was a tall cappuccino.

"So, Counselor, what is it you want to share? You turn up something I missed that proves this wasn't suicide?"

"Carson, enjoy your coffee. I don't think you missed anything. Newman shared things with me he didn't share with you, that's all. He was a cop. He wouldn't tell you things you'd include in your report he didn't have evidence to back up. What he shared with me were suspicions, based on his experience and observations. I think you need to hear what he was worried about."

Carson ran a hand over his bald head and forced a smile.

"Drake, the man committed suicide. He must have been worried about a lot of things."

"Carson, if you want to write this off as suicide, be my guest. I'm not going to let my client be smeared in the press when they run wild with a story based on your incomplete investigation. If I prove this wasn't suicide, and you've closed the case, my only recourse will be to let the press know how you botched the job. You think your career will stand another embarrassment?"

Drake noticed Carson's clenched jaw and thought he'd just wasted a good part of his morning. He could manage without Carson's help, it would just take him a little longer. He got up to leave.

"Sit down, Drake. Tell me what you think Newman was worried about, and then get the hell out of my investigation. This isn't the only case I'm working."

Drake sat down and leaned forward onto his forearms, holding his coffee in both hands in the middle of the table. He didn't want the rumor of the day at Starbucks to be his mention of ex-cons at Martin Research.

"You can spot an ex-con walking down the street, and so can I. Newman could too, and thought some of the ISIS security guards had the look. When he checked, he found their records were squeaky clean. They all had new Muslim names and weren't from around here. He suspected their IDs were phony. I interviewed the ISIS manager to check it out, and got nowhere. I thought the manager looked like a felon too, although he's damn good at hiding it. I, for one, do not buy suicide. I talked with Newman around noon, and he was not depressed. He was tired and pissed that someone had messed with his company. He was blaming someone, ISIS predominantly, but not himself."

"Drake, I talked with Newman, too. He was anxious, upset, and distraught. That sounds like someone capable of suicide to me. If I'd banked a hundred thousand dollars for selling company secrets, I'd be anxious, upset, and distraught."

"Were you able to find out where the hundred thousand came from?"

Carson took a drink of cappuccino and looked out the window.

"Not yet. Looks like the money came from some offshore account. I'll admit it's a little troublesome the money was deposited after the secretary was killed. Just to humor you, let's say Newman's suspicions are true, why would the security company be involved?"

"I don't know. We know the security system was turned off. Only two people had the code to do that, Sam Newman and ISIS. Newman's dead, and I don't believe he committed suicide. I can't rule ISIS out, can you?"

Carson took another drink of cappuccino. When their eyes met, Drake could see Carson was considering what he was saying and didn't like where it might take him.

"I'll see what I can find out about the ISIS guards, the hundred thousand and sit on my report for now. You find anything that'll support your suspicions, let me know. Thanks for the coffee," Carson said as he stood and walked out.

Drake watched him walk to his unmarked Crown Victoria. He didn't think Carson was convinced that Newman hadn't committed suicide, but at least he seemed to be willing to dig a little more. It will be interesting, Drake thought, to see if he has the same impression of the ISIS manager. Carson's bullying manner should allow him to see the man's true colors, given what Drake had seen of Kaamil's arrogance.

Chapter 15

It was ten after two in the afternoon and Kaamil hadn't heard anything about Sam Newman's unfortunate suicide from his source in the police department. His source at KOIN, the CBS Portland affiliate, hadn't heard anything either.

Kaamil stopped pacing in front of his office window, returned to his desk, and picked up his phone.

"Get me that detective out in Hillsboro, Carson, I think. Tell them it's about the Martin Research investigation and don't let them tell you they'll give him the message. I need to talk with him today."

He didn't have time to play phone tag with the police. He had to report to Malik that he had the situation covered, or he would have to send a team to take care of the nosey attorney. If the man wanted to stick his nose where it didn't belong, he was all too happy to cut it off, along with the rest of his head.

"Sir, Detective Carson's on line one."

"Detective Carson, Kaamil Sayf. I'm the regional manager of ISIS. I wanted to check in and see if you needed anything from me for your Martin Research investigation. I know you probably want to wrap that up as quickly as possible."

"I think I have most of it worked out, Mr. Sayf. I am curious about one thing, though. As I understand it, there are two people who have the code to turn off the security system at Martin Research, you and Sam Newman. Is there anyone else who might have access to that code?"

"We have the code, certainly, we installed their system. There are several of my employees who have access to the Martin Research system codes in case there's a need to get into their system for some reason, but it's not something that's just lying around in our office. Why do you ask?"

"The system was turned off the night Mr. Martin's secretary was killed. I'll need the names of your employees who have access to those codes."

"You're wasting your time if you think someone here turned off that system. How about Sam Newman? What's he saying?"

"Unfortunately, he isn't saying anything. He's dead."

"How unfortunate."

"You knew the man, you know any reason someone would want to see him dead?" Detective Carson asked.

"You think someone killed him?"

"Could be. You going to give me the names of your employees with access to that security code, or do I need to get a court order?"

"Don't threaten me, Carson. Do your job. Stop looking for some nigger to pin this on," Kaamil said, and slammed down the phone.

Damn it, he thought, if the police weren't buying Newman's suicide, he'd just have to give the lazy cop a little more evidence to convince him. And now, there was clearly a need to take care of the attorney. Even if his death raised suspicion, they were too close to be stopped now by some snoopy counselor who wouldn't let well enough alone.

Chapter 16

Drake was tired. Since his drive to the coast two days ago, it felt like a week had been crammed into the last forty-eight hours. After a tedious morning and most of the afternoon, he decided to head home early.

He relaxed a little as he drove toward home, settling into the slow flow of traffic. On the weekends, traffic from the city to the winery tasting rooms was becoming so heavy the state was considering building a bypass and putting a toll booth on the old highway to take advantage of the area's attraction. Drake hated the idea. The charm of the place wouldn't last long if it became as accessible as a shopping mall.

The red hills around Dundee and Carlton had vineyards before the Prohibition years forced farmers to switch to crops they could sell. The region flourished again after a couple of UC Davis pioneers re-discovered the area in the 1970s. Since then, the valley running south for a hundred miles was home to over two hundred vineyards growing pinot noir, pinot gris and chardonnay grapes that wine lovers couldn't seem to get enough of.

When he reached the old farming town of Dundee and drove past the tasting rooms flanking the two-lane highway, the fire station, and the lone store, he turned off on Worden Hill Road and followed it past the old red barn at the Maresh vineyard. His twenty acres were just around the bend. They rose above the road on a southeasterly sloping tract that caught both the morning sun and the ripening warmth of afternoon rays. Perfect for growing grapes, as soon as the old vines were pulled out and new ones planted.

A sigh of relief escaped his lips as he slowed and turned left up the long gravel driveway of his property. Midway, an old barn hunkered down near a stand of oak trees. Beyond it, the driveway ended in a turnaround below the front of the old stone farmhouse.

Behind the house was a building that had been originally built to house a small winery. There were steps leading down from it to a wine cellar that connected the winery building to the main house. Drake used the winery building to garage the 993 and Kay's Land Rover LR3, but he didn't keep wine around long enough to need a wine cellar. The wine cellar had proven, however, to be a handy way to make it to the house when it was raining hard.

As he stepped out of the car, Drake heard Lancer charging toward him from the back porch of the house.

"Hello Lancer," he said, reaching down to scratch behind his ears. "How was your day? Run off any of those pesky deer trying to eat our grape vines?"

Standing with his head almost to the tips of Drake's fingers, Lancer stood still except for his tail. Bred to be a world-class personal protection dog, and with rigorous training for *Schutzhund* competition, he was the perfect home security system. Pity the poor intruder who mistook his calm manner and underestimated his violent capabilities.

"Come on boy, let's get you some dinner."

After changing into an old pair of jeans and a dark blue polo, Drake filled a dog dish with the high energy food Lancer favored and poured a glass of 2001 Beaux Freres pinot for himself. Watching Lancer devour his meal, he settled into his dark brown leather chair next to the river rock fireplace in the kitchen and thought about dinner. Maybe broil a salmon steak, steam some rice, and make a salad sounded about right, if he could muster the energy to get up and fix it.

With a shake of his head, he got up, refilled his glass, and took a salmon steak out of the refrigerator. He splashed lemon-dill sauce over the salmon, started water to boil in a saucepan for rice and put the oven on broil.

As he sat on a stool at the kitchen counter, he thought about his new client. Richard Martin was a good man as far as he could tell. He was doing important research, and thought he'd hired the best security service his company could afford. Still, his secretary had been murdered in his office. Now his brother-in-law was dead. None of it made much sense.

He was missing something. The part of the puzzle that troubled him most was ISIS. If Sam Newman didn't have a reason to shut off the security system, neither did ISIS. There had been no apology for the system malfunction, if that's what it was, just an attitude that was strangely disconnected. If Martin Research was one of my major clients, Drake thought, I would sure as hell be more involved in the investigation. Maybe tomorrow he would see it differently, but right now he was trying to see to the bottom of a very muddy pond.

After dinner, he went outside and sat on the covered front porch that spread across the front of the house. From there, he could see down to the road and beyond to the Cascade mountain range in the east. To the south, the neighboring vineyards were identified by green rows of grape vines stretching across their acres. For him, it was like being at the beach, mesmerized by the waves.

When the shadows started to lengthen, Lancer finished patrolling his domain for the day and returned to the porch. Drake was asleep in one of the two Adirondack chairs, his chin down on his chest. After standing next to his master patiently, Lancer finally licked his left ear and growled softly. His master opened his eyes and smiled.

"You might cut a guy a little slack. You do this all day, if you want. I try it for a few moments, and you wake me up. I get the message. Tomorrow, when I'm rested and run your butt into the ground, you're going to wish you had let me sleep."

At 2:00 a.m., Lancer was again trying to wake Drake, his muzzle nudging Drake's left shoulder insistently.

Drake was awake instantly. He recognized his dog's signal there was a threat outside somewhere. He quickly pulled on a pair of jeans, a T-shirt and his running shoes in the dark. From the dresser next to his bed, he took his Kimber .45 in its soft leather holster and stuck it in his jeans. He also put his Harsey tactical folding knife in his right front pocket. When he was ready, he extended his right hand palm down and waited for Lancer to touch his nose in its middle. When Lancer returned the ready signal, Drake snapped his fingers softly with the search signal.

He knew Lancer would silently locate the threat, inside or out, and wait for his command before taking any action. It was up to Drake to decide what that action needed to be.

Chapter 17

Drake followed his dog through the house to the front door. Lancer stood pointing outside. From his still and steady stare, Drake knew the intruder was somewhere in front of the house.

He reached down to pat Lancer and considered his options. He could wait for something to happen, turn on the floodlights, or slip outside to identify the intruder. Since Lancer rarely alerted him to the occasional black bear that wandered across the farm, it wasn't likely the visitor was four legged. Using the floodlights would probably scare the intruder away before Drake had a chance to see who it was. That left slipping outside, and choosing action over anxiety.

He turned and ran to the stairs leading from the kitchen to the basement, and then to the tunnel and the winery building. In less than a minute, Drake cracked open the side door on the north end of the building and peered out into the darkness. Over the pounding in his ears, the first sign of an adrenaline rush, he heard a car somewhere in the distance and a whisper of breeze in the tops of the tall fir trees behind the building, but nothing in or around his house.

Thirty yards across an open grassy area, a small copse of oak trees stood on the northern edge of his property. From there, he'd be able to see ninety percent of the sloping ground in front of the house. Drake kept Lancer at the heel, and ran across to the oak trees. The short, early summer grass absorbed the sound of their movement and cushioned his knee when he knelt in the trees' cover to search for the intruder. When he reached out to Lancer, he felt the raised hair on the back of his neck.

Drake looked for any movement around the house. Lancer's body stiffened against his leg and turned to the right, toward the gravel driveway leading up to the house. Drake focused his eyes in that direction and spotted three men moving single file in the grass along the driveway. With the light of a thin crescent moon, he could see that the two men in front carried rifles. The third man had something shorter, stockier, maybe a MP5 submachine gun.

When the group reached the point where the driveway began its sweep to circle in front of the house, they paused for a moment, then separated. Two men broke off from the group to circle the house, while the third crept toward the front. Drake thought the third man was the leader, from the way he directed the other two with a wave of his hand. By separating, they gave him a chance to pick them off one at a time. He felt his training take over and, magnified by the rush of adrenaline, a sense of confidence he hadn't experienced in a long time. He didn't welcome the confrontation, but he knew his chances of prevailing were as good as theirs.

Drake moved down through the oak trees, keeping his eyes on the man circling the house on the north side. When the man stopped beneath his bedroom window, Drake gave Lancer a finger-down, palm-back signal in front of his nose. Lancer would stay and protect his back as he crept forward to deal with intruder number one.

With a slow, deep breath, Drake moved within a yard of his first target. The man was looking to his right and left, carrying an AK 47 at port arms. A bulge beneath its barrel identified a grenade launcher. Whoever these guys were, they weren't here for a routine burglary. Nothing he owned was worth killing for, and no one knew enough about his military training to bring this kind of fire power.

Drake leaped forward and drove his right fist into the man's kidney. As the intruder bent backwards from the blow, he swung his left forearm around his neck and his right hand behind his head. When he was able to hook his left hand in the crook of his right elbow, he pulled back in a stranglehold. The man dropped his rifle but fought to escape. Drake pulled him backwards off balance and whispered in his ear.

"Keep fighting and I'll break your neck. Who sent you?"

The man answered by throwing his left elbow over his shoulder at Drake's head, violently wrenching his body from side to side.

Drake tightened his hold, to choke out his attacker.

"Keep fighting, and you're going to take a long nap."

The man dropped to his knees and tried to pull Drake over his shoulders. The maneuver was a military move taught in third-world countries, and when he whispered *"Allahu Akbar,"* Drake realized the man was prepared to die before surrendering.

"One last chance before I break your neck."

When the man threw his hands back to claw at Drake's face, Drake powered his right forearm down and pulled quickly back on his left, breaking the man's neck.

As the body went limp, he softly snapped his fingers for Lancer to join him. The man circling the house on the other side wouldn't stay there long before getting a signal to enter.

Drake ran quietly across the parking area at the back of the house and peered around its corner. The second man was standing with his back to the house, looking to his left, waiting for a signal from his leader. In the shadows, Drake saw the man wore the same dark clothing and carried the same weapon as the first man. What were they after? Perhaps he could learn the answer from this second man.

He patted Lancer's head, signaled for him to stay and protect, and slipped around the corner of the house. The second man was a foot taller than the first, but slower in his movements. Drake had moved to within six feet of the killer when he turned and started to swing his weapon around.

Before the man could warn his leader, Drake took a quick step forward, knocked the weapon aside and head-butted him on the bridge of his nose. While the man was still stunned, Drake slipped behind and applied the same stranglehold he'd used a few moments before.

Refusing to be subdued, the man struggled to claw at Drake's eyes. In less than ten seconds, he also lay dead.

Drake ran back to the other side of the house, away from the gravel drive. If he could slip back into the oak trees and get behind the man at the front of the house, he had a chance to neutralize him and find out what this was all about. That chance was slim, however. The leader would be suspicious by now that something was wrong.

Staying next to the back of the house, he ran until he again reached the stand of oaks. From there, he could see the third killer walking slowly toward the veranda in front of the house. He was twenty yards away, two first downs, about the distance he used to run to chase down quarterbacks who tried to run away from him before they were sacked. The only difference was this QB was armed.

Instinct and old training prevailed. Drake charged at the man with his .45 drawn and pointed center mass. As a Delta Force operator, he'd learned to run, shoot, and keep shooting until the target was down. Now, he just wanted to get close enough to gain the advantage and convince the man to drop his weapon.

The man finally reacted to the sound of the charge, and started to turn around.

Lancer was five or six feet to Drake's right, ready to launch himself at the intruder when Drake gave the signal.

"Lancer, kill!"

Drake wanted Lancer's attack to knock the man down. Once he was on the ground, he would have a chance to reason with him. But the man brought up his MP5 to shoot the closer of two moving targets.

Big mistake, Drake thought. No one shoots my dog. He fired twice and dropped the man before Lancer landed at his throat.

In the silence that echoed in his ears, Drake called off his dog.

"Lancer, leave. Good boy," he said, patting his head until he felt him start to relax.

After he kicked the MP5 away and couldn't find a pulse, he pulled off the killer's black ski mask. He was a black man, mid-twenties, with a scraggly goatee. There was nothing in his pockets except a blue, prepaid Motorola TracPhone.

Drake circled the house and searched the other two men, while Lancer sniffed their bodies. Like the first, both carried no identification and were also black men in their twenties. By the time he finished, the adrenaline rush hit and he willed his muscles to relax.

He needed to stay focused. It wasn't unusual to hear gunshots where he lived, but the last thing he needed was a zealous neighbor calling the police. He needed to decide what to do with three dead bodies.

Drake listened for sounds of any remaining intruders. When Lancer stopped casting his eyes back and forth and sat next to his right leg, he started over to the driveway where a black Suburban was parked next to the old barn. He moved at a fast walk, with his .45 drawn, until he reached the right rear of the SUV. Satisfied that the SUV was empty, he opened the door. No light came on and the interior was empty. Whoever these guys were, at least they were smart enough to shut off the interior lights. They had even left the keys dangling from the ignition.

Drake relaxed and holstered his .45. On the way back to his house, he considered the situation. The approach to his house by the three was military style, albeit crude, and they weren't there to rob him. So who were they?

If they were any of the felons he'd convicted while a prosecutor, they would have waited and tried for him in town, drive-by style. Those men, though convicted, weren't street stupid. They would leave calling cards and make sure everyone knew it was them. There were no personal enemies he knew of, so what was this about?

By the time he reached the house, he decided his situation was too complicated for local law enforcement to handle. The City of Dundee relied on the Yamhill County Sheriff to enforce its laws. He'd spend the next week trying to convince a room of deputy sheriffs he hadn't mistakenly killed three trespassers. If he got Detective Carson involved, and there was any possible tie to Martin Research, he'd probably wind up in jail. That left the Senator. He'd want to know if this somehow involved his friend, Richard Martin, but maybe he could pull a few strings and get him out of this mess.

Chapter 18

In the next half hour, Drake loaded the three bodies in the Suburban and drove them into the outbuilding. When the sliding door was closed, he laid each of them out on the concrete floor and placed their weapons beside them. He'd leave the forensic stuff to others, but at least for now, they were out of sight.

Back in the house, he made sure Lancer had a full bowl of water, and went directly to his study to call his father-in-law. It was 3:00 a.m. He hoped the Senator was a light sleeper.

"Don't think you've ever called me this early. You all right?"

"Not exactly sir, can we talk?"

"Give me a moment to get downstairs."

While he waited, Drake thought about what he should say over an unsecured phone line. He'd be careful, but the Senator needed to know his predicament.

"Okay, fire away, while I start some coffee. Something tells me I might not get back to bed for a while," Senator Hazelton said.

"Three uninvited visitors came calling an hour ago. Unfortunately, this was the last call they'll ever make. I could use some help deciding how to clean up the mess they left."

After a long pause, the Senator asked, "Their intent wasn't friendly?"

"You could say that. My reception wasn't either."

"You think this is related to the matter I asked you to look into?"

"Possible."

"I see." After another long pause, the Senator said, "Are you saying your visitors will be staying for a while? Maybe permanently, if we're not able to make other arrangements?"

"I don't see them going anywhere," Drake said.

"Let me make a call or two and see if I can help. You all right in the meantime?"

"I'm okay. I've stored their things. I'll wait for your call. Use my cell phone number."

Drake didn't know who the Senator would call, but he was relieved to know help might be on the way. He started his own coffee maker, and suddenly realized he was hungry. He poured a tall glass of orange juice, filled a bowl with Cheerios and milk, and sat down to refuel himself.

With a shudder, he felt anger boil up. He had controlled his emotions because he knew, unleashed, anger got you killed. Now it raged within him, like a rogue wave smashing against the rocks. Whoever was behind this would regret it. He was trained to hunt and he was starting to get a scent again.

Drake was drinking his second cup of coffee when the Senator called.

"I have arranged for transportation for your guests. In maybe thirty minutes, you'll get a call. The person will ask you to confirm that there are three passengers and a dog named Lancelot to be picked up. Correct her mistake about your dog's name. After you've bundled your guests off for the night, call me. We'll find time for coffee tomorrow."

Drake almost smiled. The Senator sounded as if he'd been handling cleanup operations his whole career. His years on the Senate Intelligence Committee certainly would have exposed him to the ways of covert ops. Perhaps there was a side to the Senator he needed to know a lot more about.

Thirty-five minutes later, Drake's phone rang.

"Mr. Drake, I've come to pick up three passengers and someone named Lancelot. Does that mean I will have four passengers?"

The voice was soft and meant to sound servile, but the tone of authority came through loud and clear.

"The name is Lancer. He's my dog. He'll be staying with me, so there are only three passengers. Is that something you can handle?"

"Very good, sir. I think we can handle your problem. We should be there in another five minutes," the female voice said. "It would be helpful if you would leave a light on for us."

Drake put the phone down, hoping he hadn't made a mistake asking the Senator for help. The woman he talked to had handled the call efficiently. There was something in her voice that said she didn't appreciate what she was being asked to do.

In less than five minutes, Drake spotted two white Suburbans pulling into his driveway. They slowed as they approached the turnaround in front of his house. When the lead vehicle stopped, the front passenger door opened and a woman stepped out.

She was tall, with long brown hair. In khaki pants and blue windbreaker, she looked law-enforcement confident walking his way.

He stepped out his front door and walked down to meet her.

"I'm Liz Strobel, Mr. Drake," she said as she reached him. "I'm told you have a problem and need our help."

Drake shook her outstretched hand. Her eyes were light blue above high cheekbones, and her lips were full but pressed tightly together. Ice Lady was the identifier that first came to mind, but maybe cold and tough better described the woman. Whatever she was, she wasn't wasting any time taking control of the situation.

"Who are the men you brought with you?" Drake asked.

"The men are Secret Service. We're handling the advance for Secretary Rallings's Seattle and Portland visits. We were closest when Senator Hazelton called him and asked for help."

"And who are you?" Drake asked.

"I'm the Secretary's executive assistant. I was FBI before the Secretary asked me to help him pull together DHS. Don't worry Mr. Drake, I've been around. I have field experience. I know what I'm doing."

"And what are you doing here, on behalf of the DHS Secretary and Senator Hazelton?"

"Mr. Drake, I was told you might have killed three men you think might be connected to the murder at Martin Research. Your father-in-law and the Secretary think if there's anything to your suspicions, they should look into it. If it turns out you killed men who didn't have a clue the Secretary was coming to town, we'll turn it over to local law enforcement. If there is a connection, we need to know it, so the Secret Service can protect the Secretary."

"I didn't know the Secret Service protected Cabinet heads," Drake said.

"After 9/11, the Secret Service reports to the Secretary, not to Treasury. The Secretary has declined full protection, but a small detail accompanies him when he makes public appearances. Now, why don't you tell me what happened," Strobel said, stepping back and crossing her arms across her chest.

Drake knew about VIP visits from his days in the D.A.'s office. Protection details didn't have time to investigate ancillary matters when they were in the field. Something else was going on, not just the murder of Richard Martin's secretary.

"You got here pretty fast," Drake mused. "Is there something you know about these guys that I should know? Has someone threatened the Secretary, or the Senator? Do you think this is somehow related?"

"Mr. Drake, the sun will be up in two hours and ten minutes. I'd like to be out of here by then. I'll tell you what little I can. U.S. and Canadian intelligence agencies believe terrorist cells are planning assassinations of North American politicians, in response to our targeted killings of terrorist leaders around the world. The Secretary of Homeland Security is a natural target. We're looking into every possible threat real aggressively. Now, will you show me the bodies and explain what happened?"

Drake nodded and motioned for her to follow him around the house to the outbuilding behind. Liz Strobel, in turn, signaled her team to drive along behind them. He was stalling to some extent. He wasn't sure how much he should say, in case Miss Executive Assistant decided this was a local matter and didn't want to be involved. She hadn't Mirandized him, but everything he told her would wind up in a report, somewhere. On the other hand, if he didn't convince her this was connected to Martin Research, and therefore somehow involved the Secretary or the Senator, he'd find himself explaining it to other investigators. Better to trust the Senator, he decided, and tell the lady what she wanted to know.

Chapter 19

Drake led the procession to the outbuilding, pulled the sliding door aside and allowed Strobel and her entourage to inspect the three bodies. After a quick look, three of the men knelt down and began a careful search of the bodies. One man started recording images with his digital Leica, while another stood aside, speaking softly into a personal recorder. The two remaining Secret Service men searched the Suburban and examined the weapons on the ground next to it.

Liz Strobel watched the men work for a moment, then walked over to Drake's side.

"Let's go inside and talk. I could use a cup of coffee if you have any," she said.

Drake stepped aside at the door and let her walk ahead of him into the kitchen.

"Nice place. You don't see many stone farmhouses around here," Strobel said.

"My wife gets all the credit for the house. She loved this place. So you don't scare yourself, that large dog standing silently behind you is Lancer. He won't hurt you."

"Is that right, Lancer?" Strobel asked, and slipped off the stool to pet him.

Lancer didn't move, except for the hairs that spiked up on the back of his neck as he growled deeply.

"Lancer, down," Drake commanded quickly. "Sorry, forgot you might be armed. He's trained to smell guns and attack if he thinks there's a threat. After what he's experienced tonight, I should have taken time to introduce you."

Drake walked over and patted his dog's head.

"She's okay, Lancer. Kiss and make up."

Lancer did as he was told and held up his right paw, which was gingerly shaken once by Liz Strobel.

"Lancer was quite a hero tonight. He probably saved my life when I ordered him to attack the third man. The guy tried to shoot him instead of me. But as you can see, he's just a marshmallow."

"Had me fooled," she said, moving quickly back to her stool.

Drake poured them each a cup of coffee and sat down across the breakfast bar.

"All right, Ms. Strobel, what would you like to know?" Drake asked. "Do you need background about my work for Martin Research, or just information about tonight?"

"Why don't you tell me why you think these three men came here tonight," Strobel said, sipping coffee from the cup held in both hands in front of her face.

"I don't know why they came here, but I think I may know who sent them. I think it's the security firm that Martin Research uses. I visited their Portland office yesterday afternoon to question them about the security system failure right at the time Richard Martin's secretary was killed. The manager tried to throw the blame on Martin Research's head of security, man named Sam Newman. Within hours, he had committed suicide.

"I met with Sam Newman yesterday. He was convinced the security firm, ISIS, was responsible for the security system being turned off. He also thought ISIS was sending felons to work security details there.

"By the time I got back to my office today, there was a large, black weightlifter staking out my front door. Tonight, three black men, with scraggy beards, come gunning for me. I don't know how it's all connected to Martin Research, but the dots do seem to connect."

"And you think this security firm is somehow involved with the murder at Martin Research?" Strobel asked.

"Yes. And that's what their head of security thought, as well."

Strobel set her coffee cup down and walked to the window, looking at the Secret Service agents working in the outbuilding. He knew what she must be thinking. How had he killed three men who were heavily armed, in the middle of the night, two of them with his bare hands? Why hadn't he just called the police and waited for help?

Drake wasn't prepared to answer those questions. Some of it, she might learn, if she looked in the right places. Most of it, she would never understand. Strobel said she had "field experience." But his field of experience and hers were miles apart. She was trained to protect herself when in harm's way. He was trained to be the harm in his enemies' way. He was the hunter, and hunters didn't sit around waiting to be hunted.

"Why did you kill these men, Mr. Drake?"

"I think that's obvious, don't you? They were trying to kill me."

Before she could ask another question, one of her men came to the back door and asked her to step outside where John Mason stood waiting.

"I don't know what's going on here, but it doesn't look like these three came to steal his TV. They were armed like a team of S.E.A.L.s. From some of the tattoos, I'd say they've seen hard jail time. What does he say happened?" Mason asked.

Mason was the senior member of the Secret Service detail handling the advance preparations for Secretary Rallings. With his bald head and barrel chest, he looked like an old professional wrestler who became a bouncer. His voice, however, carried all of the authority of a drill sergeant.

"Without a trace of remorse, he said he killed them because they were trying to kill him. He thinks it's related to a murder at Martin Research, the place the Secretary is visiting. He thinks it may involve the security firm the company uses."

"Well that's just swell. We have less than a week before the Secretary gets here. Now, a murder at one of his stops, and the company's attorney kills three black men on his farm. Three possible Muslim ex-cons, judging from some of their tattoos and facial hair. We don't have time to sort this out. Can we change his schedule, come back later in the summer?" Mason asked.

"He won't go for it, John. The monitoring system Martin Research has developed is one of his pet projects. The dedication ceremony at the chemical weapons depot is a big deal in this part of the country."

"Then you better make sure you convince me this situation isn't a threat to your boss or I'm calling the whole thing off. You know I can," Mason said over his shoulder, as he walked back to his men.

Strobel went back into the house. Drake was still seated at the kitchen counter drinking his coffee.

"I'll need some time to sort this out, so I'm going to take their bodies, weapons and vehicle. The Secret Service will handle this initially, but I don't want anyone else knowing about it until I get some answers. If this is leaked, I'll have to turn it over to the FBI. Do you understand?" she said abruptly.

"Does this mean you're not going to be finishing your coffee?" Drake asked.

"Mr. Drake, I'm doing your father-in-law a favor. I honestly don't care if you spend the rest of your life in jail for using deadly force here tonight. My only interest right now is finding out if this poses a threat to my boss. Here's my card. Call me if you learn anything," she said, as she laid her card on the counter, and left to join the men waiting in the Suburbans idling outside.

Drake looked at her card: Special Executive Assistant to the Secretary of Homeland Security. Impressive, for such a good-looking, conflicted young woman. Beauty and brains, tough outside and yet she was puzzled by how he could actually kill someone instead of waiting for the police to arrive. She'd handled things with obvious authority tonight, but Drake wondered how long her position could protect him when pressure started to build. If ISIS was behind the men sent to kill him, it wouldn't be long before they were missed and someone started asking questions.

If he wanted to stay ahead of this mess, he needed some answers, fast.

In the lead Secret Service Suburban, John Mason unloaded on Liz Strobel. "Liz, I'm not sure what we're doing here, but I think we just stepped in a big pile of shit. We're removing evidence from a probable crime scene. We can't hide these bodies for long, and I don't know what to make of this guy Drake. You don't take out three men the way he did without special military training. That dog looks like it's just about as well trained as he is. We're going to have to know a hell of a lot more about Drake and the men he killed tonight, before I'm willing to let the Secretary come here," he said.

"I know, John. When we get back to the city, I want you to take the bodies to our field office. See if we can identify any of them. I'll request a full background check on Drake and arrange to meet with the local Joint Terrorism Task Force sometime today. We have some leeway here, but I want to make sure we're not just doing a political favor for an old friend of the Secretary."

In fact, that was one of her biggest concerns. The Secretary and Senator Hazelton were allies in the battle to make the country safer from terrorism. She knew they traded favors from time to time, but that was the way things worked in Washington.

What concerned her now was that Secretary Rallings had involved her in something that might not have anything to do with national security. Drake was smart enough to get his father-in-law to help him cover up manslaughter, at the very least, by pretending it had something to do with terrorism.

She wished she knew more about the man. When she was with the FBI, she'd been around men who had killed in the line of duty. Tough as they were before a shooting, she'd seen numb shock on their faces afterwards. None of them had been as calm as Drake. He didn't seem to have any reaction or feelings about what he'd done. The only thing she'd noticed was a smoldering look of controlled anger in his eyes.

He hadn't tried to impress her in any way. She was used to the effect her looks had on men, especially when she was flashing her DHS credentials. Drake hardly seemed to notice. He just made sure she understood what had happened on his farm.

Fascinating, she thought, as she settled back in her seat beside Mason in the lead Suburban. She had a job to do, but if getting to know Adam Drake was part of it, well then, that was just a plus.

Chapter 20

Kaamil stood in the dark, looking down at the lights along the street below that wound through the office park. It was the quiet hour before sunrise. He had spent the night in his office after leaving the house where his three jihadists were preparing to go after the attorney. The three were among the first group of ten trained at their facility east of Mount Hood. Each had proven to be proficient with the weapons they were provided, from knives to rocket-propelled grenades. There was no reason they should have had any trouble killing one attorney asleep in his farmhouse.

But something was wrong. They should have called as soon as the man was dead. A slight delay might be expected, but not a delay of two hours. Kaamil felt the creeping dread of failure swirl around him, like fog rising at sunset.

His cleanup team handled the security chief at Martin Research without a problem, and he expected this team to dispose of the attorney just as easily. If they were arrested, they had the number of an attorney who would immediately notify him. If the mission had to be called off for some reason, they were instructed to call before turning back. None of these things had happened. None of them.

Kaamil took a deep breath and turned back to his desk. He sat down and began another encrypted email to Malik.

The men I sent after the attorney haven't returned. They haven't contacted me and I fear they won't. What do you suggest? K

Twenty minutes after he hit send, his screen signaled a message.

These men must not be traced back to us. Find out what happened and where they are. If they aren't dead, make sure they are. If they are dead, create a diversion. Call our friends and have them protest Muslim discrimination, profiling and police abuse of deadly force. Turn up the heat and the media will do the work for us. We only need less than a week without interference. Use the fear of bad publicity to slow the police down. M

Kaamil pulled up the list of friends Malik referred to, and began a series of calls. By the time the morning commute was over, there would be an outcry from the Muslim community about three brothers who were missing. The media would pick it up in time for the evening news, and would make the weekend a busy one for every law enforcement agency eager to prove they weren't responsible.

Once again, Kaamil marveled at the wisdom of their leader.

Chapter 21

Drake woke, after three hours of sleep, and headed to the kitchen for a cup of coffee. Most of what he'd brewed the night before was still in the pot. After two minutes in the microwave, it almost tasted fresh. He added a splash of milk and sat down at the counter to think.

He'd replayed the night in his mind over and over again, from the moment Lancer alerted him to the moment when the Secret Service left. It wasn't the three men he killed that had troubled his sleep. It was the unknown person who sent them that kept his mind racing through the night.

That and the anger he felt at the return of violence to his life. He had walked away from it in disgust after politics took over the war in Iraq. Now it had returned, uninvited. Tonight had been about reacting, a response learned from experience, and he didn't regret what he had done. They just picked on the wrong guy. What bothered him most was knowing it wasn't over, and that he couldn't walk away from it this time. It wasn't going to leave him alone until he put a stop to it.

Which meant he had to find out who killed Richard Martin's secretary. If he found her killer, he would also find out why someone wanted him dead. The only lead he had was ISIS and its manager. He would just have to keep an eye on them, especially the manager.

After a shower and shave, Drake dressed in his casual best—jeans, dark blue T-shirt and his favorite Nikes. He reloaded his .45, threw two spare clips in his gym bag, along with half a dozen protein bars, two liters of bottled water and a pair of old Zeiss binoculars. On the way out, he made sure Lancer had food and water for the day, and left for town in Kay's Land Rover LR3. If they were watching for his Porsche, her white Land Rover wouldn't attract their attention.

It took him almost forty-five minutes through morning traffic to reach the office park across SW Meadows Road from the ISIS office building. He found a parking spot with a clear view of the underground parking entrance and exit for the ISIS building, and settled back to watch. It was something he had done many times before.

For an extraction or targeted killing, he and his team would spend weeks watching their target before they made their final plans. In the Middle East, they often watched from a distance, sometimes as far away as half a mile. In Europe, they were able to set up surveillance much closer, being able to blend into the environment. It had been much the same in Central and South America. But the watching was always the same, learning the movements of their target, the comings and goings of the people around him, the routines they followed. Some of the time there were unexpected occurrences, and plans had to be adjusted. But they usually knew enough to know how the target would react to the unexpected.

This time, Drake didn't know anything about his target, if that's what he was, and didn't have a clue about his routine. All he had was a hunch that the ISIS manager, or his company, was somehow involved. Drake watched as cars started driving into the underground parking lot of the ISIS building. Just before the cars turned to descend the ramp, Drake had a full frontal view of the car's passengers. Through the Zeiss lens, he could clearly see the face of each person. So far, he didn't recognize any of them.

Just before 9:00 a.m., two black Suburbans turned into the parking lot and headed toward the underground parking ramp. Drake sat taller as he focused on the driver of each SUV. None of the men looked familiar, although the Suburbans were identical to the Suburban that came to his farm, minus the gold ISIS logo.

By 10:00 a.m., Drake still hadn't seen the black Mercedes SLS roadster he thought the ISIS manager was driving. The roadster had been parked in the only reserved spot, and had to belong to Kaamil. He was the only one Drake had met with an ego big enough to drive the powerful and expensive car. If anyone was going to show him what ISIS was up to, it would be its manager.

Drake was so caught up with his surveillance of ISIS that he almost forgot to let his secretary know where he was. With one hand, he scrolled to his office number and called Margo.

"I didn't want you to worry, but I may not be coming in today. I'm looking into the security company Martin Research uses. Not sure how long I'm going to be tied up. If you need to reach me, though, I'll be available."

"This is a new pattern, you not coming in, and calling me after the fact. Does this have something to do with that goon waiting outside yesterday?"

"I don't know, maybe. I had some trouble at the farm last night. It might be better if you didn't go out a lot until I get back. Let Paul know you're alone in the office today. I'll explain when I get back. If you get a call from Detective Carson, or a Liz Strobel, from the Department of Homeland Security, give them my cell phone number. Otherwise, just take a message on the rest of the calls. Tell them I'll call them back next week."

"What's going on, Adam? I don't like what I'm hearing."

"Everything is going to be all right, Margo. Just make sure you know anyone you let in the office. Wait for me to report in. I should be finished with this by sometime this afternoon."

He hated making her worry, and he didn't want to involve her any more than he had to. If the Secret Service couldn't keep things quiet for a little longer, Margo would bear the brunt of the initial questioning. The less she knew the better. He didn't think she was in any danger, but if she had to be somewhere, she was safe in his office. The office had steel doors with electronic locks, both front and rear, and she could monitor the surveillance cameras.

For now, all he could do was sit and watch. If ISIS was involved, someone was going to get nervous when their boys didn't report. Maybe they would do something that would lead him to whoever was responsible for the murders.

While he watched the ISIS building, he turned on the radio and took a bottle of water from his gym bag. It was going to be a long day. He settled back and turned on the news. What he heard made him sit up and crank up the volume.

"KEX news has just learned that a crowd of Muslim protesters is rallying outside Portland police headquarters, protesting the disappearance of three young Muslim men after being detained by the police. The spokesman for the group, the imam of a local mosque, is claiming that the three young men were detained by the police and haven't been heard from since. Portland Police Bureau spokesman, Brad Williams, told our reporter they don't know anything about three Muslims being detained, for any reason. He said they definitely do not have any information about three Muslim men disappearing while in police custody. Williams said, however, they are looking into the allegations."

You smart SOBs, Drake thought. If you don't know what's happened to your men, get the media involved. Claim the police are responsible and let the police do the work for you. Since 9/11, no one wanted to be accused of discriminating against Muslims. Even if there was evidence the men he'd killed were terrorists and posed a threat to the Secretary of DHS, Strobel wouldn't be able to hold off a police inquiry for long.

He had less time now to find out what the hell was going on. It was almost 11:00 a.m. He hadn't seen anyone of interest, coming or going into the ISIS building. He'd give it another hour, and then he would have to figure out another way to get inside ISIS.

At 11:15 a.m., a black Suburban pulled out of the underground garage and turned east on SW Meadows Road toward Lake Oswego. Drake decided to let it go. It was just a hunch, but everything involving Martin Research was located to the west. He didn't think Kaamil would drive one of the Suburbans when he could take his roadster. The black SLS was a driver's car, and there was no reason to choose a glorified station wagon over a real car, if you had the choice.

At the bottom of the hour, Drake watched the second black Suburban leave the parking garage and turn west. Just before it turned out of the ISIS lot, Drake caught a glimpse of the driver and decided to wait a little longer. The man behind the wheel was at least sixty and looked like an accountant, not someone Kaamil would send on an important errand.

Just before noon, the black Mercedes roadster pulled to the top of the underground ramp, hesitated for a moment, then accelerated out onto the road in front of the ISIS building. It was Kaamil. Drake started the Land Rover and fell in two cars behind the black roadster as it turned west onto Kruse Way and then north onto I-5, headed into the city.

The roadster maintained a steady speed through the Terwilliger curves and continued on toward downtown Portland. Part of him wanted to pull alongside, wave, and see how Kaamil reacted when he saw that Drake was alive. Instead, he followed at a distance to keep from being noticed.

When they neared the Markham bridge crossing over the Willamette River, Drake allowed a couple of cars to cut in front of him. I-5 continued over the bridge, but the freeway also split left into the city center and onto I-405 toward Mount Saint Helens. If Kaamil didn't want to be followed, all he had to do was wait until the last moment and swerve to the left or to the right up over the bridge.

The roadster waited until the last moment, then crossed over into the right-hand lane, taking I-5 over the river. Drake followed, and watched a minute later when it took another right onto I-84, heading toward the airport.

Traffic on I-84 was more congested than on I-5, and he had to pay more attention to his driving to make sure he wasn't spotted. He maintained pace with the Mercedes, but changed lanes frequently, and accordioned the space between the two cars. Kaamil, however, continued at a steady sixty-five miles per hour in the middle lane. Before much longer, Drake knew he would either take the exit to the Portland International Airport or continue traveling east.

When they reached the exit to the airport, Kaamil stayed on I-84. The freeway soon opened up and became a two-lane, winding speedway following the Columbia River up the gorge to Hood River. It was just the road for a car like the Mercedes SLS.

Wherever Kaamil was going, Drake was committed to following him. One way or another, he had to know if Kaamil was the man who sent killers to his farm.

Chapter 22

Despite the opportunity to drive faster, the black roadster held to a steady seventy miles per hour. Drake hardly noticed the Columbia River as it sliced through towering cliffs on either side. It was the only river that cut through the Cascade mountain range and allowed passage to the Pacific. Its beauty was lost on Drake, however. He had slipped into the role of the hunter.

When he was with Delta Force, he pursued the targets his government provided him, without question and without emotion. It had simply been his job. Now, he was pursuing someone and it wasn't his job, and there was a lot of emotion.

As he drove past the Cascade Locks and the Bridge of the Gods, two hundred yards behind Kaamil's roadster, his vibrating cell phone startled him back to the moment.

"Can I assume I won't be seeing you later today?" Margo asked.

"I'm sorry, I should have called. Something's come up. Everything okay there?"

"If you mean, do I have any more threatening men sitting around, the answer is no. Unless you count my husband, who's mad as hell you didn't let us know someone tried to kill you last night. Where are you?" she demanded.

"Margo, you and Paul have every right to be angry. I'm sorry. I'll explain everything, as soon as I can, but I need to know how you heard about last night. Is Paul there?" he asked.

"No, he isn't. A friend of his from the FBI called and asked if we were okay. He asked if there had been any trouble at the office that we needed help with. He assumed we knew what was going on, since we might be in danger, living in the condo above your office and all. Good thing we have friends, don't you think?" she asked.

Her anger stung him, but he didn't have the time to make amends.

"I'm on I-84 in Kay's Land Rover following the ISIS manager up the Columbia. I said I was sorry, and that's all I can say right now," he said, in a voice that didn't invite a response. "If that woman from DHS calls, don't tell her where I am. I don't need any interference. Everything is going to be all right, I promise. I'll call you when I'm headed back to town," Drake said and ended the call.

Everything will be all right, Drake thought, just as soon as I find the SOB who tried to have me killed.

Kaamil was still holding to a steady seventy miles per hour as they passed Viento State Park, and then began to slow. Seven miles later, he slowed even more and pulled off I-84 into the small town of Hood River, self-proclaimed windsurfing capital of the world. Apples and pears had been the main staples of the local economy before the fierce winds blowing down the Columbia started drawing windsurfers from all over the world. The town was now dominated by board shops, restaurants and microbrew pubs. There weren't many businesses, however, big enough to need a security firm like ISIS.

Drake stayed a block behind Kaamil's roadster when it turned left at the first intersection and drove down toward the river. Kaamil continued on, past a vast parking lot that served as a staging area for the windsurfers. Vans and

SUVs with roof racks, and old Volkswagen campers were everywhere. Beyond them, a couple hundred colorful sails skimmed back and forth across the water. For a moment, Drake had the sinking feeling that maybe it was Kaamil's day off, and he was here to meet someone for an afternoon of board sailing.

Kaamil drove past the parking lot and pulled up in front of what looked to be an old, abandoned warehouse. The warehouse was surrounded by a chain link fence topped by barbed wire, with a gate that appeared to be locked, blocking Kaamil's entrance.

Drake pulled to the curb just beyond the town's riverside Expo Center and watched. Within a minute, a man dressed in a dark blue shirt with lettering above the left pocket, a dark blue baseball hat with matching lettering, and jeans hurried out and opened the gate. When Kaamil pulled through the gate, the short Hispanic man stood at attention with his head bowed, and then stayed at the gate as Kaamil drove in and stopped next to the building.

When the guard stayed at the gate, Drake drove to the end of the street and made a U-turn that brought him back past the warehouse. He pulled into the parking lot of the Expo Center. He pulled out a map and looked over the top of it toward the warehouse. Moments later, Kaamil came out of the warehouse with another man and got into Kaamil's car. For a second, Drake had the feeling he knew the other man. Thick black hair, stylishly trimmed, sunglasses, and a gold chain flashing at his throat, the man looked like a Latin movie star dressed in a denim shirt and blue jeans.

There was one street leading away from the warehouse, and it ran right in front of the Expo Center parking lot. When Kaamil and the warehouse man drove past, Drake lowered the map and followed in the Land Rover. Up the hill to State Street, and then left on First Street, Kaamil drove slowly, looking for a parking spot.

The light traffic in the small town and the two turns Kaamil had made left Drake only one car behind the black roadster. If Kaamil pulled into an open space, he would have no choice but to drive by to keep from being spotted. If that happened, he'd be lucky to find a space of his own close by.

At the next intersection, Kaamil turned left onto the one-way Oak Street. Midway down the block, he pulled into an open space in front of a restaurant called Taco Del Mar. It was the only open space on the block. The only thing Drake could do was drive around the block and hope to catch sight of them, or find somewhere to watch Kaamil's car until he returned to it. Either way, he'd come too far to lose the man now.

Drake drove back to Second Street, then an extra block down State Street and tried again to find a place to park on Oak Street. Every parking space was full on both sides of the street. It was looking like finding somewhere to watch Kaamil's car was his only option, when a pickup pulled out from the last space on the left side of the street. Drake quickly pulled into the vacated space and searched for Kaamil or his passenger. He couldn't see either man, but he did have a clear view of Kaamil's black roadster parked on the other side of the street in front of the restaurant.

Tourists moved up and down both sides of the street, in and out of the sport shops and T-shirt emporiums. Drake noticed some of them checking out sandwich board menus displayed in front of several of the street's restaurants. That had to be where Kaamil went, he thought, taking his Latino friend to lunch. There were three restaurants he could see, but only one offered him a full view of its occupants. Taco Del Mar was an unpretentious fish taco stand with a counter along the back and wooden picnic tables scattered throughout the seating area. The front of the restaurant was open, with a pull-down overhead door to close up at night.

Two of the first tables were occupied by young couples wearing short wetsuits turned down to the waist and T-shirts. A couple of families took up another three tables, with the adults at one table and the kids at the other two. At the last table in the rear, two men sat with bottles of beer in front of them. Kaamil had his back to the street, leaning across the table to talk with his passenger, who sat facing toward the street. The man still had his sunglasses on, but Drake again had the feeling that he knew the man somehow.

He was tempted to use the binoculars he'd brought along, but decided it might attract too much attention from some passerby. Instead, he dug out Kay's digital camera from the center console and switched it on. He focused the zoom lens on Kaamil's car. When its image was clear, he set the camera on the dash and flipped out the side LCD screen. He could see Kaamil's table clearly without having to hold the camera.

Drake sat back in his seat and watched the two men. They were still talking and drinking their beer when a waitress brought two plates of tacos to their table. Kaamil didn't acknowledge the waitress, but his passenger removed his sunglasses and smiled broadly, saying something that made the young woman laugh. With his sunglasses off, there was no question in Drake's mind where he'd met the laughing Latino. He had convicted the man of meth production and distribution, the attempted murder of a prostitute, resisting arrest, and assaulting a police officer. He was surprised Roberto Valencia was out of prison. He had been sentenced to fifteen years, and even with good behavior, should still be behind bars.

Young Valencia was the son of Armando Valencia, one of the drug-smuggling kingpins operating out of Mexico.

Armando had been a top lieutenant of Amado Carrilo Fuentes, when *El Jefe* died accidentally after a botched plastic surgery operation in 1997. Armando moved aggressively out on his own, and was soon moving tons of drugs from Columbia through Mexico into the United States. He was also the first to recognize the tremendous profit potential in manufacturing and distributing methamphetamine in large quantities, along smuggling routes already established for other drugs.

Meth, produced in sophisticated super-labs capable of turning out enough for sales of $750,000 to a million dollars a day, soon became Armando's largest income producer. When the super-labs were targeted by the DEA and frequently raided, Armando used his Mexican gangs to smuggle the meth and allowed others to take the risk of production.

Armando's son, Roberto, was born in California, the first child of his first wife. Armando had a habit, however, of marrying the prettiest girl wherever he lived. He remained faithful until the police were too close to capturing him. Then he moved on. Each time he settled down after escaping capture, he celebrated his freedom by starting over, with a new wife.

After Roberto graduated high school in Los Angeles, he tracked his father down in Mexico and told him he wanted to learn the family business. Four years later, Armando sent his son to the Northwest to oversee his meth network there. That's when Drake met the young man. He had been arrested for trying to kill a prostitute who failed to please him. Further investigation connected him to a number of other crimes, including the sale of methamphetamine. Drake convicted him of attempted murder and assorted drug charges.

That was five years ago. Drake saw Roberto had lost his youthful appearance, but he still had style. Even in jeans and a denim shirt with the sleeves rolled up above the wrist, his heavy gold chain and gold Rolex made him look like a rich playboy. What he and Kaamil had in common, Drake could only imagine. Whatever it was, he doubted it was legal.

~~~

Kaamil wasn't a huge fan of Mexican food, but Roberto loved fish tacos. Roberto said it reminded him of growing up in Los Angeles. So, they ate fish tacos. Roberto was too valuable to their plan to upset.

"Are you ready?" Kaamil asked, drinking a little of his Corona.

"Don't worry, enjoy your taco. I know the routines of the security guards, and their families. My men have even been in their homes. My men will do what I tell them."

Kaamil watched Roberto carefully. He wasn't concerned about Roberto. The man would put a bullet between the eyes of any man in his gang who disobeyed him. Behind the good looks and quick smile was a man who enjoyed inflicting pain and killing people, especially young women. Kaamil had buried enough of them at the ISIS ranch, as a favor for Roberto, to know. He was concerned about Roberto's men. They were the ones who had to blackmail the targeted security personnel, and maintain control of them when their families were taken hostage.

"Do they understand there can't be any witnesses, not even children? We'll have to leave the country if there's anyone left to identify us."

Roberto finished his second taco and lifted his Corona to his mouth, running the rim of it back and forth over his lips. Kaamil thought his eyes looked like the eyes of a rattlesnake, unblinking and deadly.

"What is it you're worried about, Kaamil? Are you worried my men won't get your guys in, or that your young martyrs will chicken out? Decide Paradise isn't worth dying for?" Roberto said, with a sneer. "You would do better to worry about your own men."

Kaamil forced himself to remain calm. He thought, when this is over, I'll kill you myself. What could you ever know about dying for a righteous reason? The only god you're willing to die for is money, or maybe good sex. That's why we will win, Roberto, that's why we will win.

"Oh, I do worry about my men, Roberto. I worry their sacrifice will be wasted if you let me down. If you do, I will have to kill all of you. That's just my worry. I need to get back to Portland. You need to get to the ranch and make sure everything is prepared for Malik's arrival tomorrow. If you let him down, make peace with your god, you won't live another day.

Chapter 23

While the two men were busy eating, Drake called his secretary.

"Mr. Drake's law office. He's not practicing law this week, he's out pretending he's Superman. May I help you?"

Drake suppressed a smile. "You know you weren't supposed to tell anyone about the Superman thing. If it'll make you feel better, this is all on the clock, so there's a possibility you'll be paid this month. Is your husband there by any chance?"

"Just one moment please," she said, mimicking a receptionist at the D.A.'s office they used to joke about.

Drake knew she used humor to cover her feelings. He imagined this time those feelings were probably anxiety and fear. He had to stop thinking he was the only one involved in what was happening. Margo was more than his legal assistant. She and her husband were friends.

"Afternoon, Adam. Margo tells me you're in Hood River. What's up?" Paul asked.

Drake pictured him standing ramrod straight next to his wife's desk, with his square jaw clenched, waiting for an answer.

"Sounds like I have some fences to mend when I get back."

"She's worried about you. We both are. She's not used to guys gunning for you and hanging around the office. She wasn't exposed to that, even when she worked for you in the D.A.'s office," Paul reminded him.

"Paul, I'm sorry. I had no idea this was going to turn out this way. Margo told you, I followed Kaamil, the ISIS manager, to Hood River this morning. Well, I'm watching him have lunch with someone you may remember, Roberto Valencia."

"Sure, I remember the punk," Paul said, after a moment. "Young Mexican drug dealer, son of that Mexican cartel leader. I thought he was still in prison. What's he doing with the ISIS guy?"

"I don't know yet. I'm not getting warm fuzzies, watching these two breaking bread together. Valencia's sentence was fifteen years. Can you find out when he was released and what his parole officer says he's supposed to be doing? I saw him come out of an old yellow warehouse here in Hood River, down on Portway Avenue. Maybe someone in the department knows someone up here who can tell us who owns the building. Don't tell them why you're interested. Valencia may have bought some friends here."

"I'll make some calls. If things take a turn, let us know what's happening, or Margo says don't come back. I guess she means she wants you to keep in touch," Paul said.

"Tell her I promise."

Drake focused again on the two men. When Valencia turned toward the street, to watch two young women in cutoffs and bikini tops walk by, he took two quick pictures of his leering face. Both men then got up and strolled toward Kaamil's black roadster.

Before the two got there, Paul called back.

"Valencia was released six months ago. Good behavior apparently means you get ten years off your sentence. His parole officer thinks he fled to Mexico, only reported in once. The warehouse you had me check belongs to ISIS, according to the Hood River PD."

"What a surprise, Kaamil's in business with Valencia."

"Well, there's more. The warehouse is leased to a farm supply company. One of its key customers is a ten-thousand-acre ranch that ISIS owns and uses as a regional training facility."

Strange that an international company like ISIS would locate a training facility in such a remote area, Drake thought. Even stranger that it had connections to a known drug smuggler.

"Paul, I have to go. Kaamil's leaving with Valencia. Find out as much as you can about this training facility and call me back."

Drake watched the roadster pull away from the curb and followed in the Land Rover. Kaamil turned right at the light on North Second Street and retraced his route back to the old warehouse. There, he pulled through the gate and let Roberto out. Kaamil didn't get out of his car, and as soon as Valencio entered the warehouse, made a U-turn and drove back out of the fenced warehouse yard.

At the Expo Center where he'd parked again, Drake decided to stick with Kaamil. He knew about the warehouse. Now it was time to see what else Kaamil was doing in Hood River. As he started to pull out, he saw a yellow Hummer H2 drive out of the warehouse from the delivery bay.

Drake hung back until the Hummer drove by. He could see both cars ahead of him and hoped they were both going the same way. That hope didn't survive for more than a minute. Kaamil pulled onto the I-84 ramp back to Portland. Valencia continued on to Hood River.

Now what, he thought. Follow Valencia and see what he's up to, or stay with Kaamil. As much as he wanted to stay with Kaamil, his instinct told him to follow Valencia. Besides, Valencia was making it easy for him, driving the biggest SUV you could buy, painted bright yellow.

Valencia turned onto I-84 headed east, and then took the exit for Hwy. 35 heading south toward Mount Hood. Drake hung back a hundred yards or so as the highway passed through the outskirts of Hood River and then became a two-lane highway running through farmland. The twists and turns of the winding road interfered with his line of sight at times, but he was able to stay close enough to catch occasional glimpses of the yellow Hummer.

Leaning down until his nose almost touched the steering wheel, he could see the snow-capped peak of Mount Hood rising above, dominating the skyline through his windshield. From his farm, he could watch the distant peak turn pink with a good sunset. When you were near the mountain's base, it dwarfed everything around it.

Before they reached the small town of Mount Hood, maybe ten miles from Hood River, the Hummer's brake lights flashed. Drake was two hundred yards behind when it turned left, off the highway. As he passed by, he saw a manned security gate, a twelve-foot cyclone fence with a barbed wire crown stretching out on both sides of the gate, and an enclosed guardhouse. Next to the cement and river rock guardhouse, an elegant sign made of black lava rock with brass letters announced the location of the ISIS Pacific Northwest Regional Training Facility. Admittance was by appointment only. Before the gate disappeared from view, Drake watched in his rear view mirror as the Hummer was waived through.

He drove on until he saw a gravel road where he was able to turn around. Before he pulled back onto the highway, he called his office. Paul answered.

"Glad you're still there. This is really starting to smell. Kaamil headed back to Portland, so I followed Valencia. He drove south of Hood River, and right into a restricted area operated by ISIS, their Northwest Regional Training Facility. Security guard, cyclone fence, the works. Valencia was waived right through. You ever heard of the place?"

"No, but if they're hiding something there, they're smart enough to keep under our radar. I was able to find out that the Hood River PD does a lot of their training there. It has a practical firing range, a shooting house that simulates real urban situations and a tactical driving course. We've never used them, but a lot of the smaller police departments do," Paul answered.

What's going on, Drake wondered. ISIS trains cops but lets a convicted felon drive right in with a wave of his hand. He rubbed his face for a moment, then turned to look down the road toward the ISIS facility.

"Okay, find out whatever you can about this training facility. Anything else on Valencia?"

"Nothing new, but I generated a lot of questions about why I wanted to know as soon as I started asking around. My guess is there must be a current investigation under way. Guys who were always straight with me got real vague when I asked for specifics. Pissed me off, to tell the truth. The guys I called owe me. One of them asked if I was making inquiries on your behalf."

Drake was quiet for a moment. The Secret Service must have enlisted the help of the FBI, and details of the attack on his farm had gotten out. He'd have to see if Liz Strobel could keep a lid on things a little longer.

"I can't get involved in a criminal investigation right now. If you're asked what you know, say it's all privileged, attorney-client work product, that you're helping me on your off-duty time, okay?"

"I will," Paul said, "but I'm not sure I like it. Margo works for you, and you know we'll do anything we can to help. But I can't put my job on the line."

Drake heard the concern in his voice and understood it for what it was.

"Paul, I won't ask you to do anything that puts your job in jeopardy. I'm not paying Margo enough to support you both. I'll make sure you and Margo are kept out of it."

Drake stared in the direction of the ISIS front gate after he ended his call. He was promising the two people he was closest to that there wouldn't be unintended consequences that involved them. There were always unintended consequences. The only thing he could think of to prevent there being too many was to find out what was behind the security gate down the road.

Chapter 24

Roberto Valencia was still fuming as he drove through the gate at the ISIS Regional Training Facility. Having to pimp for wannabe black jihadists and bringing in young women to pose as virgins, for a taste of Paradise, was bad enough. Having to suffer the condescending manner of Kaamil was more than he could stand.

If his father hadn't ordered him to cooperate with these Muslim clowns, he would have killed the first one of them to disrespect him. He knew their kind. He saw them in prison, getting special privileges, eating special food, having special prayer time. They even got special shower privileges, so they could shower without being seen by other inmates. If he'd had his way, his prison gang would have shanked all blacks hiding behind their prison-found religion.

But, business was business. The Middle Eastern jihadists controlled a lot of the drug supply his father's cartel moved into America. Meth wasn't the only thing that made them money. Heroin was still popular, and the terrorist presence in South America was starting to limit the number of cocaine suppliers. If he had to put up with fools who wanted to take over the world, so be it, as long as they kept him in business.

He did have to give them credit, he thought, driving along the paved road leading to the heart of the training facility. The old cattle ranch had been turned into a first-class operation. The two-story red brick operations center, with its state-of-the-art communication capabilities, was one of the finest facilities of its kind. There was a firing range, a one-thousand-yard-long sniper range and a shooting house for live-fire practice. It also had a landing strip, long enough for private jets, a dormitory and a military-style mess hall.

Pulling up in front of the operations center, Valencia smiled at the clever deception of the place. In addition to its legitimate purpose training ISIS personnel and selected others, ISIS had a secret underground facility. It was used to train and house its own cadre of terrorists. That's where he was headed, to make sure everything was prepared for a last supper for the three men starring in next week's attack.

The front lobby was manned by a uniformed security guard, controlling entry to the offices and classrooms above ground. He also made sure no one wandered into the research lab below, where Valencia ostensibly worked as a contract research chemist. What a joke, he thought, passing him off as a chemist. The only chemistry he'd been around was in the meth labs he operated for his dad. If that's how Kaamil wanted to pass him off, it was okay with him. All he wanted to do was provide the cooperation his dad had promised ISIS, and live to enjoy another day.

The security guard looked up just long enough to recognize his security badge and wave him toward the sign-in roster on the counter. A retired cop who seemed unaware of the secret nature of the company he worked for, he had always been respectful.

"Afternoon Mr. Valencia, working today?" the man asked.

"For a while, Ken. I have some tests to finish, then I'm out of here. How about you, *como esta, bien?*"

"Sure, I'm okay Mr. Valencia. My son is bringing the grandkids to visit this weekend. The wife has been getting ready all week. Don't see them nearly as often as we'd like," the old man said.

"Have a good weekend," he said, walking to the elevator.

He knew what the man was talking about. He dreamed of being back in Mexico with his dad, and hoped he would be soon. The odds of pulling off Kaamil's plan successfully were slim to none. Maybe he even wanted it to go wrong, just to prove Kaamil wasn't Allah's chosen.

The elevator descended a floor and opened to a lab on the left, and storerooms on the right. Next to the lab door was a keypad and a handprint scanner that opened the electronic locks. He didn't know how many others were cleared to enter the lab, but from the look of the place, he was the only one to enter recently. Half windows ran the length of the front wall on either side of the door. There were two island counters inside, with all the usual lab equipment. Another door at the back of the lab was marked "Supplies."

Valencia pulled down the Venetian blinds on the front windows and went directly to the door marked "Supplies." When he entered the code into the keypad, the green light came on. He then placed his hand on the handprint scanner and placed his right eye onto the iris scanner. Ten seconds later, the lock on the door clicked open and he entered the secret lair ISIS used to hide and train its jihadists.

The lair consisted of a long hallway with two classrooms, four sleeping bays, a large locker room with showers, an exercise room, and a dining hall. The walls throughout were bare cement, and the gray vinyl floor tiles did little to brighten up the place. It resembled an old fallout shelter.

At the end of the hallway, another secured door led to an escape route. A tunnel ended at a ladder to a locked manhole cover. It opened at the base of a tree near the barbed-wire fence on the southern end of the ranch. If the underground facility was discovered, trainees could make their way to a nearby trailhead and disappear in the national forest that bordered the ranch.

There was also an armory with another tunnel leading to the airstrip, that allowed personnel to come and go without being seen.

Kaamil's plan for the big evening was to decorate the dining room to look like a harem's quarters. Fragrant garden flowers, screens depicting tiled harem walls, and satin pillows under soft lights were to be brought in. Natural-colored tent canvas would drape the concrete walls, and Persian rugs would cover the floor. No expense was spared to create the right atmosphere for the three young martyrs.

Valencia thought it was a waste, trying to create a fantasy for men who were certain to be killed. Even if they believed they were going to be met by adoring young virgins in Paradise, why give them their prize before they got there? Malik had developed a designer drug for Kaamil's men that combined the sense of confidence ecstasy provided, with the energy and aggression produced by meth. He doubted the men would need anything more to motivate them.

He was upset, though, that he would be wasting three pretty young girls. None of them would survive the evening. The effects of the drug potion and the stimulation of the evening would make their lovers hard enough on them. He knew Kaamil would not let them live to connect ISIS to the assassination plot.

Valencia quickly checked the armory, where the supplies and decorations for the send-off feast had been delivered. Everything was there and organized, just as he had ordered. With any luck, he thought, I won't have to come back here after next week. Partnering with these crazies was too dangerous. If they weren't killed, they'd wind up in jail, or hung. Either way, it was bad for business.

Chapter 25

When Valencia didn't come out of the ISIS training facility after half an hour, Drake drove back to Hood River. He hadn't eaten since breakfast. After picking up a sandwich and some ice tea at a drive-through Subway, he headed back to Portland.

Kaamil was up to something, that much was clear. He and Valencia appeared to be friends, but even that didn't explain what Valencia was doing at the ISIS training facility. Kaamil could be in business with Valencia, letting him use the warehouse, and ISIS might not know about that. But the security guard waved him through the gate, so someone at ISIS had to know about the drug dealer.

He hadn't learned anything today that got him any closer to tying Kaamil to the men sent to kill him. Hell, the most he could prove was the guy kept bad company. His instinct, though, told him Kaamil was behind it all.

The trick would be to get someone with the resources to investigate Kaamil and ISIS. For that, he needed something he didn't have—evidence of a security threat involving the Secretary or the homeland. Liz Strobel was only interested in protecting the Secretary, and then the country, in that order. He still wasn't sure he could trust Strobel, though. She hadn't done a very good job keeping his name out of things.

He would just have to go it alone for the time being. He'd operated solo before, and with the restraints on law enforcement, he might even be more successful. Things like search warrants and probable cause didn't apply to private citizens, as long as you weren't breaking the law. If you were real careful, no one would know even if you did.

As he drove past the historic Columbia River Gorge Hotel in its manicured gardens perched high above the river, Drake decided to call Liz Strobel. Even if he didn't trust her, she may have learned something that would help.

She answered on the first ring.

"I've been waiting for your call. Where are you?" she demanded.

"Hey, calm down. Was I supposed to take you to lunch or something? If so, I'm truly sorry. I forgot. How can I make it up to you?" Drake asked lightly.

"I'm not in the mood to play games with you, Mr. Drake. I'm the one that got stuck answering questions you should have been here to answer. Half the imams in this city are demanding to know what happened to three Muslim men they claim have disappeared. The press is demanding to know what we know. I'm trying to keep you from being arrested for murder."

"We need to meet. I stumbled onto something this morning you need to know. Can we meet for a drink, say in an hour? It's important."

There was a long pause. She was either trying to compose herself or considering whether to have him arrested.

"I've borrowed an FBI office in the Crown Plaza building. Is there somewhere close?" she finally said.

"Yes, but I don't want to be questioned by anyone from that office just yet. I know most of those guys. We need somewhere a little farther away. Are you staying downtown?"

"I'm staying at the Marriott."

"Why don't you go there? I'll meet you in Champions, the sports bar, say 4:30 p.m."

"All right, I'll be waiting to hear what you've learned. We've discovered a few things ourselves."

Drake hoped the things she'd discovered were more than just the names of the three dead guys. He didn't care who they were. He was anxious to know who sent them and why. That would give him a target.

Before he turned off I-84 an hour later, in Portland, Drake called his office. The afternoon traffic was starting to build, slowing him to thirty-five miles per hour as he crawled along through the east side of the city, with the bright afternoon sun in his eyes.

"Margo, I'm meeting the person from Homeland Security at the Marriott in a few minutes. I'll be back before the end of the day."

"Everything's quiet here. I may be gone when you get here. Paul's taking me to the coast for the weekend and wants to beat the traffic."

"Great idea, Margo. Tell Paul I said so. We'll pick up the pieces at the office next week when you get back."

"I'll try. Sorry if I've been snippy, I wasn't prepared for all of this. I'll be better next week."

Drake could hear the relief in her voice that she was getting out of Dodge for the weekend.

"You've been great, Margo. I wasn't prepared for it either. Have a glass of wine, enjoy a sunset and don't worry about any of this."

Margo had worried through too many nights, wondering if her husband would come home. Worrying about her own safety was something new. He was proud of the way she was handling it.

The Marriott was only a block away from Drake's office, but he decided to park the Land Rover at the hotel. The only place to park at his office was his reserved space, labeled with the unit numbers of both the office and his condo, where Paul and Margo were living. If someone ran the plates on the Land Rover, he didn't want them crashing through Margo's door to arrest him.

He tossed the keys to the valet parking attendant and walked directly to the elevator on the south side of the lobby. The hotel was busy for an early Friday afternoon. While he waited for the elevator, he looked around and saw the reason why. The hotel was hosting a day-long seminar with the catchy title "21st Century Health Insurance Trends." Most of the attendees were wandering around, probably looking for the nearest bar. Who could blame them, he thought. The best speakers never got scheduled last on a Friday afternoon.

When Drake's elevator stopped on the second floor, he saw that Champions wasn't crowded yet. Windows ran along the length of the east wall. Bar-height pub tables were placed to take advantage of the view of the river, and Mount Hood in the distance. The other walls were covered with sports posters, framed Trail Blazer uniforms, and sports memorabilia. Drake chose a table towards the rear and sat facing the door to watch for Liz Strobel.

Portland was known as America's Microbrew Capital, but when the waitress asked him for his order, he asked for a pint of Full Sail Pale Ale, brewed in Hood River. Should have joined Kaamil and Roberto and had a glass there, he thought. It might have saved a lot of time, for all of us.

Drake took a drink of beer and saw Liz Strobel walk in. With a quick look around the bar, she spotted him and walked briskly to his table before he could wave to her. She was wearing a black skirt and a creamy, long-sleeved blouse, and didn't look like someone who had just left her office. She looked like someone going out for dinner. Drake wondered if she had changed her clothes just for him. Whatever the reason, she had most of the men in the bar watching her walk to his table. If they knew this was just business, he thought, most of them would be lining up to introduce themselves the moment he left.

"Thanks for coming. I appreciate it," he said, as he stood and pulled out a chair for her. "Get you something, or are you still on the clock?"

"A glass of wine, please. Yes, I'm on the clock. I still have quite a mess to clean up, thanks to you."

"I didn't invite them to pay me a visit, remember? What's this about the imams raising hell? I thought you were going to put things on ice for a while."

"We tried," she said. "Someone with the FBI or the morgue must have tipped the press and the press contacted the imams for a comment or something. I don't know. My relationship with the FBI isn't as smooth as it could be. They think we're poaching on their turf. Someone in the office may have leaked it, to make us look bad. Your sweet little Portland hasn't helped the situation much either by ending their partnership with the FBI in the Joint Terrorism Task Force. Now the FBI is afraid to offend anyone in this city, especially Muslims," Strobel said.

The waitress returned and asked for her order.

"Wine please, 2002 Chateau St. Jean Chardonnay Reserve, if you have it," she said.

"You know your wine. You will have to try Oregon's chardonnays. We have some excellent ones," Drake offered.

"I grew up in California. Sonoma wines have always been my favorite. Didn't mean to offend Oregon," she said. "So tell me what you think you stumbled onto. I'd like to think there's something that makes sense of all of this."

"In a moment," he said as the waitress set her glass of wine on the table. "First tell me what you found out about my three visitors."

"The JTTF would like to meet with you tomorrow morning at 9:00 a.m. They're going to tell you what they want you to know. I can tell you that your three visitors have criminal records and were Muslim men who apparently converted to Islam while in prison. That's no surprise. We're trying to find out what they were doing here in Portland, but the imams are making that difficult with the ruckus they're raising. No one in the Muslim community is willing to talk to us. Now it's your turn."

It was about what Drake expected. Sam Newman had suspected a couple of the ISIS security guards were ex-cons. The men he'd killed had the scraggly facial hair of young Muslim men. He couldn't connect the two directly, but he doubted it was a coincidence Kaamil was a Muslim. All Muslims weren't criminals, of course, but it was a connection.

Drake took a drink of his ale and told Strobel what he'd seen in Hood River.

"You know about my suspicion that ISIS and its manager are somehow involved. I followed their head guy up to Hood River today. It's about an hour or so up the Columbia River Gorge. When he got there, he drove to an old warehouse down by the river and picked up a man for lunch. Someone I know, because I prosecuted him for smuggling drugs. When they finished lunch, Kaamil headed back to Portland. I followed the other guy out to the ISIS Regional Training Facility. The drug smuggler drove right in, past the security guard at the gate. There's no way in the world this guy should be anywhere near a legitimate security firm."

Liz Strobel turned to look out the window toward Mount Hood.

"Who's the guy you saw up there?" she asked, turning back.

"His name is Roberto Valencia. He's supposed to have skipped on his parole and be in Mexico, with his dad. I could report him and have him arrested, but we might never know what he's doing with Kaamil and ISIS."

"And his dad, who's he?"

"Armando Valencia, head of a powerful drug cartel in Mexico," Drake explained.

"And you think this guy or his dad is somehow involved? That's all I need right now. Drug cartels and terrorists trading drugs for weapons is one of our biggest headaches."

"I don't know much about his dad these days. That's something you could check out."

"I'm starting to wish I'd said no when you asked for this meeting. What do you know about this training facility ISIS has in Hood River?"

"Not enough. It's located on a big ranch. They train their guys for executive protection work and even do some training for law enforcement. It's got firing ranges, a track for evasive driving training, and an airstrip for small planes and executive jets. I had a friend check it out," Drake answered. "It sounds like a big-time operation."

"Anything else you think I should know before the meeting tomorrow? I don't want any surprises, after the problems I created when I agreed to take those bodies off your hands. The FBI hates it when we step in, then leave them holding the bag when we leave town."

"No, that's all I know. If you learn anything about ISIS or the Valencias before the meeting, I'd appreciate a call."

He watched her walk out before taking out his wallet to pay for their drinks. She reminded him of Kay in a lot of ways. She was tall, beautiful, and self-confident. Kay was passionate about teaching and Liz seemed passionate about her work with DHS. He hoped her passion was more about protecting the country than her career, though. If it was just about her career, she wouldn't risk it to save his neck. He would know tomorrow, one way or the other.

Chapter 26

Saturday morning started out to be a warm day. After a decent night's sleep and a run with Lancer, Drake treated himself to a chorizo scramble breakfast with chorizo sausage, red potatoes, sweet onions, jack cheese and three eggs at the nearby Black Walnut Inn and Vineyard. The scramble was only on the menu during the winter months, but he knew the owner, who was also the Inn's chef.

The Inn was designed to look like an old Tuscan villa, with ochre walls and a red-tiled roof. Set atop a south-facing ridge with a new vineyard planted below, it was one of the newest attractions in the area. Drake was able to enjoy it all without being a guest at the inn. To be neighborly, he had offered to cut his hourly rate in half if his legal services were ever needed. So far, he had the better end of the deal.

After fortifying himself for his meeting with the JTTF, he took his time driving into the city. Driving usually relaxed him. Today, his mind was wrapped around the puzzle of ISIS.

Thirty minutes after leaving the Black Walnut Inn, Drake pulled into the parking garage across the street from the Crown Plaza building and found a parking spot on the top floor. Shoppers were out early this Saturday morning, eager to work off their pent-up need to spend their week's earnings.

Walking across the street brought him to the security guard station just inside the building that housed, for the most part, government offices. Drake signed the register for visitors, took off his watch, put his wallet and keys in the tray, and walked through the metal detector. On the other side, he collected his things and took the elevator to the fourth floor. The elevator opened onto a reception area for the Portland FBI office.

"Adam Drake," he told the young receptionist behind a bulletproof glass enclosure, "I'm here to meet with Liz Strobel and the JTTF."

"I'll let her know you're here," she said, and punched an extension number into her console before saying, "Mr. Drake is here to see you, Ms. Strobel."

Before he had time to sit, a metal door with a security pad opened and Liz Strobel motioned for him to follow. She looked every bit the executive assistant of the Director of DHS this morning. She wore a camelhair jacket over a dark brown blouse and striped slacks. Her tightly pressed lips didn't allow a word of greeting to escape them.

Following her down a long hallway, Drake entertained the thought that her passion for her career had probably triumphed. Strobel walked ahead of him into a conference room where three men sat at a long mahogany conference table. There were only two pictures on the walls, a picture of the president and a picture of the twin towers before they collapsed. The American flag stood in the corner beside the two pictures. It was an appropriate place to meet with the terrorism task force.

Bruce Burton sat on the right side of the table across from where Drake stood. He had met Burton before, but hadn't dealt with him since he took over the JTTF. Six feet tall, probably two hundred pounds, he looked like someone who had played football in college, which he had. Burton played halfback at Notre Dame.

"Hello, Bruce," Drake said, reaching across the table to shake his hand.

"Adam," Burton said, shaking his hand without standing. "You've met John Mason from the Secret Service and on my left is Robert Jorgenson. He works with me on the task force. Have a seat. We have a few questions for you."

Jorgenson was the youngest of the three men on the other side of the table. A gung-ho FBI newbie, from the looks of him. Crew-cut blond hair, and a dark gray suit that didn't conceal a body hardened by hours in the gym. Baby-blue eyes he was trying his best to make look fierce. Drake gave him a nod that wasn't returned.

"Perhaps you could start by telling me why you killed the men who came to your farm last night?" Burton began.

"Self-defense, Bruce," Drake answered coldly.

"You could have called nine-one-one and waited for help. Maybe there'd be someone alive to question besides you," Burton responded.

Drake felt his pulse starting to race. It was always the Monday-morning quarterbacks who wanted to know why you didn't retreat.

"If I had waited, Bruce, the person alive right now wouldn't be me. Besides, the law doesn't require me to retreat before using deadly force against the imminent use of deadly physical force, and you know it," Drake said, quoting Oregon's law regarding deadly force. "You've read the reports by now, you know what happened out there."

"Oh, I think I have a pretty good idea what happened all right," Burton said. "You did what you were trained to do—kill the enemy before he kills you. John got the Secretary to obtain your service record. You might be a little rusty, but I'd say you're still an efficient operator."

Drake looked at the man across the table without reacting to his statement. Delta Force soldiers were known as operators. Their records were supposed to be sealed, to protect the identity of men who did things the government needed done. He wasn't happy that Burton knew enough about him to call him an operator.

"Look, I'm not here to bust your balls, Drake," Burton said. "But before we stand up for you with the press and the Muslim clerics, I have to be convinced there was no way you could have avoided killing those three men."

"My dog woke me up, signaling danger outside. I saw three men surrounding my house, armed with AK 47s and one MP5. Those are weapons I recognized. They are not used for peaceful purposes in the dead of night. My only chance against all three of them was to take them out one at a time. I tried to subdue them, but they kept fighting. One whispered *'Allahu Akbar'* with his last breath. The last one, the guy I thought was their leader, turned his MP5 on me at the last second. I didn't have a choice," Drake explained.

Glancing briefly at each of the others seated at the table, Burton said, "Why don't you tell him what we learned about these three, John."

John Mason leaned forward, opened the file in front of him, took out three photos clipped to NCIC printouts, and slid them across the table to Drake.

"You don't need to read their rap sheets," Mason said, "mostly robberies, assaults, carjackings and drugs. We identified them from their fingerprints, which were about the only things they hadn't altered since leaving prison. They converted to Islam in prison, took new Muslim names, and disappeared. Their parole officers didn't know where they were and had no idea why they were in Portland. They haven't broken any laws that we know of, since they left prison. Until last night, that is. That's all we know at this point. We don't know where they were living or how they've been supporting themselves."

Drake was surprised they had all been living with no known means of support and no new crimes they were being sought for. Usually felons either tried to go straight, at least initially, or reverted to their old ways of supporting themselves.

"Okay," Burton said, after Mason closed his file and sat back in his chair, "so these guys were bad guys, despite what the imams are telling us. You have any idea why they came after you?"

Drake met Burton's gaze directly and shook his head. "None of my old cases or anything I'm working on now would give these guys any reason to want me dead. The only possible connection, and it's nothing I can prove, is my poking around the murder at Martin Research, starting two days ago."

"Liz told us about you following this ISIS guy yesterday and the drug dealer he met for lunch. Why do you think this has anything to with the other night at your farm?"

Drake looked at Burton and smiled. "I don't believe in coincidences, or random acts of violence. I doubt that you do either. I visited the ISIS office Thursday afternoon, trying to find out what caused the security lapse at Martin Research. At about the same time, the head of security at Martin research was killed. Whoever did it, tried to make it look like a suicide. That same night three guys came after me. The next day I see the ISIS manager having lunch with a felon I convicted, who apparently has access to a private ISIS facility in Hood River. That's why."

"It's not against the law to have lunch with a parolee," the blond kid injected, rolling his eyes. "Maybe he was interviewing the guy for a job at their ranch up there, you ever consider that?"

"No hotshot, I didn't," Drake said, tired of the hostile looks he'd received from the kid since entering the room. "And if you were using the brain the FBI hired you to use, you wouldn't consider it either. ISIS can't hire felons and have firms that do secret research for the government as clients."

As the kid started to get out of his chair, Burton took control of the situation. "Sit down Jorgenson, and keep quiet. Maybe you can learn something."

Looking back at Drake, Burton continued, "The ISIS manager's meeting with someone you know is a felon doesn't impress me. Maybe he doesn't know the guy's a felon. I'm more interested in any information you might have that warrants my involvement. We're sitting on three bodies in the morgue. Ms. Strobel is concerned there might be a connection between the murder at Martin Research, these dead Muslims, and the Secretary's visit next week. You have anything that indicates a terrorist threat is mixed in with all of this? Anything that I should let the Secret Service worry about?"

Burton was a good man, but Drake could see why this meeting had been called. The JTTF and the FBI weren't about to jump into another terrorist investigation. Their last one blew up in their faces. They had arrested and jailed a Portland lawyer after a misread fingerprint linked him to a terrorist train bombing in Madrid. It cost the government two million dollars when they settled his lawsuit.

"You know the terrorism angle better than I do, Bruce. The dots are possibly there, but I don't see how they're connected," Drake admitted, and watched relief flood over Burton's face.

"Good. Glad you agree with us. We'll do everything we can to smooth over the killings on your farm. Ms. Strobel will keep you advised about that, and we'll back up your story about when and where things took place. If there's anything we can do to help with the police investigation, you call me," Burton said as he stood, signaling the end of the meeting.

Drake left, realizing he was on his own. If ISIS sent the three gunmen his way, as he suspected, it was up to him to prove it.

Chapter 27

David Barak, aka "Malik," left his twenty-seventh floor penthouse, one block off the Las Vegas strip, to head to the airport. He was accompanied by his personal bodyguard, Jamal James, a former defensive tackle for the San Diego Chargers. At six foot eight inches and three hundred fifty pounds, Jamal was a menacing presence that Barak was proud to have in his employ. Jamal wasn't just a big body. His eyes shined with intelligence, his movements were both graceful and quick, and he was loyal. People were impressed that a man of such obvious strength and quality was his servant. Barak was most impressed with the man's unswerving loyalty. The President of the United States might have his Secret Service to stop bullets for him, but Barak had Jamal.

"Jamal, when we get to Oregon, I want you to have the biggest steak the chef at the ranch can find," he said, as they took the elevator down to the waiting limousine. "You've been a loyal friend. Is there anything you might want to do while I'm busy for several hours?"

"No sir, dinner will be enough. I thought I'd just wait for you in the plane. Still haven't gotten used to flying around in so much luxury," Jamal said with a wry smile on his broad face. "The quarterbacks always got the private jets."

In America, Barak had learned that symbolism was everything. Bodyguards, expensive cars, private planes, big homes, and clothing and watches that cost as much as two-thirds of the world earned in a year, were symbols of achievement, worth, and superiority. He had chosen to put his headquarters in America's gaudiest city, where symbolism was everything. It reminded him every day why America was a fraud and had to be destroyed. A country that celebrated actors above teachers, banned its religions from public places and catered to man's most basic instincts, in the most vile and public ways, could not be allowed to remain the world's leader.

So he put on the symbols America cherished and was recognized as a business leader, a man of means. His company, ISIS, was a world leader in security services and executive protection. Because of its success, he had access to the secrets of many of the world's largest corporations and its most famous and influential people. Soon, he would make use of that access to shock the rich and powerful. He would make them all wish they had not allowed their governments to make war on Islam.

Barak was concerned about the developments in Oregon. It was where he had chosen to make his first strike, and he couldn't afford to fail. As he made his way to the Las Vegas Executive Air Terminal and his private Gulfstream G650, he knew he would have to do something about the attorney Kaamil had allowed to live. He could not be permitted to jeopardize their plan. He would have to find a way to throw the man off their track.

In four short days, when the Secretary of Homeland Security was assassinated, the world would learn that the jihad could reach everywhere. Then, those on a list of twelve of the most influential American leaders and celebrities would receive an invitation to convert to Islam—or face the consequences. He had the means and the ability to make sure they understood that opposing Allah meant a swift and sure punishment. He smiled, as he thought about headlines announcing the beheadings of Hollywood stars, television anchors, politicians and a few billionaires. People who thought they were above the violence their government's bombs had brought to so many in Arab lands.

As his plane took off for the flight to his training facility outside Hood River, Barak stared down at the flat land that reminded him of his homeland, and the life, war with the Jews had taken from him. He had vowed at his father's funeral that he would avenge his death a thousandfold. With Allah's blessing, and the Brotherhood's support, he was close to keeping that vow and getting his revenge.

Chapter 28

As Drake left the Crown Plaza Building, he ran through his options. He didn't have anything but his suspicion that ISIS was behind Janice Lewellyn's murder. He didn't have evidence the three gunmen sent to his farm were connected to the murder, and nothing that linked Kaamil and ISIS to either. He understood that. The FBI investigated federal crimes and domestic terrorism, and neither of those two categories appeared to be involved. The Secret Service had come to his aid only as a favor to his father-in-law, and they had no reason to help him any further.

The only thing he could think to do was to take a closer look at ISIS. To do that, he needed some help. A little help from someone who thought like he did, someone who had some of the same skills. Someone he trusted, a friend.

When he got back to his office, he found he had the place all to himself. Margo had left for the weekend with her husband. At his desk, he called his friend.

Mike Casey was a brother in arms, as loyal a friend as a man could have. They had served together in Delta, where Mike was the long gunner, or sniper. He'd saved Drake's life more than once when an enemy unexpectedly stumbled onto their mission. Drake always felt more confident when Mike was providing him cover from a rooftop, a building, or a ridge, even a half mile away. Tall and gangly at six foot six inches, with red hair, he drew too much attention in their assigned fields of operation to be at Drake's side. But from a distance, he was always there as his unseen partner.

Before Mike became a Delta operator, he flew helicopters for the 160th Special Operations Aviation Regiment (Airborne). Its sole purpose was to deliver and pick up Special Operations commandos. Because they often flew at night, the unit was known as the Night Stalkers. They were the aces of military helicopter pilots. Mike was a natural pilot who flew by the seat of his pants and made landings and evacuations other pilots wouldn't attempt. He was quickly picked up by Delta Force for its own aviation platoon. When they learned he was a great sharpshooter, a tribute to his misspent youth in Montana hunting varmints, he was also accepted as one of their snipers.

After leaving the Army, Mike settled in Seattle, working for a small security firm. Five years later, he was chosen by the firm's retiring founder to run the operation. He became the major shareholder, by virtue of stock options he'd earned and had been given with his promotion. Married, with a wife who adored him and three young children, Mike Casey remained a close friend and confidant.

"Casey residence," Mike said when he answered. In the background, children were splashing in a backyard pool and something was sizzling on a grill.

"I take it I'm interrupting one of your deck parties," Drake said, "want me to call back later?"

"Hell no. I don't know how I get stuck doing all the cooking around here, on the weekends anyway. Give me a minute to find someone to burn these burgers," Mike said. "Megan, honey, could you take over for a minute? Drake's on the phone."

Drake smiled, listening to the sounds of his friend's

normal life. There were times when they both thought such a life was too much to hope for. They had lived so far beyond normal they thought they would never make it back. They both had, though Mike's normal life was lasting longer than his had.

"When you coming up to see us again?" Mike asked, after a minute or so. "The kids keep asking when they get to see Uncle Adam."

"I was hoping I could talk you into coming down and spending a day with me. A new client's secretary was murdered in his office and a couple of yo-yos came gunning for me on the farm. I could use a friend to help sort things out. Maybe get out of town, go hunting some varmints like we used to."

From the tone of Mike's voice, Drake knew his friend understood what he was saying.

"Nothing I'd like better. Varmints, you say. What would you like me to bring along for this little outing? I have an M24A2 I picked up from one of our old friends. Will that do?"

The M24A2 was an improved version of the M24 sniper weapon system Mike had used in Delta Force. With a detachable 10-round magazine and barrel modifications to accommodate a sound suppressor, the rifle had proven itself in Afghanistan and elsewhere.

"If you think you can hit anything with it, bring it along. We might get to do some hunting at night, so if you have any of those special binoculars or scopes, they might come in handy as well," Drake suggested.

"Can do. When do you plan on having this here soiree?"

"Tomorrow night," Drake said, and listened patiently for his friend to calculate the domestic damage his request was sure to cause.

"Tomorrow night, huh," Mike repeated. "If I'm able to make arrangements for this adventure, when would I be able to get back to burning burgers?"

"If your kids like burned burgers for breakfast, I'd say sometime Monday morning. Is that soon enough?"

"A man ought to be able to get out of the house once in a while. It'll just have to be. Do me a favor, go out and buy a box of chocolates I can take back to my wife. I'd like to have a bed to sleep in when I get back," Mike chuckled.

Drake put the phone back in its cradle and swiveled his chair around to look out over the marina below. Weekend boaters were moving up and down the river. He'd accomplished as much as he could for the day, it was time to go home and get some work done on the farm. Get on his old, red Massey Ferguson tractor and pull out another row of the dead grape vines left to rot by the previous owner. The work would help his mind settle into a planning mode for tomorrow night's soiree, as Mike called it.

Chapter 29

It was an hour before sunset when Barak felt the nose of the Gulfstream dip. The white snowcap on Mount Hood glowed pastel pink out the window as the plane banked to the left. When it straightened out for the runway below, Barak could see the nearby Columbia River off to the right. Pretty country, he thought, just the right place to teach America how ugly war is.

He had regional training facilities like this one in four other areas around the country. They were all legitimate training centers and respected members of their local business communities. They also secretly served as quarters for the finest assassins assembled under one banner in a thousand years. With ISIS offices around the globe, there wasn't a person of significance anywhere in the world he couldn't reach.

After twenty years, he had created a privately-held corporation worth a hundred times the twenty-five million he'd been given. His resources were as great as the armies of half the countries in the world. The best arms and munitions, a fleet of private jets, armored vehicles, state-of-the-art communication systems, his company had it all. But his plan didn't rely on any of that.

One dedicated, well-trained assassin was all he needed to terrorize any nation he wanted. Blow up fifty people in a shopping mall and America would mourn for only a moment, just as Israel had learned to do. But kill the leaders and icons of a nation, and the white flag of surrender would be raised before the first funeral was held.

When his plane rolled to a stop at the west end of the runway, Barak saw that Kaamil and Roberto Valencia were standing next to one of the company's black Suburbans. The sprawling ranch house he stayed in whenever he visited was only a short walk away, but he appreciated the respect their attention provided him.

"Kaamil, Roberto, I hope you have good news for me. Bad news spoils my appetite, and right now I am very hungry," he said, as he stepped out of the plane. "Come, let's relax and eat, you can tell me of your progress."

When he was in the Suburban beside Kaamil, he remained silent. The silence would serve as fertile ground for nervousness to grow, which is what he intended. Kaamil had made mistakes, and he needed to know if there had been more. Calm men can tell lies, but men who are afraid tell you the truth. Both Kaamil and Roberto were afraid of him because he gave them reason to be. On separate occasions, in front of each of them, he'd shot one of their men for a mistake the man had made. Neither of them had the courage to tell him their men weren't responsible for the mistakes.

Of his training facilities spread throughout America, this ranch was his favorite. The mighty river and the vast gorge it ran through were spectacular. Something about the majestic mountain that seemed to hover over the ranch made him relax. It would be a pity if he could no longer come here, he thought.

After Kaamil pulled up in front of the ranch house, Barak led them in past the massive river rock fireplace to the game room. He called it the game room because it had a bar, a small fireplace, leather chairs and a poker table. The scent of good cigars permeated the knotty pine paneling. It was easy to imagine neighboring ranchers sitting around the poker table drinking whiskey and swapping tales. It was the only room in the ranch house he hadn't remodeled.

Barak took a new bottle of Herradura Anejo tequila off the shelf behind the bar and poured two fingers in each of three crystal tumblers he set on the bar.

"Join me, gentlemen, in a toast to our success. While we eat, you will tell me what a fantastic job you are doing. But allow me to relax a little first."

He saw that both men were still nervous, Roberto more than Kaamil.

"So, Roberto, how are you finding life in this little paradise by the river? Have you found the women here satisfactory?" he asked. He knew from his investigation of the man that young girls were his weakness.

"Girls seem surprised when the goods they offer find a taker," Roberto said, with a small smile. "They wear cut-offs and bikini tops everywhere. It's like going to market. The shopping has been good."

"And how is your father's business doing? Is he still number one in the Northwest?"

"Don Malik, I can assure you we are. The old warehouse you lease us down by the river has worked out well. We hide our product in the farm materials and supplies we ship out of there. None of our shipments have been intercepted. My father asked me to thank you for your assistance," Roberto answered.

"I am glad to hear it. Tell your father, I look forward to working with him on the matters we discussed. Kaamil, how are you doing? Are you having the same success as Roberto with the ladies?" Barak asked, more for Roberto's benefit than any real interest in Kaamil's love life. Kaamil preferred prostitutes and, while there were several favorites, he was discreet and careful in that respect.

"I'm not complaining. Women are sometimes necessary, but who could keep up with Roberto," Kaamil said with a shrug.

"Well then, let's go see if our chef is ready for us. Leave your drinks here. We'll have some wine with our meal."

Barak led them to the dining room, where a platter of steaks sizzled next to a large bowl of mashed potatoes and a Caesar salad on the table. A decanter of red wine sat in front of Barak's plate, and the chef stood with his chair pulled out. When he had tasted the wine, he dismissed the chef with a wave of his hand.

"Now, gentlemen, I want to hear about each of your assignments," he said, as he forked a large steak onto his plate and waited for the bowl of mashed potatoes to be handed to him.

Kaamil went first. "The men are prepared and know what to do. We have trained for two years, the last two months in the mock-up of the Emergency Center. They are proficient with their weapons and anxious to fight. You'll see when you meet them."

Barak accepted his report with a nod of his head, and turned to Roberto.

"Roberto?"

"The men you require are ready. The civilian security guards at the chemical depot are customers of mine. They are black, like your men, and about the same size. They have each given me one of their uniforms in exchange for a month's supply of my product. They won't live long enough to use that much, of course."

"Are you positive we can trust them?"

"As positive as I can be. I have compromising pictures that would cost them their jobs. They have all received pictures of their wives and children to remind them how serious I am. One man I approached refused me. He and his family suffered a most horrible fire in their home that consumed them all. No one else will trouble us. They think I just want to steal from the depot."

Barak met Roberto's steady gaze and was satisfied he was telling the truth. He still seemed nervous about something, though. Maybe it was the operation itself that gnawed at the man's nerves. He would have to talk to Kaamil about it.

"Fine, I am satisfied both of you have done what I asked. Kaamil, is the team assembled in the dormitory or the bunker?" Barak asked.

"They are waiting for you in the bunker."

"When we finish our meal, I will go and meet them. Now, eat, enjoy the food Miguel fixed for us. It is one of the things I most look forward to when I visit—his steaks and these marvelous mashed potatoes," he said, as he dug into the small white mountain of them on his plate.

Chapter 30

Barak and Kaamil left Roberto with a second tequila and walked down a graveled path to the operations center. The path was lined with pink rhododendrons, and daphne scented the air.

"Roberto is nervous about something. Do you know what it is?" Barak asked.

Kaamil hesitated a moment, deciding whether or not to divulge what he suspected. "There are rumors about young girls disappearing in Hood River. Who knows, Roberto may be involved."

Barak turned to look at his protégé in the soft evening light. There was something that Kaamil knew and wasn't telling him.

"Are you sure that's all it is? We have heard those rumors before. We have three days left. If you have any reason to think Roberto may fail us, I need to know. I could get his father to send someone we can trust. There's still time."

"He'll be fine," Kaamil said as they reached the front door of the operations center. "We had a disagreement. He blasphemed our religion, made fun of kissing the Black Stone of Kaaba. I set him straight."

"And how did you do that? Did you fight with him?"

"No, I told him if I repeated his words to you, he and his entire family would be killed as infidels." sacrificing their lives was an honor. The games they played as children mimicked suicide bombers killing Jews. Pictures of *shaheeds*, hung on the walls of their homes. American jihadists didn't have that background. Their motivation, for the most part, was not to honor their god or protect their way of life. It was to hit back at the country they blamed for their miserable lives. Hatred was their motivator, and he was not sure hatred was enough.

The Brotherhood had loaned him an Egyptian psychiatrist to oversee their mental conditioning. They had been broken, made to feel guilty about their country, and offered a way to redeem themselves. They had posters in their rooms proclaiming the honor of those willing to die for Allah, sessions of hypnotism and nightly sleep programming. But Barak knew it wasn't the same as growing up dreaming of dying as a martyr.

Kaamil held the back door in the lab open and let Barak walk ahead to the first classroom where they were waiting for him.

Three men sitting in the first row in the classroom jumped to attention when the door opened. They stood stiffly, staring straight ahead, wearing green camouflage fatigues and combat boots. Aside from their beards, which would be gone before Wednesday, they looked like well-trained and disciplined soldiers. They would easily pass for civilian security personnel at the depot.

"At ease," Barak said. "You have finished training. I am proud of you. You act and look like the holy warriors you are. Three days from now, you will have the honor of striking fear in the hearts of every man, woman and child in this country. You will be remembered with fear and trembling. That's something you were never allowed to achieve before. Allah has chosen this for you."

Barak then stepped in front of each man, looking deep into his eyes. "There is no God but God, and Mohammad is

149

his Prophet. Do His will, as you have been trained, and He will reward you in paradise. Are you ready to do that?"

Each man, in turn, said he was.

"From this moment on, you will remain here to prepare. Tomorrow night you will be allowed to celebrate at a feast we have prepared for you. It is a small taste of the pleasures that await you. Then you will have two days to purify yourself and write letters to family or loved ones, and make your video statement. Wednesday is the day you have been waiting for, and it will be glorious. I envy you and I salute you," Barak said, holding a salute similar to the Nazi salute, before he turned and left the room.

Back at the ranch house, Barak joined Roberto for another tumbler of tequila in the den.

"Kaamil will be back in a couple of minutes, he's inspecting the men's rooms. We have time to talk. I can see you and Kaamil are wary of each other. Will you have a problem working with him these last few days?"

"I don't have to like a man to work with him," Roberto said, with a shrug. "There are many men I deal with in my business that I don't like. Kaamil likes to intimidate people he orders around. I don't take orders from anyone but my father. He asked me to cooperate with you. I am doing that. Now, if you'll excuse me, I have a young lady waiting for me. Thank you for the excellent tequila and dinner, Don Malik."

"Good bye, Roberto. When your men have finished what I have asked them to do, you should take the opportunity to visit your father in Mexico. Can that be arranged?"

"I was thinking of taking a short vacation myself. I'm sure my father will be happy to see me," Roberto said, and left.

Four more days, Barak thought, and I might take a vacation too. What better time to celebrate than after you have assassinated an American Cabinet member.

Chapter 31

Mike Casey drove up Drake's long driveway at 7:15 a.m. Sunday morning. Drake had just returned from a morning run with Lancer and watched the dust rise behind his friend's SUV. When it stopped in front of the old farmhouse, Drake gave his friend a friendly salute and went to greet him.

"Thought I'd see you for lunch, not breakfast."

"I slipped out before the kids were up. Thought it would save me from making excuses for not being home," Mike said, swinging his long legs out of his white Yukon. "Fix me that breakfast you just mentioned and tell me what's going on, 'cause I suspect I'm going to need my strength today."

Drake led the way into his kitchen and started pulling items from his refrigerator.

"Coffee cups are in the cupboard to the right of the sink. Some scrambled eggs and toast enough, or do you want me to pull out a steak to go with your eggs?"

"Scrambled eggs and toast will do for now, but save the steak for lunch," Mike said.

Drake smiled as he started cracking eggs in a small mixing bowl. Mike's youth, spent on his folks' Montana ranch working long days, taught him to eat big meals when there was time.

"Thanks for coming on such short notice, Mike. I seem to have kicked over a hornet's nest when I started poking around a murder at a client's place," Drake said, adding a little milk to the bowl, along with a pinch of fine herbs. "If I don't get ahead of this thing, I'm going to wind up being sucked into a homicide investigation that could cost me my practice."

"And you think this has something to do with that varmint you want to hunt?"

"I do," Drake said, pouring the egg mixture into a large skillet. "The security firm at Martin Research is ISIS and it's involved somehow."

"Whoa, you're talking about ISIS? I know those guys. They're the big kids on the block of corporate security and executive protection. Why do you figure they're involved?"

"Too many coincidences. Rich Martin's secretary was murdered when the security system crashed or was turned off. After I questioned ISIS about the security breach, my client's head of security at Martin Research supposedly committed suicide, hours after I met with him. He was okay when I talked to him, and he was the one who first pointed a finger at ISIS. I woke up that night with three guys surrounding my house for a turkey shoot. I'm the turkey."

"You're taking so long on those eggs, I'm really hungry now," Mike moaned. "So I assume you took care of the shooters in your usual way and want to find out if ISIS is involved. You have any bacon or sausage to go with those eggs?"

"Not all of us can eat like you, Mike. You'll have to make do with some chorizo I have in the refrigerator. I'll throw in some chili peppers. Start the toast. Bread's in the pantry."

Mike came back with the chorizo, a can of black beans, a loaf of bread and a smile on his face.

"If you're going to add peppers, I thought these beans might be tasty as well. So what's this little adventure tonight all about?"

While they ate what turned out to be a pretty decent egg scramble, Drake continued the briefing and told Mike about following the ISIS manager to Hood River, the drug dealer he had lunch with, and the training facility.

"I've heard about the ranch. Supposed to be a small version of the Blackwater facility in North Carolina that trains private military personnel. But ISIS can't have a convicted felon running around on its ranch. They'd start losing business, big time, if anyone reported it. What did you say the felon's name was?"

"Maybe you'll get to meet him, name's Roberto Valencia. That's where I want to go tonight, the ISIS ranch. Do a little recon, like we used to," Drake said, watching for his friend's reaction.

The wry smile he always wore slowly faded from Mike's face.

"Do you know anything about this ISIS facility? Like, are there guards, security cameras, dogs, you know, some of the basic things we used to look for? 'Cause I don't need to get caught and wind up in jail. We can't shoot our way out of things here in the States."

"I don't plan on getting caught. I just want to look around, see if I can find out what Kaamil's up to. I know I'm not wearing the uniform again, but it's sure starting to feel like someone has me in their sights. All I want you to do is cover me, like old times."

"So you're thinking about going in alone and blind? When was the last time you did something like this, ten or twelve years ago? We're not kids anymore."

"Some things you don't forget, Mike. I'm still in good shape. I just want you watching my back. Something's not right about ISIS. You up for one more soiree, amigo?" Drake asked.

Mike's curiosity overcame his reluctance. "Let's say I am up for one more little adventure. What's the plan?"

"I walk in, you cover me, I walk out and we drive home," Drake answered, holding a serious look on his face as long as possible. "Of course, we may have to tweak that plan a little."

Mike let out a long, slow sigh of relief. "Whew, for a minute I thought you were crazy like when I first met you. Course then you'd have just said, 'let's storm the place.'"

"I'm older now, so I'm thinking we should storm the place carefully."

For the next two hours, they went over all the possible scenarios. What was the best time to visit the ranch? How would they communicate? How would they deal with security measures? What would they do if guards were encountered? What about dogs, did they need tranquilizer darts? What did they do if he was caught? If he found something incriminating, did Drake take it with him or capture it digitally?

Then they went over the equipment they needed. Mike had brought most of it with him, including night vision goggles and tactical headsets.

"I've mounted state-of-the-art communication equipment in the Yukon. With these headsets, we can communicate up to a half mile away from it, no problem. The headsets are configured to use with optical head bands. I'll be able to see what you see at all times, and you'll be able to see whatever's out there," Mike said proudly. "I've tried to make sure my guys have the best equipment available when they work."

With Mike's M24A2, they agreed to limit their firepower to the handguns they were used to carrying—the .45s they had been trained to use as Delta Force operators.

"How far are we taking this thing tonight?" Mike asked.

"I'm just going to take a look around. I don't plan on making things worse by shooting anyone. Don't worry about it, Mike, they're not even going to know I'm there," Drake said, sounding as confident as he could. "Look, I have some work to finish in the vineyard. You can help me, or take a nap. It's your choice. I'll take you to dinner around 6:00 and we'll leave for Hood River around 7:30."

Drake spent the next three hours on his old tractor, pulling out another row of old grape vines, alone.

Chapter 32

After a late breakfast and a walk around the ranch facilities, Barak headed back to the ranch house for Kaamil's final briefing before he returned to Las Vegas. His plan was flawless and would succeed, if all his players did their part, especially Kaamil.

Over a cup of Turkish coffee in the den, he ran down the list of things he wanted Kaamil to do, and then asked about the attorney.

"What success have you had with the man you wasted three men trying to kill?"

Kaamil's eyes flared before he answered.

"He hasn't shown his face again. The imams are putting pressure on the cops to find out what happened to our brothers. My source says their investigation is also looking into his role in their disappearance."

"Find a way to turn up the heat. If he comes around again, make him disappear. The police will think he's running from their investigation," Barak said. "Don't you like the coffee? Drink up, you'll hurt my chef's feelings."

"I was waiting for it to cool," Kaamil offered. "It's very hot and very strong."

"That's the way I like it, hot and strong. Great Turkish coffee is supposed to be 'Black as Hell, Strong as Death, and Sweet as Love' according to an old saying. Are you comfortable with the arrangements for tomorrow's party?"

"Everything is set. Roberto is bringing the girls and the food. None of the regular staff is here, because it's Sunday, and I didn't want your chef involved. Their juice will be laced with the drug you designed, and it will be in their meals until Wednesday. They'll be as courageous as lions and have the time of their lives."

Barak finished his cup and nodded his approval. "What have they been told about the plan for their extraction?"

"The truth. I'll be there in the Medevac helicopter to pick them up. I don't expect they will make it that far, but if they do, we don't want them captured."

"And are you willing to do what's necessary, if it looks like you might be captured?"

Kaamil met his leader's gaze directly. "You don't have to worry about me. I'll never let them take me alive."

"Good. That's what I expect of my leaders. In this fight, the price may be death. If you're not willing to pay it, you will remain your country's slave. Remember that."

On his flight back to Las Vegas, Barak thought about his young lieutenant, and how easy he was to motivate. Telling him that jihad was his way to take revenge against whitey was all it took. Inflaming his anger had been easy, once he discovered Malcolm X was the young man's hero. Convincing him that martyrdom was noble had been harder, but Kaamil's fear of returning to prison guaranteed the end would be the same.

Looking out his plane's starboard window at the verdant mountains stretching south toward California, Barak wondered how America was going to react when it realized the racial violence rising up against it was being mobilized by its enemy.

Chapter 33

After dinner in Dundee, Drake answered Mike's careful questions about life as a widower and his law practice as they were driving to Hood River. When they arrived, he gave his friend directions to a drive-thru coffee shop just off the interstate.

"Sunset's at 8:59 p.m. tonight, so there's time to kill before we head out to the ISIS ranch," Drake said. "It's not your beloved Starbucks, but maybe it'll keep you awake while I'm prowling around."

"Forty-four million customers, ya gotta be proud. Changed the world since 1987, that's more than we were able to do."

"Yeah, but we sure tried, didn't we?"

A sunset painted thunderheads pink and purple as they piled up against the eastern flank of the Cascades. Mike drove them through the old downtown section of Hood River until they turned south onto Highway 35. The scattered lights from rural homes and small ranches soon gave way to the darkness of forested land, broken only by the headlights of the SUV.

"There's a road just south of the ranch. It ends at a trailhead into the national forest. We'll park there. If we see anyone, we're hikers out overnight," Drake said. "We'll hike in and when we get as close to the ranch buildings as possible, I'll make a quick insertion. We'll be back in Portland by breakfast."

"Plan's a little short in details, but then yours always were. Let me hear your voice now and then, in case I get scared out here with the coyotes and such."

Mike had concealed himself as a sniper for days, while snakes and all sorts of insects crawled over him. A night in the open, for him, was a piece of cake.

When they drove past the unmanned ISIS guardhouse a short time later, a surveillance camera tracked their passage. A quarter of a mile beyond the guardhouse, a country road turned east, and ran parallel to the southern boundary of the ranch. When they found the trailhead, Mike pulled his Yukon into the small graveled parking area. The darkness of the night was brightened only by a panoply of stars. A new moon did little to help illuminate the ground. Both men moved silently to the rear of the Yukon where Mike unloaded their gear. They pulled on black balaclavas and positioned the headset headbands on their heads.

After a final check of their equipment, Drake spoke softly into the boom-arm mike of his tactical headset.

"This headband is new. Wish we'd had something like this when we were running around in Iraq."

"Latest equipment, designed for special ops, private security and private military work. I'm looking into some of the Blackwater-type contracts available around the world. Thought I'd better check out some of the equipment they use," Mike said.

"You sure you want to get into that line of work?"

"Have to. If you do executive protection work these days, clients want to know you can mount an operation if one of their people is kidnapped. You remember the hand signals, in case you can't talk to me?"

Drake raised his hand to his forehead, as if he was

looking into the distance, the signal for "watch." He then signaled "sniper," by making a looking glass with his left hand at his left eye, and pointing his right hand like a pistol ahead at the ground. With his left hand he made the A-OK sign for "I understand."

"Let's stay together until we reach the decline that slopes down to the ranch buildings. From the topographical map I bought, it looks like there's a fairly steep drop-off ahead. From there, we're below the tree line. Find a high point where you can cover me, and I'll move in."

"Ready as ever," Mike said, tapping his chest twice with a closed fist. "Just don't take too many chances."

"If I run into trouble, you'll be the first to know."

A carpet of pine needles provided silent passage. When the pine trees began to thin out and the lights of the ranch buildings were visible three hundred yards away, Drake told his friend to cover him.

"I'll work my way down through the boulders and sagebrush below us. When I get to the bottom, tell me what you see ahead."

Drake moved down through the large boulders scattered just below the timberline, looking for signs of intrusion detection devices. Mike had told him about the newest perimeter security devices he wouldn't be able to spot. With the size of the ISIS ranch and its extensive perimeter, they were fairly confident he wouldn't be detected, if at all, until he got close to the ranch buildings.

When he reached the bottom of the slope below the timberline, he keyed his mike.

"You seeing what I'm seeing?" he asked Mike.

"Looks like the flat area ahead of you might have a few surprises. Twenty-five yards across, flat like it's been leveled and treated with weed killer. I can't see anything growing on this side of that barbed-wire fence."

"You see anything on the other side of the fence?"

"Can't see anything, but I suspect it's infrared. The open area must have sensor pads."

"I'm going to my left, by that small cluster of trees. From here, it looks like that's the end of this open area. Maybe I can find a way in from there," Drake said.

Moving laterally, he worked his way through the sagebrush until he reached the small cluster of juniper trees. From there, he could see the ranch house and other buildings clearly.

"What are you scoping?"

"I don't see anything between those trees and the fence. From the fence to the buildings, it's clear. No one's moving around. There are lights on in the ranch house and the largest of the three buildings below it."

Drake studied the open ground ahead of him, sector by sector. He didn't see anything to contradict Mike's assessment.

"I'm going to chance it. If there are sensors on this side of the fence, deer and coyotes would drive whoever is monitoring their system nuts. They're probably trying to make us think there are detection sensors out here."

"Of course, they could just use dogs to keep people out," Mike suggested, knowing how Drake loved Bullmastiffs, Dobermans and Rottweilers trained as guard dogs.

"Thanks for that, bolsters my confidence immensely. I'm going over to the fence to see what it looks like."

Drake moved quickly to the fence. He was in the open, but unless someone was watching this particular sector of the ranch perimeter with night vision binoculars, he wouldn't be noticed. The fence was a typical barbed-wire fence, four strands running between cedar fence posts.

Crawling under the bottom strand of barbed wire, Drake stood up and whispered into his mike.

"I'll stay here for a couple minutes to see if that triggered anything."

When Mike saw no activity below, he directed Drake to move to his left to a slope that ran down to the ranch house and other buildings.

"It looks like that's your safest way in," Mike said.

Drake ran across sixty yards of old pasture land to the bottom of the slope before he crouched and scanned the area. Ahead at ten o'clock, he saw the outline of the largest of the three buildings on the lower level, below the ranch house.

Vectoring back from right to left, Drake thought he saw the glow of a cigarette midway between the two-story building and the fence line he'd just crossed.

"Mike, put your scope on that small stand of trees directly in front of me. I thought I saw something there."

After a moment, Mike confirmed it.

"You have a man smoking a cigarette in the middle of that stand of trees. I don't know how he got there. I've been watching that area from the buildings to the fence since you went in. He wasn't there a minute ago. I would have spotted him."

"I'll head his way and see what he's doing. If they have guards posted, I may be wasting my time. If he's just taking a smoke break, maybe I can follow him and find a way in. If he looks my way, signal."

Drake moved quietly forward, keeping his eyes on the stand of trees faintly illuminated by the stars overhead. Growing up in the city, he never got over how bright the stars were in central Oregon, east of the Cascade mountain range. After covering the first fifty yards of open rangeland, he stopped and looked again for the red glow of the cigarette he'd seen earlier.

"Mike, is he still there? I can't see him."

"Neither can I," Mike said. "I watched him until a minute ago when I looked away to check for activity down around the buildings. When I looked back, he was gone. Stay put until I find him."

Drake dropped to the ground and searched the area ahead of him. All he saw with his night vision goggles were a few gnarly juniper trees bunched together. The trees were only seven or eight feet tall, but their twisted shapes provided excellent cover for a man sneaking a smoke or standing guard duty.

"He's not there," Mike reported. "Unless this guy is a world-class sprinter, and ran back behind one of those buildings when I looked away, he just disappeared."

"Not possible, I would have heard him. I'm going to take a look." He wasn't going to risk getting any closer until he knew where the smoker went. A posted guard doesn't smoke, and no one was that fast over uneven rangeland.

Drake stood and moved ahead, watching for movement. When he was twenty yards from the junipers, he checked with his spotter again.

"Still clear?" he asked.

"Go. I don't see anyone from here," Mike reported.

Drake moved forward and stopped behind the first juniper large enough to provide cover. He could still smell the tobacco smoke hanging in the night air. He was alone amidst the ancient shapes of the junipers, with no sign of danger until he stepped down on a metal surface and froze.

Chapter 34

Drake's first thought was that he had stepped on a mine. He'd worked around mined areas along the border between Iraq and Iran, seen hundreds of boys and men missing arms and legs. Then he started remembering what he'd been taught about land mines. He squatted down without shifting his weight and gently felt the surface around his feet. It felt like a manhole cover. Feeling around the circumference of the metal plate, he found an opening, wide enough for four of his fingers to lift the cover.

"Mike, you won't believe this. I know how our smoker disappeared. I'm standing on top of a manhole cover. He must have surfaced from somewhere underground for a smoke break."

"If they're hiding something underground, they're not going to be happy the hired help is using it to sneak out for smokes."

"I'm going to try and lift this cover, see if he left it open for his next break. It might be my way in," Drake said.

"You sure you want to do this? If you trip an alarm, you'll have a hell of a time getting back out."

"If I'm wrong and ISIS is running a legitimate operation, they'll just call the cops. You can bail me out. If I'm right and don't make it out, you'll know my hunch was right. We win either way."

Drake stepped off the manhole cover and wedged his fingers in the half-inch crack around the edge. He lifted the cover and saw a soft red glow lighting a concrete shaft with a steel ladder leading down.

"Mike, I'm going in. The cover wasn't secured. Looks like a tunnel leads back toward the buildings. I'll be back in fifteen minutes, or signal I'm in trouble."

Drake climbed down the ladder, closing the cover behind him. The tunnel led to a metal door fifty yards away. He moved quickly down the tunnel, took a moment to slow his heart, and pulled the door open with his right hand.

He saw a long hallway with unfinished concrete walls, doors on each side, and industrial-type lighting overhead. Drake moved quietly to the first door on the left and listened. Easing it open, he found the room empty except for a bed, a small desk and a military gray, portable metal closet against the far wall. It looked like some of the barrack quarters he'd occupied over the years.

The door across the hall opened onto a large sleeping bay, with enough empty bunks lining each wall to sleep twenty or thirty men. He saw showers and sinks at the far end. Whatever this place is, Drake thought, it's built to accommodate a lot of people.

Back in the hallway, he checked the next two doors on the left. Both rooms looked like the first he had entered. The next room on the left, however, looked like it was being used. The bed was made in military fashion, and on the desk was an open Koran. He saw a prayer rug on the floor and, on the side of the gray metal closet, a uniform was hung. Stepping closer, he saw that it was a security staff uniform with a Umatilla Depot patch on the left shoulder. The name tag sewn above the right pocket said the uniform belonged to Jameer Williams.

Drake felt a chill run up the back of his neck. The Umatilla Depot was one of seven U.S. Army installations in the United States currently storing chemical weapons. It was located two hours east, six miles south of the Columbia River. A new chemical agent disposal facility had been built in 2001, to incinerate the twelve percent of the nation's chemical weapon stockpile housed there. So far, only thirty percent of the stockpiled Sarin (GB), nerve agent (VX), or mustard blister agent (HD) had been destroyed.

While he didn't consider himself Islamophobic, learning that ISIS was housing or training security personnel from the nearby chemical weapons depot unnerved him.

In the next room, Drake found another prayer rug and another security staff uniform belonging to one Mohammed Marcus. As he started to search Mohammed's desk, he heard voices in the hallway. Two men, who sounded like they were headed his way.

"You see them girls? Those brothers having themselves a time tonight."

"Just a taste of paradise, like Kaamil said. Gonna be all I can do to let them party alone."

Drake stood behind the door, hoping he wasn't in one of their rooms. When the two men passed, he eased the door open and watched them walk toward the sleeping bay. They were wearing tricolor camo fatigues and desert combat boots, like the ones worn by the National Guard units in and around Portland. Both men were tall and appeared to be in their twenties, black, with close-cropped hair.

Before they entered the sleeping bay, one of them said "Kaamil only gave us five minutes to hit the head, we better hurry. Hope Yousef hurried up his smoke break. He won't wanna miss the show."

As soon as both men were out of sight, Drake slipped out and turned left. He wanted to see the party area the two men were talking about. Just then, the double doors at the end of the hallway started to open. Another man in camo fatigues was backing through the door, holding a large cardboard box in his hands.

Drake had just enough time to open the next door on his left and duck into the room. It was the same as the other two, except for a framed picture of a beautiful woman on the dresser.

When the man with the box passed the room, Drake inched the door open and snuck a quick peek down the hallway. The first two men were just coming out of the sleeping bay. The man with the box stood waiting for them to clear the doorway.

"You two better hurry, you're going to be late. I'll make sure Yousef is back."

Drake pulled the door closed as the two men came running past. If someone went looking for Yousef and found the manhole cover unsecured, he'd have to find another way out. He had to make a run for it and hope the man with the box didn't come out before he reached the other end of the hallway.

In college, he was first team, weak side linebacker, and the quickest on the team in closing a hole or chasing down a runner. He could still run a mile in five minutes and fifteen seconds. But tonight, when he needed to reach the tunnel in a hurry, it seemed like he was running in quicksand.

"Hey, what the hell you doing here," the man with the box yelled, as Drake ran past the sleeping bay door. "Stop or I'll shoot your ass."

Drake barely broke stride, seeing the box man wasn't armed, and pushed through the steel door. He ran down the long tunnel and scrambled up the ladder out of the underground bunker.

"Mike," he whispered loudly, as he threw open the manhole cover and broke into a run, "I'm gonna have company shortly. Where should I go?"

"I see you. Lights are going on all over. Angle to your left, toward the shooting range, where it's dark. From there, you have a pretty clear path to my ridge."

Drake ran toward the covered firing line of the shooting range, then angled up toward the ridge. No one seemed to be chasing him. Another hundred yards and he would reach the fence, then the ridge beyond.

"Bad news, Amigo. They're sending dogs. Three packs of Dobermans, one of them is headed your way, be there in half a minute. You want me to take them out?"

"No, I'm gonna make like Mel Gibson," Drake said between pants, "and stare them down. Hell yes, shoot them."

From the ridge, Drake was two hundred yards away and covering ground quickly. The Dobermans, though, were closing faster. The problem was one of timing. Mike would have to hit all four dogs in a matter of seconds.

"If I say 'down,' get behind a rock or something. You may have to help me here. Commencing fire now."

Behind Drake, four large Dobermans were running straight at him, like greyhounds chasing a mechanical rabbit. The lead dog was slightly ahead. The other three were flanking him.

Twenty yards behind Drake, the lead Doberman went down in a rolling tumble, knocking the dog to his right momentarily off course. Then the dog on the left did a somersault when his head exploded.

Drake didn't turn to look, but he heard the sound of another dog fall. He knew he wouldn't hear the whisper of the 7.62mm rounds coming from Mike's suppressed M24A2.

"Down," he heard, and dove behind a small boulder. He looked up as the last Doberman went airborne, like a guided missile aimed straight at his face. He rolled to his right, looking up in time to see the last dog's head explode.

"Come on, *Kemo Sabe*," Mike said, "no time to be lying around. You have more dogs headed your way."

Drake got up and ran for the fence, deciding to tell his friend he thought he'd cut it a little close with that last dog.

Chapter 35

In the ISIS command center, Kaamil stared at the surveillance monitors. Someone had broken into the bunker and wandered around in the martyr's rooms. Malik would kill him for allowing this to happen. Kaamil moved closer to the monitor and replayed the video. The hooded man entered from the steel door that was supposed to be locked. He had come down through the escape tunnel, which was never to be used unless their survival required it. How had this happened? He watched as the man moved from room to room, until he was frightened off.

He replayed the video once more, this time running it back ten minutes before the intruder entered. There, six minutes before the intruder entered, one of the new trainees opened the steel door a crack to make sure no one was in the hallway, and then dashed into the sleeping bay. Unbelievable! After all the screening and tests the men went through, how had one so stupid made it this far?

Kaamil slammed his hands down on the console and punched on the computer audio microphone.

"Abed, Rashid, get to command center immediately. Bring Ibrahim and the new man Yousef with you. Now!" he shouted.

The problem was twofold; find out who the intruder was, and make sure Malik didn't hear about him before he returned to Las Vegas. The first problem was the hardest by far. The intruder wore a black balaclava and black clothing. There was nothing obvious in his outward appearance. He looked fit, over six feet tall, and he moved like some of the combat instructors he'd trained with. The man could be one of Roberto's competitors, someone who learned about the ranch and came to spy.

It could also be someone Malik had sent to test them. Which meant it was already too late to keep Malik from hearing about the intruder. There was one thing he wasn't concerned about, though. The intruder wasn't from the government. A government man would get a search warrant first and come in through the front door. And he wouldn't wear a balaclava, he'd have FBI, in big white letters, on his jacket.

Before his two lieutenants arrived, Kaamil took a 9mm Glock from a drawer in the command console and stuck it inside his belt. When they entered the room, he watched each of them carefully. He'd known both men in prison, and they had proven their loyalty to him time and time again. But, he'd put them in charge of the dormitory wing and ultimately they were responsible. They were nervous. The small movements of their hands and the stiffness in their postures gave them away. They were not so afraid they refused to meet his withering glare, and he knew it was because they trusted him.

The other two men were also nervous and afraid. Kaamil addressed them first.

"Someone broke into our bunker tonight, and was allowed to escape. Do either of you know how that happened?"

Ibrahim, the one carrying the box into the sleeping bay who had confronted the intruder, stared at the wall behind Kaamil and said, "No."

Kaamil stepped in front of Yousef. "Do you know how the intruder got in?"

"How would I know?" Yousef said, with a shrug of his shoulders. "Maybe he got in when the Mexican brought the girls."

Kaamil wanted to laugh at the man's stupid attempt to blame his action on someone else. The smell of tobacco was still strong on him.

"Do you know the Koran, Yousef? Do you know that the Prophet commands us to do what is just and forbids us to do what is evil? You know that, Yousef?" Kaamil asked quietly.

"Of course, and 'allows them as lawful what is good, and prohibits them from what is bad,'" Yousef said, finishing the sura Kaamil had paraphrased.

"And do you consider lying something that is good, or is something that is bad?"

In that moment, the look in Yousef's eyes signaled he understood Kaamil knew and that he was about to die. It was also the moment Kaamil whipped the Glock around and shot the man in the heart, took a step to his left and shot Ibrahim.

"Let that be a lesson," he said to Abed and Rashid, as he put the Glock down on the command console. "Lying to me will kill you. Not being a warrior and stopping an intruder when you have the chance, will kill you as well. Now, no one else knows someone broke in tonight, and no one else is ever going to know. We failed to secure this facility. It will not happen again. Keep these two here until the men are in bed. Then remove them with the party trash. If anyone asks, they were selected for a mission and haven't returned yet."

Kaamil walked out of the command center and headed back to the ranch house. He had a growing suspicion that someone had him in his sights, and was about to pull the trigger.

Chapter 36

It took twenty minutes to reach the Yukon and another fifteen minutes for Drake to walk point and lead the way back to Hwy. 35. When he climbed in, they turned left to follow the Mount Hood Loop back to Portland.

Drake pulled off the balaclava and sat back in his seat for a moment with his eyes closed.

"You were a little slow with that last dog. Just wanted to mention that, in case there's a next time. Age and all, though, you did all right."

"Come on, man, you gotta love the beauty of it all. I waited until that last dog was in the air, so you'd remember how much you need me. How much fun would it have been for you, if I'd shot those dogs when they were a hundred yards back?"

"You're right, Mike. Foolish of me to think you'd take the shot when it would be a challenge, when you could wait and take the easy shot."

"Oh, man, that is not fair. I had your six. You used to sneak into a place and not wake everybody up." Mike laughed when he glanced over and saw the feigned look of hurt on his friend's face. "So, what'd you see down there?"

"Not what I expected. There was a sleeping bay, like on a military base, then a string of private rooms. Reminded me of our old Delta quarters—a bed, a small desk and a wall locker. In two of the rooms, there were Korans on the desks and prayer rugs on the floors."

"So what's ISIS doing, training Saudi security guys?" Mike asked as they drove past the Mount Hood Ranger Station.

"I don't think they're training Saudis. The guys I saw are American blacks. The rooms with the prayer rugs had security staff uniforms for the chemical weapons depot in Umatilla hanging on the lockers."

In the ensuing silence, both men thought about what that could mean.

"You're going to have to tell someone about this," Mike said. "We've had enough homegrown terrorism in the Northwest to know these nut cases are a menace. They're just stupid enough to hit an Army chemical depot. I have clients in and around the depot red zone. I know how dangerous that shit is. With thirty-seven hundred tons of old chemical weapons stored there, an explosion or fire in the storage area with a strong wind blowing and a lot of people are going to die."

They were driving through a primeval forest, with canopies of towering, old fir trees almost blotting out the stars as they drove down the old Barlow Road. It was the last leg of the Oregon Trail that had brought settlers to the fertile Willamette Valley. The thought of thousands dying from one of man's modern inventions of war seemed inappropriate in a place of such dark and ancient beauty.

"Who can I tell?" Drake asked, staring ahead into darkness beyond the headlights. "I broke into the place. By the time anyone could serve a search warrant, they won't find Korans, prayer rugs, or depot uniforms. Maybe there's an explanation I'm not seeing. ISIS does train security personnel, there's no reason they can't be training people to work at the chemical depot. Who's going to do anything, just because I say I saw some Korans and prayer rugs? They'd just say I'm an Islamaphobe."

Mike turned to look at his friend. "When did you start worrying about what other people think? We used to throw together mission plans on a lot less. ISIS and this ranch operation smell, and you and I know it."

He was right. Drake's suspicions and anger at being targeted had propelled him this far, but he felt a deep and foreboding reluctance to getting involved with his government again. He'd been a pawn on a chessboard when he was an operator in Delta Force. He didn't have any desire to get involved with the FBI or DHS and be a tool for someone else again.

He also couldn't stand by while Kaamil and Roberto Valencia and their crew might be planning something that would endanger thousands of innocent people.

"Okay, you're right. Just because my little sneak-and-peek at the ranch won't convince anyone, it doesn't mean I shouldn't try. If they won't listen, then we'll have to see if my father-in-law can help, as a last resort."

Drake opened his cell phone and scrolled down to the number Liz Strobel had given him. It wasn't midnight yet, and he hoped she was in her room and not out partying somewhere.

Six rings on her phone and an invitation to leave a message told him she was either out, or choosing not to answer his call. He knew he could call the Senator at any hour, but that would only lead eventually back to Strobel. He would wait until tomorrow.

"She's not answering. Let's get back and get some sleep. I have a feeling we might have a busy schedule the next couple of days, once I raise an alarm. Any chance you can stay around for a few more days?" Drake asked.

"Why, you planning on going it alone like we used to, if you can't get anyone to listen? I need to get back to the office tomorrow, but I might be able to return to keep your ass out of trouble."

Drake smiled at his friend's subtle reminder of past close calls. Mike had an uncanny ability to lay down covering fire that had allowed him to escape many a kill zone. Mike was the best partner he'd ever worked with, and in Delta Force there weren't any bad partners.

"Let me see what Strobel says, and I'll call you. She might find my charm irresistible and forget she stood by while the Secret Service and the FBI threw me under the bus. If she doesn't, we'll proceed with Plan B, just as soon as I figure out what Plan B is."

Chapter 37

Early Monday morning, after four hours of sleep and seeing Mike off, Drake called Liz Strobel. When she answered, her gravelly voice said she'd been sleeping soundly.

"'If this is your idea of a sick joke, guys, I'll make you pay," Strobel said.

"Good morning, Sunshine. Adam Drake. I need to talk to you."

"Yeah, but I don't have to listen. It's early. Why are you doing this to me, Drake?" she whined.

"Whining doesn't become you, Sunshine. Meet me downstairs in an hour for coffee. I may even buy you breakfast. I have some news you need to hear," he said and hung up.

Strobel slammed down the phone and pulled the covers over her head. Her job required her to be as tough as the men she ordered around, but keeping up with them when they started drinking was still a skill she hadn't mastered.

An hour later, Drake watched Strobel walk into the coffee shop of the Marriott, dressed like she was headed to the White House to brief the President. Navy blue jacket, tan skirt, a soft cream-colored silk blouse, and heels. He was impressed.

Strobel stopped behind her chair, where she locked a brief, this better be good, stare on him before she sat down. Then she waited for Drake to talk.

"I'm sorry I woke you up. I thought you might like to know your boss may be in danger," Drake said.

"If this is an attempt to get me to interfere in the investigation of the guys you killed, you can save your breath. It's out of my hands, as you no doubt saw the other day."

"This isn't about that, although there may be a connection. What if I were to tell you that at a location close to the chemical weapons depot, there are men living in an underground bunker. They have uniforms that will identify them as security guards at the depot. Your boss speaks there day after tomorrow."

"My first question would be, why you think these men pose a danger to Secretary Rallings? The second would be, how did you learn about some underground bunker?" she said, sitting back in her chair while the waitress put her coffee on the table.

"First, just to be clear, I said your boss might be in danger. The reason is simple, but then I'm a fairly simple guy. The men in the underground bunker are black American Muslims, and they're hiding underground," Drake said.

"But you don't know why they're in this bunker, and they're a threat because they're Muslim and black?" Strobel asked, with her eyebrows raised. "You'd be popular in Washington with that kind of logic, Mr. PC."

Drake shrugged, "If it walks like a duck and quacks like a duck, out here we call it a duck. Most of our homegrown terrorists in the Northwest have been black Americans who converted to Islam. When they're living in a secret underground bunker, with uniforms that provide access to a chemical weapons depot, I think the threat possibility should at least be explored."

"You haven't told me how you know about this bunker."

Drake studied her face. He hadn't decided if he could trust her with the truth. "I can't tell you that, and you don't want to know. Look, my father-in-law will be with your boss Wednesday at the dedication ceremony. I have no reason to make this up."

"So what am I supposed to do with your suspicions? I can't get a FISA warrant with what you've told me. And I won't get the FBI involved, not when they're trying to hang me out to dry because I helped you."

"What good is Homeland Security when you won't investigate a threat like this? You have something suspicious going on near a chemical weapons depot with enough chemical munitions to wipe out the west coast," Drake threw down.

"You know damn well why we can't help," she said, standing up. "If you or your source doesn't have the guts to tell us about this bunker, don't expect me to send in the cavalry."

Drake knew she was right, just as he knew that getting her involved would have slowed him down anyway. He had to warn her, but hadn't expected her to do much. If America wouldn't do everything possible to protect itself at home, he would. He wasn't afraid to do it again, Strobel's accusation notwithstanding.

He finished his coffee and walked back through the hotel lobby on his way to his office. If the Senator would go along with the plan forming in his mind, he would conduct his own investigation.

Chapter 38

As soon as Drake got to his car, he called the Senator at home.

"Good morning, Senator. I need to talk to you, as soon as possible. Will you be in your office this morning?"

"Fortunately, no. I'm taking the opportunity to enjoy a late breakfast at home. I don't get many of these opportunities. Want to join me?"

"I'd like that. I'll be there in twenty minutes," Drake answered.

On his way to the Senator's house, he thought about what he should tell him. He wanted to trust the Senator, but the first thing the Senator did when he'd called for help was call the Secretary of DHS. Would he feel obligated again to pass along whatever Drake told him?

He liked the Senator, both as the father his wife adored and as a politician. He seemed to do what was right more often than he did what was politically expedient. But, Drake reminded himself, the Senator was a Washington insider. He remained in office because he knew how to play the game. He didn't have a choice, Drake concluded. There wasn't much more he could do on his own.

When he pulled up in front of the Senator's home, the Senator was waiting for him at the front door.

"I'm not used to my new security system yet. Every time it tells me someone is coming, I think I need to get up and see who it is. Meredith just checks the video monitor. Our breakfast won't be ready for several minutes, so let's walk. You can tell me what we need to talk about."

They walked from the front drive around the eastern perimeter of the Senator's estate toward the lake. Drake told him about following ISIS's manager to the warehouse in Hood River, seeing Kaamil meeting with a drug dealer, and his sneak-and-peek on the ISIS ranch.

"I met with Secretary Rallings's assistant this morning and told her what I suspected. I didn't tell her what I'd seen. I don't know her well enough to tell her I broke into the bunker so she can add another crime to the list being investigated. She told me unless I had the guts to come forward, she wasn't going to call in the cavalry."

"That sounds like Liz," Senator Hazelton said. "She was in the background of the Brandon Mayfield fiasco. She's not anxious to let the government step into another mess like that without rock-solid evidence. Sum up your theory for me."

"At first, I was just curious about why Richard Martin's secretary was killed, and how the security system failed to identify her killer. Then, I had a bad feeling about the ISIS manager and saw him meeting with the drug dealer. Now, I'm suspicious on a whole different level. I think there's a possibility ISIS is planning something that involves the chemical weapons depot, maybe your visit there."

"And this is based on what you saw on this ranch in Hood River?"

"Everything I've learned about ISIS really, but yeah, what I saw up there. There isn't a legitimate reason I can think of for hiding that bunker underground. There are several buildings where they could house personnel for training without hiding them. ISIS trains security types from all over the world. I doubt any of them would put up with the facilities I saw. I thought of one other thing on the way here. It was bothering me, back of my mind, and I just remembered what it was. The two chemical depot uniforms I saw looked legitimate, but the patches on the uniform weren't permanently sewn on yet. They were being prepared to look like the real thing," Drake said.

"Is it possible this has something to do with drugs, smuggling them into the chemical depot? You saw the manager with the drug dealer."

Drake watched a ski boat drive past on the lake for a moment before answering. "I'm not sure what any of this has to do with the chemical depot. I know a lot of terrorists would like to get their hands on our old chemical weapons. On the other hand, the uniforms I saw could be nothing more than a prop to let them smuggle drugs into the depot."

"But you think it's more than just drugs?"

"Senator, there are just too many things happening for all of them to be coincidental. Richard Martin's secretary was killed for a reason. The head of security, who's supposed to have killed her, conveniently commits suicide before he could be questioned. Then, after I confront the manager of ISIS, three men show up at my farm and try to kill me. I see ISIS friendly with a drug dealer, and hiding Muslims in an underground bunker. I think this is about more than drugs."

The Senator turned to face Drake. "What do you want me to do?"

"I don't think you can do anything, just yet. We don't know enough. What I'd like to do is visit the chemical depot. I know how to spot weaknesses in a facility's defenses. If you could arrange for me to visit there tomorrow, say as the head of your personal security detail, I'll say I'm coming to check out arrangements for your visit. Maybe I can make some sense out of all this."

"I hope you're wrong about this. It's one thing to think Richard Martin's research project is in trouble. It's an important part of our homeland security effort. It's an entirely different matter to think a chemical weapons depot is being targeted. We've protected those old weapons since the end of World War II, and we're finally getting rid of the damn things. I'll arrange for you to visit the Umatilla Depot tomorrow, just as soon as we finish brunch," Senator Hazelton said, putting his hand on Drake's shoulder and turning him toward the house for their breakfast.

Chapter 39

Eight-thirty Tuesday morning Drake flew out of the nearby Hillsboro airport, one of the busiest executive airports in the country. His chartered plane flew east up the Columbia Gorge. On his left, Mount Saint Helens was crestless after the volcano of 1980, and on his right, the towering peak of Mount Hood.

Drake tried to relax on the short flight and think about what he needed to look for at the depot. He told the Senator he knew how to spot security weaknesses. When he did it before, the enemies were regional warlords and third-world military forces, not the security force of a highly guarded and sensitive American military depot. He didn't even know what high-tech measures the military used today, especially since 9/11. If security was a lot better than it had been on bases when he was in the military, maybe there wasn't a lot to worry about.

When he landed at the small airport in Hermiston, he was impressed to see that the Umatilla Depot Commander had a white Suburban and driver waiting for him. Drake identified himself and got into the passenger seat of the Suburban. The depot was located twelve miles west of Hermiston and the short drive through the sparse, high desert landscape didn't take long. Not long enough to develop much of a conversation with his driver, who appeared to have been instructed to keep his mouth shut.

The sprawling, nineteen-thousand-acre installation, had one thousand and one concrete, steel-reinforced, earth-covered igloos stretched across the land. It stored twelve percent of the nation's chemical weapon arsenal. Originally the old weapons had been designed by the Nazis. Nerve gas and mustard gas by the tons had been made, as lethal as anything ever developed for warfare at the time. After WWII, chemical weapon plants in the Russian zone were dismantled, put on railroad cars for the trip back to Russia, and reassembled. The West had seized samples of the weapons, but when it learned Russia was reconstructing the chemical weapon factories, it had to scramble to catch up and achieve parity with its old ally, now a new adversary.

But times had changed. The stockpiles of chemical weapons that had never been used were being destroyed. The job of the new Umatilla Chemical Demilitarization Facility (UMCDF) was to destroy all of the three thousand, seven hundred and seventeen tons of chemical weapons. That was what Lt. Col. Hollingsworth was supervising at the depot.

Under his command were six hundred and fifty civilian contract employees, and a National Guard infantry company. Another one hundred personnel lived on base to monitor the chemical agents, operate the incinerator, perform security operations, and conduct a highly important public affairs program. No one wanted to live near a chemical weapons facility, and the folks around the Umatilla Depot were no exception.

When Drake neared the depot, he saw the perimeter had a fence topped with barbed wire. There was a second, inner fence topped with razor wire.

"You ever have anybody try to get through your fences?" Drake asked the driver.

The driver, a National Guardsman in his twenties, answered with a snort, "Yeah, couple of drunk assholes tried it on a dare last year. They didn't make it to the inner fence before the reaction team got there. Our electronic surveillance is the best in the world. No one's going to breach our perimeter, sir."

From the looks of the fences and the surveillance devices he could see spaced along the inner fence, he had to agree. If you were going to gain access to the depot, you weren't going to do it by crashing through the perimeter fences.

At the main gate, security guards carefully checked his ID, even though he was escorted by the Commander's driver. In the distance, an armed patrol moved along the inside of the perimeter fencing.

"You use perimeter patrols all the time, or just for the ceremony tomorrow?"

"Twenty-four seven, sir, twenty-four seven," the driver answered, as he drove on to the cluster of buildings that housed the Commander and his staff.

A guard at the front door of the depot headquarters checked his ID again before escorting him to the Commander's office. They walked down a hallway with a highly polished floor and photos of the depot's operations on the walls.

Lt. Col. Hollingsworth was younger than expected. He was short, maybe five foot nine or so, a fireplug that probably led his men in calisthenics.

The commander stood behind his desk and watched Drake with a polite smile as he entered the room. He was used to dealing with politicians. Now he was being asked to answer to some security person for a guest speaker he'd already gone out of his way to protect.

"Colonel Hollingsworth, I'm Adam Drake. Thank you for making time to see me and go over the arrangements for tomorrow, on behalf of Senator Hazelton."

"Mr. Drake, I took the liberty of calling the Pentagon to make sure the Senator had a son-in-law. I learned you were

Special Forces. Your record is a little skimpy, though. That suggests several things to me. Would you mind telling me why you're here?"

Drake smiled and said, "Colonel, you're a careful man. I was Special Forces, and I am Senator Hazelton's son-in-law. I'm also an attorney. I help the Senator from time to time."

"That doesn't tell me why you're here, does it? But if the Senator is worried, I'm sure your trained eye will spot something my staff may have missed."

The twinkle and challenge in the Commander's eyes said, as clearly as anything, take a look, you won't find anything even if you were Special Forces.

Commander Hollingsworth called his aide into his office, introduced her to Drake and then dismissed them both. His aide, Capt. Martinez, had short black hair, beautiful brown eyes and wore a uniform that sported airborne wings. She didn't waste any time letting him know she was efficient, and more than qualified to serve as the Commander's aide.

"Commander Hollingsworth told me you're interested in our security arrangements for tomorrow. This depot covers a rectangular area of nineteen thousand, seven hundred and twenty-eight acres. There are two outer fences and roving security patrols. Two hundred reservists augment our civilian security force, and all of them are armed. Surveillance cameras monitor K Block, where the chemical weapons are stored in bunkers that have detectors for leakage and security breaches. This is a secure facility, Mr. Drake. I'm not sure what it is you want to see," Capt. Martinez said stiffly, as they walked toward the Commander's Humvee.

"Relax, Captain. I'm just here to see that the Senator is in good hands tomorrow. The curiosity is my own—call it professional interest. Where do your reservists come from?"

"The current rotation of reservists is from the Texas National Guard. They're here for one year. They've been through the Army's Special Reaction Training for this type of facility, and they're good people."

"I'm sure they are, Captain. What about your civilian security force? Do you hire and screen them, or does someone do that for you?"

Capt. Martinez looked away and briefly glanced down at her boots before she answered. Her right hand rested on the passenger door of the Humvee she was about to open for him.

"We screen and hire them ourselves. We only hire people with prior security training, mostly from the military, but some from the private sector. Not all of them have Special Reaction Training, if that's what you're asking. We run enough drills to make sure they know what they're supposed to be doing. This isn't everyone's dream job, but we do get good people."

"There's not a lot to do out here, are there any problems here at the depot?"

"Not more than usual. You know what it's like on an Army base. Most of the personnel who live here are young. We've had some fights in town. Some of the local citizenry don't like us much. I don't blame them. These weapons are pretty scary. We had some problems, when the incinerator was being built, with the construction workers. We've had bomb threats, because someone thought we were covering up nerve agent leaks that made them sick. But other than some minor drug use, we haven't had any significant problems."

Drake wanted to smile at the way she minimized the problems the depot had experienced. He knew, from news reports, there had been attempts to sneak into K Block. A lab worker had walked off with a vial of nerve agent by accident, causing a panic until the man was found. And, a security guard shot himself during a simulated attack on the depot.

"Tell me about your emergency planning and training," he said.

"Mr. Drake, I understand you were in the Army. What unexpected threat do you think we haven't trained for? There's a no-fly zone here. We train for someone trying to crash a plane into one of the igloos in K Block to cause a nerve gas leak. We train for coordinated attacks at multiple perimeter sites, truck bombs crashing the gates, you name it. Training is what the Army does best."

Drake knew she wasn't angry yet, but she was getting close.

"Captain, I'm not here to give you a bad time. I just need to confirm arrangements, so I don't get in your way tomorrow. Maybe you could show me around the depot and review your plans for tomorrow. I'll be out of here before you miss me."

The tight smile on her face said there was no way in hell she would miss him.

After they were seated in the Humvee and driving slowly on the depot's main road, Capt. Martinez began her review of the arrangements for tomorrow.

"The dedication of the incinerator is scheduled for ten hundred hours. There are three hundred guests and dignitaries invited, your father-in-law included. They have all been screened for us by the Secret Service. No one will be allowed to enter the depot after oh-nine-thirty hours. We've doubled the security patrols around the perimeter of the depot. The airspace is already restricted. The Oregon State Police, the Hermiston County Sheriff and the Hermiston Police Department will be on alert. Additionally, the Oregon National Guard unit in Pendelton will have their rapid response team on standby. The State of Oregon, as you probably know, developed our emergency disaster plan. It's as comprehensive as it gets. I think we've got things covered here."

They were driving by the storage igloos in K Block as Capt. Martinez concluded her briefing. Row after row of earth-covered cement and steel storage units housing the chemical weapons stretched away into the brown and barren distance.

"Who has access to this area?" Drake asked.

"Security staff patrol the area and civilian lab personnel monitor the igloos for leakage. No one else gets in here," she said.

"What happens if you have an accident here in K Block? What does the emergency plan call for then?"

Capt. Martinez stopped abruptly, next to the entrance of an igloo and turned to face him. "If there's an accident, Mr. Drake, sirens go on all over the depot. Personnel in the command structure, responsible for responding to an emergency, immediately go to the depot's emergency operations center. There are cameras installed all around K Block so command personnel can watch personnel responding. Visitors are taken to the emergency center, where they can be protected from any chemical weapon exposure. Our response teams deal with that exposure. Then, the emergency operations center determines the potential exposure to the surrounding communities. The depot's medical staff prepares to deal with decontamination and treating any victims," she said, slamming the Humvee into gear. "If you need more information, take it up with Colonel Hollingsworth."

On the silent ride continuing around the depot, they drove past the chemical agent disposal facility with its giant incinerator. Drake saw that the dedication platform had been erected in the visitor parking area. He made a mental note that the dedication platform was less than a mile from K Block.

"One more question and I'm done," Drake said, breaking the silence. "If an emergency occurs during the ceremony tomorrow, how long will it take to move visitors to the emergency center?"

"The visitor buses arrive, and then remain behind the grandstands. They'll take visitors to the emergency center. The VIPs will be brought in by assigned Humvees. Everyone will be instructed to return to the vehicles they arrived in if an emergency siren goes on. Our rehearsals require twelve minutes to return everyone to the emergency center," Capt. Martinez said, without turning her head from the road.

If rehearsals took twelve minutes, Drake knew the real thing, with all the confusion that sirens would cause, would take twice as long.

"I'd like to see the emergency center, and then I'll be out of your hair, Captain."

When he was returned to headquarters, after a quick tour of the emergency center, Lt. Col. Hollingsworth was in a meeting. Drake was left alone in the Commander's office to look at the books in his glass door barrister's bookcase. They were mostly biographies and civil war histories. The pictures on the walls were of ceremonial poses with senior officers the Commander had served with. Some were pictures of young soldiers in fatigues, in unnamed places around the world, including one of a much younger Lt. Col. Hollingsworth. Drake wondered how Hollingsworth had wound up in charge of a chemical weapons depot, far away from the action.

Based on his tour of the depot, it was clear that the facility was well guarded against an attack from outside the perimeter fences. If an airplane violated restricted airspace and attempted to crash into an igloo, the earth-covered bunkers were reinforced to withstand the impact. No, if the depot was exposed to a serious threat, Drake concluded, it would come from within—from the civilian security force or some reservist.

"Well, Mr. Drake, did Capt. Martinez convince you we're secure here?" Lt. Col. Hollingsworth asked when he returned to his office.

"That's one straight aide-de-camp you have there, Colonel. Yes, she did her best to convince me you're one hundred percent secure here. But we both know that's rarely the case."

Lt. Col. Hollingsworth sat down in his high-backed chair and studied Drake. His look was not defensive, but coolly appraising.

"If you think you spotted something, lay it out for me. Protecting this place and the people who live around here is my job. I take it seriously, but I don't believe any place is one hundred percent secure."

"Colonel, I can see you take your job seriously. Just a couple more questions and I'll be on my way. What identification is required to get into the depot for your civilian personnel and reservists?" Drake asked pointedly.

"The two hundred reservists stationed here all have military ID they were issued by their units. Our security and civilian personnel have security badges we issue. If they have business here tomorrow, they'll be admitted as always. None of them will want to be here, unless they're working, believe me. Did you ever attend a ceremony you weren't ordered to attend?" the Colonel asked.

"No, I guess not," Drake admitted. "Thank you for the courtesy you extended to the Senator. I'll head back to Portland and see you when I return with the Senator and his party tomorrow."

As he was escorted back to the airport, Drake acknowledged the obvious threat. You might know who the individuals were who had access to your secure facility. How could you ever know their secret plans? ISIS might have secret plans that involved the depot, but how could you ever identify the people used to carry out those plans? The question worried him throughout his return flight to the executive airport in Hillsboro.

Chapter 40

Drake accelerated his old Porsche away from the charter service hanger and hit the speed dial on his cell phone.

"Hi Margo, anything urgent develop this morning?"

"Nothing that wasn't expected. Cutler and Whitcomb said they were reporting you to the bar. Judge Beck said he'd give you to the end of the week to respond to their motions, or he'd grant summary judgment. I'm working through the pile of work you left on my desk, but we have to do something about these motions.

"I know. I'm not going to have much time until Thursday or Friday. Give Eric Katz a call, see if he's available for some short-notice contract work. He was brilliant on the Court of Appeals brief, he can handle the motions.

"You have fun this morning?"

"More than you can imagine. Tell you about it when I get back. I'm headed to the Secret Service field office. While I'm there, would you call Detective Carson and ask if he's making any headway? I should be finished with the Secret Service in an hour or so."

"I will, if you promise you'll be back this afternoon," Margo bargained.

"Yes boss, I promise," Drake said, closing his phone. Her next performance and salary review was going to be a lot like a union contract negotiation, giving her everything she asked for.

Drake drove to the parking garage across from the Federal office building. He didn't expect them to tell him much, but he wanted them to realize he'd be along for the ride. After twenty minutes waiting in the reception area reading an old *Sports Illustrated,* he was escorted to the office of the managing agent in the Portland office.

Richard Rendell sat behind an uncluttered government-issue executive desk. Sitting across from him was the man who had warned him to stay out of the government's business. Neither man got up when he entered the room.

"Mr. Drake, I'm told you have a habit of involving yourself in things that don't concern you. I hope you're not here to waste my time on something of that nature."

Drake ignored Rendell's greeting and sat down in the other chair in front of the desk, turning to John Mason.

"Nice to see you again, John. I see you've been telling Mr. Rendell about me."

"No need to, really. He was in charge of cleaning up the mess on your farm last week. What is it you want, Drake?" Mason said, in his best, bored civil servant tone.

"I don't want anything, John. This is a courtesy call. Senator Hazelton asked me to accompany him to the dedication ceremony at the Umatilla depot. He wants to know what security arrangements you've made for the event. Have the person in charge of planning security see me, and I'm out of here. Then you two can get back to the high-level discussions I interrupted."

Mason looked across the desk at Rendell. "We don't have any security plans. The Army's in charge of that."

"What about security for Secretary Rallings?" Drake asked, with lifted eyebrows. "Surely you've made arrangements for his protection. He's your boss."

Mason bristled. "Let me tell you something you obviously don't know. The Secret Service is not authorized to protect the

Secretary of Homeland Security. Congress provides us with a list of protectees, and he's not on it. We do not implement operational security plans for dedication ceremonies, unless the President designates the event as a National Security Special Event, which he hasn't. This is an Army ceremony, on an Army facility, and they're quite capable of handling an event for a couple hundred people. Secretary Rallings has his own personal protection, just as Senator Hazelton does. Ask them what their plans are."

"You're telling me one of the most obvious terrorist targets walks around the country without your protection?" Drake exclaimed incredulously.

Mason stood and tried to stare down Drake. "I don't know who you think you are, coming here to tell me what I need to do. I don't care if Senator Hazelton sent you, we're done here."

Drake rose and stepped close, his nose inches away from Mason's. "Mason, I know more about protecting someone than you'll learn in two lifetimes. I learned from experience how to get inside security planned by little men like you. I was very good at it. You're making a mistake, letting Secretary Rallings walk around without protection. If anything happens to him that you could have prevented, I'll make sure someone who knows what they're doing has your job. Sit back down, I'll show myself out."

Ten minutes later, Drake was in his office, trying to calm down. Margo had followed him and stood in front of his desk, waiting for an explanation.

"I think it's time you told me what's going on."

"You're right. Have a seat," he said, as he turned from looking out the window at the marina below. Drake trusted her enough to tell her everything, and expected her to provide her usual, common-sense reality check. When he finished telling her about the last two and a half days, she had a few questions.

"Shall I assume you were trespassing when you saw these things at the ISIS ranch?"

"Let's just say it was night, and could have been open rangeland. Hard to tell where one ranch ends and another begins, except for the fence I had to crawl under. ISIS isn't going to say anything, but you can see why I can't explain things to the FBI or the Secret Service."

"So, how does your intuition jump from Kaamil and Roberto smuggling drugs into the chemical weapons depot to a terrorist plot tomorrow? I haven't heard much that supports your conclusion," she challenged.

"That's just it, Margo. I don't have anything conclusive. I just know something's not right and there doesn't seem to be much I can do about it."

"Can you ask the Senator to do something?"

"I can't get him directly involved. I did this on my own. I won't jeopardize his career. If I tell DHS or the FBI everything I know, I'm sure they'd welcome the opportunity to teach me a lesson, or embarrass him."

"So why did you go to Hermiston today?" Margo continued.

"I went to check security arrangements. With my concerns, I had to know how he's going to be protected."

"So if you tag along as part of the Senator's security detail, are you going to be able to do anything to protect him?" she asked.

Drake looked at her for a long moment. "I knew I could count on you. Probably not by myself. If you'd be so kind to get my friend in Seattle on the phone, I might be able to round up some help."

He thought he caught a smile on her lips as she turned and walked down the stairs to her desk. She was right, of course. If he was going to do anything more than worry, he needed his old partner along for the ride.

Chapter 41

With a rough idea of a plan in mind, Drake picked up the phone to talk with Mike.

"If you're calling to thank me for all my help over the weekend, you're welcome. The bill is already in the mail," his friend answered.

"Nice. I thought we were friends. Now I'm just another client."

"Just one among hundreds. So, what's up this time? You connect the dots yet on our friends in Hood River?"

"Not yet, at least not with anything I can take to the bank. I need your help again. I'm accompanying my father-in-law to the weapons depot tomorrow as part of his security detail. I'd like you to join me, ride shotgun," Drake said. "The Senator and the Secretary of DHS will each have their own personal two-man security detail, but if my hunch is right, that may not be enough."

"What do you think we might need?"

"I'm thinking an armor-plated Yukon, chemical protective gear for nine and a driver who isn't afraid of mixing it up if necessary. Think you can find someone like that on short notice?"

"I might be able to. The person I have in mind will require more than his usual high rate of compensation, due to the aforementioned short notice."

"If the person you have in mind can meet me at the Hermiston airport tomorrow morning at eight thirty, with the Yukon, the gear I mentioned, and the stuff that person brought with him last time, I'm sure we can work something out."

Before she died, Kay had asked if he missed being in the Army. He told her, with all the honesty he could muster, he did miss some of the excitement. He did not tell her that what he had done hadn't made a damn bit of difference, for all the risks he had taken. Now, he was thinking the risk might be worth it. If the sum of the parts added up to the whole he feared, it would be worth the risk to stop ISIS and Kaamil.

Drake sat quietly for a moment. He had never considered his own father's motivation. He must have felt the same way when he volunteered to return to Vietnam after his first tour. Why else would you put yourself in harm's way, if you didn't think you could make a difference? For the millionth time, he wished that he'd been able to know more about his Dad than stories his Mother told him and a name on the wall.

Drake broke out of his reverie, signed the letters and documents Margo had stacked on his desk, and headed downstairs.

"Margo, I signed the letters and things you put on my desk. I've got to leave for a bit. Call me if you hear from Detective Carson."

He wanted to see his pastor. The man had comforted Kay through her cancer, and had become a friend. Drake had learned he was a student of history and understood the world's religions. If anyone could shed light on how an American Muslim became a jihadist, Pastor Steve could.

Drake drove west on Hwy. 217 to Beaverton. The afternoon sun was low enough in the sky to require sunglasses on the way to the New Hope Faith Center. The church was a collection of new, utilitarian buildings scattered around a small college campus. There was an administration building, housing for permanent staff, a counseling center, a youth wing with a gym, and a main sanctuary accommodating as many as six thousand on Sundays.

A white Harley-Davidson Sportster XL 1200 was parked in the pastor's parking space by the administration building. He normally drove a green Honda, but when summer rolled around not much kept Pastor Steve off his Harley.

Drake parked next to the pastor's motorcycle, and walked into the building and down a carpeted hallway to the pastor's offices. After the secretary called ahead, he was motioned into the pastor's study. Pastor Steve sat behind his desk, holding his usual mug of coffee.

"Adam, come in," Pastor Steve said, getting up to give him a big hug. Big, because before divinity school, Pastor Steve was one of the best six-foot-eight-inch power forwards in college basketball. He'd written more than a dozen books on church history, started a food bank that served as many people as two county food banks in the area, and was a popular guest on local television news.

"I didn't make an appointment, sorry if I'm interrupting."

"Nonsense, I'm working on a speech. I could use a break. How are you getting along?"

"Some days are worse than others, but I'm doing better," Drake conceded. "I wonder if you have a couple minutes to talk about a case I'm working on."

"We can spend as much time as you need. I've missed seeing you since Kay died. Would you like some coffee? I could use a refill."

"Sure. I'm working on a case that may wind up involving some local Muslim jihadists. I'm curious about what makes a person of faith consider martyrdom, and even treason."

Pastor Steve waited while his secretary brought in a carafe of coffee and a mug for Drake, before answering.

"Is this a question about my understanding of radical Islam, or about some of the arrests that have involved local mosques?"

"Both, I guess."

Pastor Steve looked toward the books lining his floor-to-ceiling bookshelf while he decided where to start.

"Islam is the fastest growing religion in America, and the world right now. There are over two thousand mosques in our country. Most were built in the last twenty years with Saudi oil money. Wahhabism is the official religion of Saudi Arabia, and that fundamentalist sect of Islam is the principal influence in the mosques they build and finance here. It's also the subset of Islam that claimed the allegiance of Osama bin Laden, al Qaeda and most of the terrorist organizations in the world. The true radical believer pays allegiance to no country, only to Allah."

"But why is that brand of Islam taking hold here?" Drake asked.

"I can only guess," Pastor Steve said. "In our inner cities, Muslim organizations deliver materially in a way our government and churches don't. They build community centers, patrol the streets and get people organized. In our prisons, converting to Islam means you have protection when you're inside, and someone with money to help outside. When welfare reform came along, Saudi money stepped in when the government stepped out. Saudi-funded Islam has just done a better job reaching out to the disaffected and angry among our people."

"But that doesn't explain the appeal of radical Islam to well-educated, middle-class Americans. Not all the people who have been arrested on terrorism charges have been inner-city welfare types," Drake said.

"You don't have to be poor and uneducated to feel disaffected and angry. If you're told that family breakdown, racism and poverty result from Western decadence and immorality, fundamental Islam can seem pretty attractive. By converting to Islam, people who feel they're invisible and unimportant now belong to a powerful and moral civilization without borders. They're told that someday they'll rule the world, like Islam did in the days of the Caliphs. Hope of utopia has powered more than one 'ism' in the last hundred years."

"Do you think American citizens, who grew up in our culture and aren't taught in *madrassas*, to revere martyrdom, can be trained to be martyrs?" Drake asked.

Pastor Steve nodded slowly. "I'd have to say yes. Minority groups who perceive themselves as underdogs and blame America for their perceived oppression, can probably be persuaded to become martyrs. The reward of paradise, coupled with the teaching that Mohammed himself desired martyrdom, as bin Laden taught, is pretty powerful stuff."

"Are they brainwashed by this religious training, or is it hatred that motivates them?"

"Hatred and religious doctrine have motivated people for two thousand years. Do you know who the original terrorists were?" Pastor asked, getting up to walk to his bookcase and pull a volume from the shelf.

"Terrorism has been with us for a long time, but no, I don't know who the original terrorists were," Drake answered.

"Marco Polo wrote about a secret sect of Islam using murder and assassination as a weapon of terror, ostensibly to keep the religion pure. The master of the cult, known as the Old Man of the Mountain, kept young boys at his court who would do anything he asked them to do. It's said he promised them paradise if they carried out his assassination orders.

Marco Polo wrote that he witnessed young men jumping off the Old Man's fortress wall to their death to prove how the master controlled them. Does that sound anything like what we're reading about today in Iraq, Afghanistan, Israel, London? Why should America be any different?"

Drake didn't have an answer. After finishing his coffee, he left, promising he would see Pastor Steve in church soon.

Chapter 42

Drake was driving back to his office when his cell phone jarred him from his thoughts about American martyrs.

"Detective Carson just called. He's having coffee where you saw him last. Said he needed to talk to you," Margo said. "If you are still in the area, you might want to see him. It sounded like it was urgent."

"I'm on 217. I'll turn around and go meet him. If he calls again before I get there, tell him I'm on my way."

He wondered what the detective had that was so urgent. He knew more than he did last week, but he wasn't confident that Carson had made much progress. When he pulled into the Starbucks parking lot ten minutes later, Detective Carson waited for him at a window table.

Carson stood when he entered and gestured for him to have a seat. Carson didn't wait for him to get comfortable before he started.

"I'm getting a lot of heat, Drake, to bring you in for questioning about some dead guys on your farm. I don't have jurisdiction for that. I'm told it might have something to do with the murder at Martin Research. I do have jurisdiction to question you about that. I thought I'd save us both some time, and ask you up front what you might know about any connection."

"This doesn't have anything to do with your investigation, does it?" Drake asked. "You're getting pressure because of the imams' protests. Are you sure you want to hear what I might know? If you think this is going to make your life easier, you're dead wrong."

"What's that supposed to mean? You're the guy being investigated for killing three men. You think I can just ignore that?"

"If you're smart, which at this point is questionable, you'll walk away from this. Just do your job and find out who murdered Janice Lewellyn. The FBI is involved, but, if I give you some off-the-record information, will you tell me everything you've learned and leave this alone? Can you live with that, or do I walk out of here?"

Detective Carson looked at Drake with a decade of resentment smoldering in his eyes before he nodded.

"Stay. Maybe I came on a little too strong. You need to know there are people downtown who want to hang you for killing those Muslims. They don't want another scandal, or to be accused of covering up a profile killing. Me, if guys came on my farm, with the weapons they carried, I'd kill them too. Regardless of their religious persuasion."

"It had nothing to do with their religious persuasion. It was dark. All I knew was, they were armed, and surrounding my home. End of story. Except I can't believe they came after me because I was looking into the murder of Martin's secretary."

"So what were you looking into?" Carson asked. "I've run down all the leads. None of the people I talked to looked dangerous."

"Did you talk with the ISIS manager? You detect anything unusual about some of the help they hired as security guards? Sam Newman did, and he's dead. I did, after visiting ISIS, and three goons came gunning for me. That give you some clue how this all ties together?"

Drake could see Carson didn't want to hear what he was telling him. He didn't want to be on the wrong end of a police investigation that the feds would probably commandeer and then would look for a scapegoat if there was a mess to clean up. He felt sorry, for a second, for the cop who'd been promoted beyond his capabilities.

Drake softened his approach. "Look, trust me that you don't want to get caught up in the stuff that's out of your jurisdiction. But, if you share with me what you know, and it winds up that it's all connected, I'll see you get credit for all of it."

"Why would you do that? You're the one who blew the whistle on me. All I did was what any cop would have done with a scumbag like that. He was going to walk unless I did something."

"That was then, this is now. I was just pissed you screwed up my case and the guy walked because of you. I could have won that case, regardless of what you thought. This is bigger than our past differences. Tell me what you've learned."

"Martin's secretary was the proverbial straight arrow. Wrong place, wrong time. Martin's the same straight arrow and a workaholic. Logs at least eighty hours a week. His employees love him," Carson recited. "I don't think Sam Newman committed suicide. He was a devout Catholic, and his priest said he was a regular at confession. There wasn't enough gunshot residue on his hand, and we can't find his dog. According to Martin, that dog would never leave his master. There just isn't any reliable evidence that he had anything to do with the secretary's murder, or that he killed himself. Someone else was involved, had to have been."

"So, where does that leave us?" Drake asked.

"Nowhere. None of the employees at Martin Research

had any problems with Mrs. Lewellyn, as far as we can tell. The reports of earlier break-ins haven't led to anything. I'm still trying to get budget approval for an outside computer expert to go over the malfunction in the security system. The ISIS records show the entire system went down about the time we figure Mrs. Lewellyn was murdered. ISIS says it wasn't shut off, that the system just crashed. I just don't buy it."

"What do the guys at Martin Research say? Do they agree with ISIS?"

"They say they don't have a reason to doubt ISIS. Without access to the ISIS computers, they can't analyze the cause of the malfunction. Personally, I think they're scared to admit their system might not be as good as they think it is."

That could be, Drake thought, but it didn't mean ISIS wasn't lying. Sophisticated security systems are redundant security systems. If one part of the subsystem isn't working, the system knows it immediately and switches to a backup subsystem. Proving that someone deliberately shut a subsystem off, without having access to the security system itself, would be impossible.

"Can you demand access to the ISIS system, so you can check things for yourself? You don't need budget approval for that," Drake suggested. "In the meantime, I'll give you anything I turn up if you'll do the same."

Carson finished his coffee and stood when Drake did.

"That's not a bad idea—see if someone starts squirming. Something I'm good at. I'll tell the folks downtown we talked," Carson said.

Chapter 43

Wednesday morning broke with promise, another picture-perfect day. Drake arrived at the Portland International Airport Flightcraft terminal at 7:45 a.m. They were all waiting for him next to the Gulfstream Secretary Rallings had reserved.

Senator Hazelton introduced him to Secretary Rallings, his aide, and the Secretary's two-man security detail. The Secretary of DHS was shorter than he appeared in his pictures, but no less distinguished. In his late 60s, he looked every bit the former Ivy League boxer he was, powerful in his upper body, with a pugnacious bulldog face. He reminded Drake of Winston Churchill.

His aide was a bright young MBA type hoping a stint in Washington would establish a foothold for his career. The two bodyguards were the aide's perfect foil, a reassigned FBI agent and a former Hostage Rescue Team leader. They introduced themselves, and their former careers, in a not so subtle way. The message was clear—stay out of our way because we're the pros.

There was another person in the party, and from the disgusted look on her face, she hadn't been told Drake was included. Her eyes tightened when she saw him, and her mouth turned down at the corners. It wasn't a frown, exactly, but it sure wasn't a smile.

Drake shook hands with the two men traveling with the Senator. He knew them both. Bob Allen was a former Oregon State Trooper and the Senator's personal bodyguard. Tim Richards was the Senator's chief of staff.

As soon as they were all seated in the Gulfstream, the pilot announced they would be airborne shortly for the flight to Hermiston, one hundred eighty-five miles east up the Columbia River Gorge. The Secretary and the Senator were seated across from each other in the first row of seats, with their security details seated behind them. Drake and the others accommodated themselves in the remaining eight seats.

Drake made a point of sitting across from Liz Strobel. As they accelerated to lift off, Strobel lost control of her composure and hissed over the roar of the engines, "You agreed to keep me informed, and now you're trying to do my job. I resent this!"

"I'm not here to do your job, Administrative Assistant Strobel. I'm here to protect the Senator, at his request," he said with a smile. "You have the Homeland to protect, but you never know when a Senator might run into a crazy constituent. Surely you don't have a problem with that?"

"What I have a problem with is you. I stuck my neck out for you and your father-in-law. I'm not jeopardizing my career just because you're seeing terrorists behind every bush."

Drake leaned toward Strobel and invaded her personal space. "You'd better pray I'm wrong, and this is just a figment of my misguided imagination. You've never seen a terrorist, let alone fought one, and you don't have a clue how they think. God help us that you're supposed to be protecting us. All you care about is your pathetic little career. Stay out of my way, and remember the day you may have underestimated the enemy, and me."

The rest of the short flight to Hermiston was quiet. The Secretary and the Senator talked quietly while everyone else enjoyed the scenery. Strobel sat stiffly in her seat, staring out the portside window at the river below. Drake thumbed through the *Sports Illustrated* he'd brought, and hoped Strobel was right and he was wrong about seeing a terrorist in every Umatilla depot uniform.

At 8:30 a.m., the pilot announced they were approaching their destination and began their descent to the small town of Hermiston. Its small municipal airport was just twelve miles east of the depot.

As the Gulfstream taxied toward the terminal, Drake spotted Mike's white Yukon parked next to the one-story building that served as the city's municipal airport terminal and flight control tower. Mike stood next to his SUV wearing a Mariner's baseball hat, sunglasses, and a lightweight windbreaker and jeans. Drake knew the windbreaker concealed more than Mike's lean body.

When they were allowed to deplane, Drake led the Senator's small party over to Mike and introduced them. While Mike was getting everyone seated, and the Secretary and his people were escorted to the vehicles the Army had provided, Drake walked over to the pilot.

"We should be back in two hours. On the outside chance we might need to get out of here quickly, I'd appreciate it if you'd stay in or near the plane. I'm not expecting trouble, but I want you to be ready in case something happens. There are a lot of people who don't appreciate what's being done at the weapons depot. There are enough nuts around to make me nervous. If I call, or my friend Mike, next to the Yukon, calls, have the plane ready to take off the minute we get here. We'll be about fifteen minutes out."

When he got back to the Yukon, everyone was seated for the ride to the depot.

"Any trouble with the locals when you told them you wanted to park next to the terminal for a while?" Drake asked.

"Not after I told them to call the Senator's office. They've been visited by so many dignitaries, they're used to the drill. You ready to roll?"

"Roll on, amigo. Let's see if the depot security staff is as alert as the airport people were."

Leaving the terminal area, they drove past a Bell 407 medical evacuation helicopter, with letters designating it as one of the life flight helicopters from the nearby Good Shepherd Medical Center. The pilot's door on the right was open, and Drake could see the pilot sitting inside.

"Looks like they're ready for any eventuality here. Were you able to get the stuff we talked about?"

"Everything's in the back," Mike said, hooking a thumb over his shoulder. "We going to be able to get all this stuff past security?"

"Shouldn't be a problem. The Senator cleared it for us. We have ID. If we're busted, I'll just tell them I didn't know anything about the stuff you brought. At least I'll be able to get the Senator through."

"Funny," Mike said, without wasting a glance at Drake.

"When we get there, I'll accompany the Senator to the ceremony. You stay with the Yukon. My main concern is if anything happens during the ceremony, there won't be adequate transportation for everyone. They've promised VIP Humvees for the Secretary and the Senator, but I want to make sure we're able to get him out if we need to. If anything goes down, I'll get him back to you, and you get us back to their emergency center."

Mike drove out of the airport and turned onto the Hermiston Highway toward I-84 and the Umatilla Weapons Depot to the west. The flat land on both sides of the highway was colored in spring green, shading to early summer brown. Overhead, contrails of fighter aircraft flying patterns over the depot crossed the sky.

"When we get to the main gate, show our ID. Ask them to call Lt. Col. Hollingsworth and tell him we've arrived," Drake directed. "He's expecting us. We'll be escorted directly to an area behind the speaker's stage. We should be there early enough to do a quick walk around."

The drive from the airport to the main gate of the depot took ten minutes. It was nine o'clock when they arrived, and there were only a half dozen cars ahead of them at the security checkpoint. Drake was pleased to see that identification was carefully checked for every passenger in the cars ahead of them. The undercarriage of each vehicle was searched with a mirror, and a German shepherd walked around each car to detect explosives.

When it was their turn, the Army sergeant matched picture ID with every person in the vehicle and checked each of them off his visitor list before calling Lt. Col. Hollingsworth. The sergeant then signaled for their escort, and a tan desert camo-colored Humvee pulled out to lead them.

The depot grounds were inspection-ready neat for the ceremony. The few soldiers Drake saw were all wearing starched BDUs and spit-shined boots. The command center looked like it had a fresh touch up of paint, and the barracks off to the right had walkways lined with white rocks leading to their front doors. Lt. Col. Hollingsworth obviously had his command standing tall for the ceremony.

The $1.2 billion chemical incinerator the Army was dedicating rose in front of them as they drove on into the depot. It was a modern-looking complex that covered a football field with its conveyors and furnaces and miles of piping. It didn't appear that much different from newer chemical plants seen around the country.

In the parking lot, in front of the main building of the incinerator, the Army had erected grandstand bleachers, and a speaker's stage for the dignitaries. In front of the bleachers, a table stacked with programs was staffed by a young corporal standing at ease. Other soldiers stood, on each end of the bleachers, to assist guests. The Army was putting its best foot forward for the ceremony.

Mike pulled the Yukon behind the stage and got out to identify himself and his passengers to the Army sergeant stationed there. While he was talking to the sergeant, Drake turned to the Senator and explained what he wanted them to do in case of an emergency.

"If an emergency happens, for whatever reason, I want the three of you to hustle back here and get inside. Bob," he said to the Senator's bodyguard, "that's your job, to get the Senator and Tim back here. This Yukon is armor plated, and we have protective equipment for everyone. I've been briefed on the Army's emergency plan, and we'll follow it. We'll just use our own transportation. Any questions?"

The Senator, his aide and bodyguard all nodded no. They may have thought he was being a little dramatic about the whole thing, but they were polite enough not to show it.

"Good, then let's enjoy the show," Drake said, hoping that it would be one they'd all enjoy.

Chapter 44

The schedule of events called for Secretary Rallings and the other dignitaries to take a tour of the incinerator. They would then adjourn to a small conference room in the main incinerator building, for coffee, juices, and pastries before the guests arrived and the dedication ceremony began. Following the coffee break, the honored dignitaries were to move to their respective seats, arranged by strict military protocol.

Drake walked behind his charge as they toured the incinerator. Well-wishers greeted the Senator and reminded him of their undying support. He wondered how any man put up with the fawning for as long as the Senator had. Politicians were just servants of the people, no different than the soldiers who protected them. There weren't many of the dignitaries who paid any attention to the high-ranking officers who stood chatting with each other. He'd seen it all before, unfortunately, the posturing of the power seekers.

Around the conference room, Drake noted sentries posted and armed with only side arms, standard issue 9mm Berettas. Despite the assurances of the depot commander, security appeared to be concentrated on the outer perimeters of the depot.

When it was time for the coffee break to end, Drake had to interrupt a persistent county commissioner. He was trying to convince the Senator federal money was needed to find out why Hermiston watermelons were losing market share to Texas and Florida.

"Ya gotta do something, Senator. I've got farmers struggling to survive. We don't have cheap labor, like they do in Texas and Florida. Either we got to let more immigrants in to do the work, or subsidize watermelons like corn and wheat. It ain't fair to my constituents."

"Senator, I'm sorry to interrupt, but you have to go. They're waiting for you on the platform," Drake said, taking the Senator's arm and turning him toward the door.

"You're a good bodyguard, Adam, but a poor politician. The man was promising to deliver the vote of almost two percent of the population of this state. That's everyone living in Umatilla County, if I'd just pay more attention to watermelons. Not that he could deliver on that promise, but you've got to listen to everyone. I had no idea Texas and Florida were our largest producers of watermelons," the Senator said with a smile.

Leaving the incinerator building, Drake saw that the local high school marching band was in place and the grandstand was full. In the forty-five minutes since the start of the tour of the incinerator, the Army had efficiently transported and seated all of the guests. Parked behind the grandstand were ten high school buses on loan to the Army for the day. One Humvee was parked in front of the first bus and another behind the last. Drivers stood at ease beside each of them. The armed security he could see, however, was the same small cadre of soldiers that had accompanied them on their tour.

Drake felt an old, familiar sensation tingling the back of his neck, and stepped off the platform to call Mike.

"I'm not feeling good about this. You see anything?" Drake said into his lapel mike.

"Not much to see. Guests were brought in without a hitch. Activities look pretty normal, but this is the Army.

Guards posted at the main gate are still there. Fighter planes are overhead, and not many vehicles are on the roads in here. They pretty much closed things down for the day. Why, you see something you're worried about?"

"No, just a feeling. They're a little light on security. Just keep your eyes open."

"Roger that. Any of those doughnuts left? I can handle the sweets, whereas you'd have to run laps tomorrow. Might help me stay alert, since I've been up since four a.m."

"Drink some of that coffee you brought along. I'll take care of the doughnuts," Drake taunted his friend.

"Okay, okay, but you're buying dinner tonight, and I choose the restaurant."

Promptly at ten o'clock, the color guard posted colors and the band played the National Anthem. When the band marched away, Lt. Col. Hollingsworth strode to the podium to greet the assembled dignitaries and guests.

"Secretary Rallings, Senator Hazelton, Mayor Severson, Congressman Wilkens, Commissioner Hansell and distinguished guests, it's my distinct pleasure and honor to welcome you on this day we've all been waiting for. This project began almost ten years ago, and many of you here were involved in its early development. We all share a common goal, the neutralization of the chemical weapons stored here. We're honored to have representatives from our capital, our state, and our area to help us formally dedicate this facility today. At this time, I'd like to introduce … "

The boom of a nearby explosion and the sirens that immediately started all over the chemical weapons depot interrupted the commander's speech. To the west, Drake saw black smoke and flames rising from one of the igloos in K Block as he ran to Senator Hazelton.

"Senator, that's where the nerve agents are stored. Please come with me," Drake instructed. "Secretary, you're welcome to join us. I have an armored SUV and protective gear for you and your staff waiting behind the platform."

Secretary Rallings turned to his head of security. "Andy?"

"If they have protection gear, let's go with them. I'm not sure the Humvees do," the FBI agent said.

The area around the platform and the grandstand in front of it quickly became a scene of panic. The invited guests scrambled from the grandstand and rushed to the buses, where they were slowed by the narrow, single-file doors of the borrowed school buses. Lines formed in front and around the buses, and soon they were blocked from leaving by the guests who were not willing to wait behind for the next bus.

The dignitaries from the speakers' platform were being ushered behind the platform, where a line of Humvees waited to take them to the emergency center. The six available Humvees could only move eight passengers at a time. Sixty or more VIPs shoved to get one of the available seats.

Drake ran with a guiding hand on the elbows of the Secretary and the Senator. They crossed through the area behind the platform, weaving through the other dignitaries, and reached their SUV where Mike stood.

"You said nine, I count eight," Mike shouted.

Drake took a quick look around. Strobel was missing. She started off the platform with the rest of them, but as he looked back he didn't see her anywhere in the crowd.

"Throw me two protective gear sets then take them to the emergency center. I'll find Strobel and meet you there."

Drake tucked the masks under his arm and ran back through the panicked crowd. Of all the people to create an unnecessary risk for herself, it would have to be Strobel.

By the time he reached the area where he last saw her, she was nowhere in sight. The steps off the back of the platform led to where the Humvees had been parked, but there were no Humvees there now. The remaining dignitaries were lined up and waiting for their return, surrounded by a squad of armed soldiers wearing protective gear. Those standing in line didn't appear to be frightened, trusting the soldiers who looked like they knew what they were doing.

One woman stood in front of the officer in charge of the loading detail, screaming into his protective mask.

"I don't care who your commanding officer is, my boss is the Secretary of Homeland Security and I order you to take me to him now!"

The Army captain started to move the woman out of his face when Drake stepped in. "Captain, if you'll allow me, I'll escort Ms. Strobel to the emergency center to be with her boss."

The captain looked through the lens of his protective mask and nodded, as if to say, if you want to deal with this psycho, she's all yours.

Drake grabbed Strobel by her arm and pulled her away. "This isn't a drill, so shut up and put this on. The explosion was in K Block. We've got to get out of here. The Secretary's already on his way to the emergency center."

Liz Strobel glared at him and jerked her arm free of his grasp. "Drake, I hope to hell you know what you're doing. If anything you've done endangers the Secretary, I'll personally see that you pay for this."

"Strobel, if any harm comes to the Secretary or the Senator, I guarantee the Secret Service, the JTTF, and you, will never draw another government paycheck. Now put this stuff on, let's go."

Chapter 45

As soon as they put on their protective masks and made sure they fit properly around their faces, Drake pulled Strobel away from the platform staging area. He headed across the open area to the visitors' grandstand. At the rear of the line of buses, he spotted an empty Humvee. The driver was busy helping people load onto a bus, and hadn't posted security around his vehicle.

Drake slowed to a walk and led Strobel toward the empty Humvee.

"Get into the Humvee and act like you own it. No one is going to pay any attention to us in this, and we're not going to do anything to change that," Drake ordered.

When they were seated, they were all but invisible amidst the confusion and movement of other military vehicles and buses. Smoke continued to billow from the bunker area of K Block, and a plume drifted southeast toward the headquarters buildings and the emergency center. As if to accent the threat, all seventy sirens of the Chemical Stockpile Emergency Preparedness Program sounded a steady, repeating, warning tone designed to be heard for miles around.

As he pulled out and joined the line of vehicles headed to the emergency center, Drake saw panic where there should have been practiced calm and efficiency. Ambulances rushed to K Block to take anyone injured to the base contamination station. Vehicles at intersections were left on their own, and buses carrying guests were stranded in the resulting congestion. Such was the terror created by the fear of the nerve agents the depot stored.

Seeing the traffic jam ahead of them, Drake turned the Humvee and headed across the open field toward the emergency center. The protective masks would protect them from any airborne agents, but full-body protection was really needed if they were in the open. A single drop of descending nerve agent on their skin would kill them. If the explosion involved fire, the nerve agents that were viscous, like motor oil, could fall on them from the plume of smoke drifting their way. Drake knew he had to get to the emergency center. He hoped Mike was already there.

The area Drake drove across was rangeland taken over for military use. The Humvee charged across it with all the grace of an Abrams M1A1 main battle tank, bouncing and bucking like a bronco at the nearby Pendleton Roundup. Drake was steadied by his grip on the steering wheel, but Liz Strobel was taking a pounding. She had one hand on the roof over her head and the other grabbing the frame of the seat below.

"Hang on, Liz. We're almost there," he said to console her.

When they reached the main base road, Drake threw the Humvee into a slide that carried them to the far side of the paved road. There were other Humvees ahead of them, racing to the emergency center, and he was satisfied to get in line and follow them in.

Outside the emergency center, things were not as focused and disciplined as they should have been. Drake quickly escorted Strobel to the main entrance of the center and was surprised when they weren't stopped. Drake was carrying his .45 under his jacket, and they were wearing protective masks. The other evacuated guests weren't. No one searched them, or even seemed to notice as they walked past the guards posted outside.

Once inside, a soldier directed them toward a large room just beyond the exterior blast doors, where guests and dignitaries had gathered. Two security guards were posted at the exterior blast doors, armed with M16s. Inside, no one was wearing a protective mask. Just as he was about to tell Strobel she could take her protective mask off, a soldier approached and said it was safe to remove their protective equipment.

Drake noted there were only three ways out of the emergency center assembly room. In addition to the main entrance, two doors exited from the rear of the room, one on each side. Each was guarded by a security guard armed with a holstered Beretta. He couldn't tell from inside the cavernous room if there were additional guards outside the rear doors, but he doubted it.

As soon as Strobel took her protective mask off, she stormed away looking for her boss. Drake spotted the Secretary and his father-in-law standing with the depot commander's aide, Capt. Linda Martinez. While Strobel made like a boat speeding through a no wake zone, oblivious to the disturbance created, Drake turned his attention outside where Mike was stationed as his spotter.

"Mike, what's going on out there?"

"Lot of people running around. You confirm our party's inside?"

"Roger that, all safe and sound. The civilian security guards are too relaxed. They look like this is a drill, but the early warning monitors had to signal a nerve agent release for the evacuation to be ordered."

"If VX is headed this way, the guys out here are also pretty calm. A few still have protective masks on, but no one's wearing protective suits. You sure they detected a nerve agent release?"

"I just overheard an announcement that detection teams are monitoring the situation. Let me know if anything changes. If it does, come in here," Drake said.

From where Mike sat in his Yukon, he had a view of the area around the emergency center. Drake knew if the situation worsened, the security guards outside would be among the first warned.

As Drake kept an eye on the inside of the emergency center, he heard Mike signal an alert.

"I'm watching three soldiers headed your way from one of the barracks. They're wearing full-body protective suits. No one else is wearing a suit. They're armed and walking like they're on a mission."

"What's changed?" Drake asked.

"Nothing. But these three are carrying M4s with grenade launchers. They look like they've just been given some urgent order."

"Keep them in sight. I'll see if anything has changed. They could be the guys I was worried about."

Drake located Capt. Martinez talking to someone and ran to her.

"Sorry to interrupt Captain, could I have a moment?"

"Excuse me, Mayor," she said, turning to Drake with a look of frustration. "What is it, Mr. Drake? Your father-in-law is fine."

"Has anything changed since we got here?"

"Look, we have everything under control. Relax and leave this to us. We've been through this a hundred times," she said and started to turn back to the Mayor.

"Then why are three soldiers wearing full body suits carrying M4s with grenade launchers headed our way?"

Capt. Martinez took a moment to process the information. "Perimeter security carries M16s and civilian security personnel carry M9 Berettas. How do you know what these guys are carrying?"

"I have someone stationed outside," Drake said.

"Shit. I'll alert security," Capt. Martinez said and rushed off.

Drake angled toward the corner of the main set of doors and called Mike.

"Sitrep, Mike," he said.

"Twenty yards from the emergency center and headed straight toward the two guards at the main doors. What do you want me to do?" Mike asked.

"If they start shooting, take them out. I'm just inside the main doors, north side. There's a room full of people in here, so be careful," Drake said.

Before Drake could say anything to alert the security guards at the main doors, full-auto gunfire erupted outside. The sound of M4s being fired in bursts was unmistakable to his ears.

Drake moved closer to the main doors and was five yards from the center of the two doors when three men burst through.

In their protective suits, the men stood boldly with the hoods thrown back over their shoulders. Drake saw the two security personnel slumped against the outside of the main doors.

Before they could start spraying deadly bursts at their captives, Drake pulled his .45 and shot the terrorist closest to him in the left temple. Just as swiftly, he was moving toward the second man when the man's head exploded in a pink burst of blood and brain. Mike could still hit a target.

The last man turned to his left, toward the sound of Drake's .45 in time to see his executioner before a bullet entered his forehead.

For a long moment, the screaming from the startled guests echoed in the vast room along with the reverberation of Drake's shots. Then a silence settled, broken only by the sobs of grateful survivors.

Drake checked each man on the floor and made sure they were dead before he holstered his .45. He turned and saw his father-in-law and the Secretary standing safely at the rear of the room.

"Drake, you okay in there? Any wounded?" Mike asked.

"I have three dead terrorists, no wounded."

"Then you should get out here. There are plenty of soldiers headed your way. Remember the helicopter ambulance we saw at the airport? It landed when those three guys started shooting. There's a guy standing next to it, watching everything with binoculars. I think this is the ride the shooters were expecting."

"What does he look like?"

"Just a second. Black guy, tall, maybe six seven or eight, wearing a paramedic's uniform. Wait a sec, looks like he saw me looking at him. He's signaling the pilot to take off. He's not waiting around to help any wounded," Mike said.

"Get the numbers on that helicopter, it sounds like Kaamil. I'm on my way."

Drake ran to where Capt. Martinez stood, giving orders to a group of soldiers. The look on her face when she saw him said, sorry, I should have listened.

"It wasn't your fault," Drake preempted the conversation. "It was an inside job. You couldn't have seen it coming. I think the helicopter ambulance that landed just as the shooting started is part of it. It's taking off. Is there anything here I can use to follow him?"

"Commander Hollingsworth has a Black Hawk, but I don't know where his pilot is."

"That's okay, I brought my own, a former Night Stalker. Tell me where it's parked, then call ahead and authorize the flight."

Capt. Martinez nodded a quick acknowledgement. "Landing pad's that way," she said, pointing. Drake turned and ran through the main doors of the emergency center just as Mike pulled up.

"Mike, we're going to borrow the commander's Black Hawk. You remember how to fly a Black Hawk?" Drake asked as he jumped in. Mike accelerated in the direction he indicated toward the landing pad a hundred yards south of the headquarters building. "If this is Kaamil, he's headed for the ranch or their warehouse in Hood River. Can we catch him?"

"Assuming the Black Hawk is ready to fly, he'll be at least ten minutes ahead of us. Good news, the Bell 407 will only do 130 knots or so at, figure 4,000 feet. We should be able to do 160 knots if they keep this bird in good shape. We'll catch him. Are we following or intercepting?"

"Depends," Drake said. "If he has a plane at the ranch, we'll have to make sure he doesn't leave. If he's headed to Hood River, I'm not sure."

The UH-60 Black Hawk had four soldiers standing with their M4s at the ready when Mike slid to a stop in front of them. The sergeant in charge of the detail saluted and reported to Drake that Capt. Martinez had called and cleared them for.takeoff.

Mike ran ahead and jumped into the pilot's seat to run through an abbreviated pre-flight check. Drake called Capt. Martinez on the radio in the sergeant's Humvee.

"Captain, we're ready to take off. I think the guy we're after is headed for Hood River, or a ranch just south of there. Notify the police in Hood River we're pursuing a Bell 407, probably hijacked from the hospital in Hermiston. Tell them to stay away if it lands until we ask for help. This is the second time I've run into these guys. I'd like an opportunity to talk a bit before they're arrested, if possible."

Drake could hear her smile over the radio.

"Roger that, a little chat time if possible. Secretary Rallings and the Senator asked me to tell you thanks. They're heading back to Portland. We'll get them to the airport safely. Lt. Col. Hollingsworth said to tell you he'll authorize whatever you need to catch these guys. Just call and let him know."

"Tell the Colonel thanks," Drake said. Then he ran to the Black Hawk and signaled Mike to take off.

As the Black Hawk nosed down on liftoff, Drake searched ahead, hoping to see the Bell 407 on the horizon. Nothing but empty blue sky.

~~~

Kaamil sat in the left cockpit seat of the Bell 407, his Glock 9mm pointed at the pilot's head.

"Fly directly to Hood River," he commanded. "I'll tell you where to land. Then you can join your family as I promised."

Kaamil called Roberto Valencia.

"It's me. We failed. Go out through the tunnel and make sure my boat's ready. Then go to the ranch and take the jet Malik has waiting for me. I have a job to do in Portland, then I'll join you in Mexico."

"Are you being followed?"

"No, but I want you out of there. No one knows you had anything to do with this."

~~~

Miles behind, Drake searched the horizon for the smaller helicopter.

"How soon before we see him?" Drake asked again.

"This sounds like a road trip with my kids. We'll see 'em when we see 'em."

"There was a time when you were the Man, professional and all."

"Nothing unprofessional about what I said. Can't give you a better estimate than that. You have a plan?"

Mike's question caused him to think. They weren't Delta Force. They were civilians acting with the blessing of the government.

"We have to stop Kaamil. That's all I know. We capture or kill him. How this ends depends on him."

"I just wanted to know if you want me to veer toward the ranch or head straight to Hood River. Of course we're going to kill him if we get the chance."

Drake nodded. "Head toward Hood River. Kaamil probably doesn't know we're following him. My guess is he'll try to slip back to Portland, pretend he wasn't a part of this. If we catch up to him and he heads toward the ranch, we'll figure something out."

Flying at one hundred eighty-four miles per hour, they spotted the Bell helicopter thirty miles from Hood River. It was flying low, a tiny white dot in the distance. The superior speed of the Black Hawk had allowed them to close the distance.

"Stay high, see where he heads."

The smaller helicopter appeared to be headed straight for Hood River. Ten miles out, it dropped even lower and veered toward the river.

Drake keyed his GRS and called Capt. Martinez. "Capt. Martinez, Adam Drake, do you read?"

"Read you clear, Mr. Drake. We've been waiting to hear from you."

"We're five miles east of Hood River following the Bell. I think he's headed to a small warehouse down by the river where the windsurfers park. It's near the Hook and the small marina there. Call the police, have them seal off the area, but not interfere. He doesn't seem to know we're following him."

"Understood. I alerted the Chief of Police in Hood River, he appreciates our situation. The explosion killed two security guards and we have five imposters dead. Our system signaled VX was released, but tests haven't confirmed that. They may have hacked our system," Capt. Martinez reported.

"Imagine that. Over and out."

Drake summarized for Mike, who had the Black Hawk flying a thousand feet above and behind the Bell. "There wasn't a VX release, despite what the monitoring system reported. One guess who caused that. Not a bad plan, using the Army to get everyone to the emergency center. Also, not a plan put together overnight.

"Means they have money to do things on a big scale."

"Kaamil's had this planned too well not to have his escape prepared. When he lands, I'll go after him. You stay, in case he gets away before I get him. Follow him, and run the bastard to ground," Drake said.

The Bell 407 sped on to Hood River. When it reached the first of the windsurfers out on the Columbia, it abruptly descended and streaked toward the old warehouse. Hundreds of windsurfers raced across the swells below, sails pulled tight into the wind. The parking lots and streets surrounding the area were clogged with vans and SUVs.

Mike dropped the Black Hawk down to three hundred feet and hovered out over the river. From there, they had a clear view of the Bell as it landed beside the old warehouse. When Kaamil stepped from the helicopter, Drake signaled Mike to land near the warehouse.

As they descended, Kaamil waved his pilot off with the gun in his right hand, and then pointed at the departing helicopter with something in his left hand. When it was clear of the warehouse and gaining altitude, it exploded. Kaamil slipped through a side door.

Drake watched in disbelief as the helicopter erupted in a fireball and fell into the river. Windsurfers closest to the falling debris dropped into the water to avoid being scorched.

"Set me down next to the door he entered. Let Capt. Martinez know the Bell and its pilot are down. It's time to end this," Drake said.

"Be careful. We don't know anything about that warehouse, could be booby traps. Why not wait for the police, they'll be here soon."

"Just get some of them killed. I might be rusty, but I have more training than any of them. Hover over the warehouse. He won't wait around for a shootout with the police."

Mike brought the Black Hawk down to within a foot of the pavement, near the side door Kaamil had entered. As soon as Drake jumped out, Mike lifted off to hover south of the building where he could see all the exits.

Drake thought about going in through the door Kaamil had entered, but decided to go around to the front door instead. Inside, he found an empty front office. Counter, secretary's desk, posters of golden wheat and cowboys trying to ride Brahma bulls. There was a door in the back of the reception area that had to lead to the rest of the warehouse.

Drake listened for sounds. Kaamil must have given the employees the day off. When he didn't hear anything, he stepped inside. Row after row of pallets of agricultural supplies, hay and straw filled the warehouse.

On the other side of the big warehouse, Drake saw a short flight of stairs leading to an upstairs office. A broad window looked down on the warehouse floor. The shadows inside made it appear to be empty.

"The warehouse looks empty. There's an office upstairs I'll check. Any sign of him out there?" Drake asked.

"Not out here."

Drake moved down the center aisle of the warehouse, checking each of the cross aisles. No sound broke the silence as he continued to the bottom of the stairs leading to the second floor.

Chapter 46

When the helicopter exploded, Kaamil walked into his warehouse with a grim smile on his face. His team was lost, but Allah had spared him to fight another day.

As he took the stairs to his office two at a time, he turned to listen to the sound of another helicopter outside. How in hell had they found him so fast?

Kaamil dashed into his office and grabbed his laptop from his desk. The rest of the computers had records for the warehouse, but his personal computer connected him to the ISIS operation at the ranch. He'd sacrifice himself before letting it be captured.

There was no panic in his voice as he used his cell phone to call across the river.

"Rashid, meet me at the Hatch in ten minutes. Park near the porta potties as close to the rigging area as you can. Have Miguel on the shore, ready to take the boat and head down the river. We'll drive slowly out of the parking area because we may be watched. Do nothing before that to attract attention. Do you understand?"

"Yes, Kaamil, I understand. Shall I alert the others?"

"Do not communicate with the others, just get to the Hatch. Do as we planned."

Kaamil was starting down the stairs from his office when he heard a shout from the floor below.

"Kaamil, I know you're here. The building is surrounded. We have business to settle. Come out like a man, we'll talk."

Kaamil laughed to himself, talk indeed. He recognized the voice of the vermin attorney. Without a sound, he turned back into his office and made his way to a storage closet. In the back of the closest, behind a spring-loaded panel, a touch pad opened a steel door that led to stairs down to a tunnel and to his boat.

The old warehouse had only one way in and out of the fenced facility above ground. Anyone suspicious of the place could satisfy their curiosity by watching traffic come and go. They would miss, however, merchandise smuggled out the tunnel passage through an old city drainpipe. The tunnel exited underneath a dock at the marina on a beak of land called the Hook.

Kaamil's boat was a black and red Centurion 23 Typhoon, a ski boat perfect for ferrying drugs across the river. No one paid attention to the boat when it drove past, filled with loads of meth and money. It was just another fancy boat on the river.

At the bottom of the stairs, he stepped through a door cut into the side of the eight foot tall drain pipe. Inside, he ran down the tunnel through puddles of water left in the bottom of the pipe after spring rains. Just past the opening at the far end, a small video monitor in a plexiglass case was attached to the underside of the dock. A digital cam mounted above provided a clear view of the empty dock and his boat.

Kaamil climbed a ladder to the dock above and strolled the short distance to his boat, just another man out to enjoy the water and the sun.

~~~

"Drake, get out here. There's a ski boat leaving from a dock near the warehouse. I think Kaamil's in the boat."

231

Drake ran to the east service door of the warehouse where Mike had the Black Hawk waiting.

"He's in that black and red ski boat, wakeboard towers," Mike said. "I didn't see him get in the boat, but when the boat headed out, I recognized him."

Through Mike's Bushnell 20x50 surveillance binoculars, Kaamil appeared to be ten feet away, driving the high-powered boat through the swells of the Columbia River. He was headed to the Washington State side of the river, still wearing a blue windbreaker with Hermiston Air Rescue across the back. With the boat planing as fast as the waves allowed, he was forcing windsurfers to veer out of his path to avoid being run over.

"Any idea where he's going? There's no way to stop him before he reaches the other side," Mike said.

"Half mile across the river is a place they call The Hatch. It's a favorite windsurfing area with a large parking lot. That's where I would go. It'll be a zoo with all the vans and cars."

Drake grabbed a headset and radioed Capt. Martinez at the chemical depot.

"Capt. Martinez, Drake here. Our man is fleeing across the Columbia. He appears to be headed to a place called 'The Hatch.' Do we have anyone over there who can seal off the area?"

The Captain was waiting for his call. "That's one of the most congested traffic areas in the Gorge. The police in White Salmon are the closest, but they'll never get there fast enough."

"I don't want to lose this guy. Request roadblocks up and down the highway along the river, then," Drake pleaded.

"I'll do what I can, but this isn't part of our emergency planning. Everyone's responding to the attack up here. Sorry."

Through the front windscreen of the Black Hawk, Drake saw the boat turn in toward the rig and launch area of The

Hatch. It drifted toward a young man standing in the water, waiting to stop the boat before it slammed into the rocky shore. Kaamil jumped into the knee-deep water, then ran up the path to the parking area.

"Best we can do now is follow him. He has to know we're watching. Keep us over the parking area, maybe we'll get lucky," Drake said. "Can you drop me near his boat?"

"Why? You'll lose him in the crowd. We're better off waiting to see what leaves the parking area and calling ahead to have the vehicle stopped at a roadblock."

Drake knew his partner was right. The police weren't going to get the area sealed off in time, and they would probably lose him in the mass of bodies below. He wasn't ready to give up, though.

"I can't let this guy walk away. Put me down near that circular drive. Then you watch the traffic leaving the area. One of us might get lucky."

Mike moved the Black Hawk sideways until it hovered over the asphalt surface on the far side of the Hatch parking area. People below froze as they watched the large helicopter slide over their heads, and then scattered out from under it. Drake jumped when Mike had him four feet off the ground, and the Black Hawk lifted again to hover overhead.

The parking lot was crowded, bumper-to-bumper in most areas, filled with vans and campers and cars with roof racks. Those not out on the water stood watching Drake and the hovering Black Hawk. The place was a kaleidoscope of color and style—with old Vanagons with Garcia logos and newer Beetles towing retro board trailers, and every kind of vehicle in between. Tan bodies were everywhere, in all manner of beach and surfer attire.

Drake scanned the faces of everyone he saw in a parked or moving vehicle. Spotting Kaamil out in the open was too much to hope for. He knew instinctively Kaamil wouldn't even take that small chance. He'd be hiding somewhere, in something that could get him out of the parking lot.

~~~

Kaamil watched out the bubble window of a Ford van as his pursuer walked by, not three feet from where he kneeled on the carpeted floor. As long as his driver didn't attract attention to the van, he knew he was safe. The police wouldn't arrive in time to seal off the parking lot, and he only had to travel less than a mile to safety.

Kaamil and his driver waited another couple of minutes, and then drove to their safe house. Ten minutes later, they were in the building on a bluff nearby, overlooking The Hatch. The safe house was a bed and breakfast ISIS had purchased for the operation through a dummy corporation. It had an upper bedroom permanently reserved for him and members of his team.

From the room's balcony, Kaamil watched as the helicopter continued to hover over the parking area. They were determined, he'd give them that, but he would see to it personally that the last round of this match was his, by a knockout.

The depot attack had been entrusted to others. This time, he'd lead the attack himself. Malik would not forgive another failure, even though it hadn't been his fault. He was a warrior, deserving of praise, but he was also realist. If he could still kill the Secretary, he might postpone his punishment and restore himself.

From his rimrock perch high above The Hatch, with the enemy so close, he knew it was time to leave before the police could set up roadblocks.

Chapter 47

Drake crisscrossed the parking area one last time before signaling Mike to pick him up. Most of the vans and SUVs had darkened windows, and more than a few of their owners had prevented him from even looking into them. They suspected he was a cop, and were fairly blunt in asking him to get away from their vehicles without a warrant.

Whatever means of escape Kaamil had waiting, it effectively concealed his presence. The whole operation had been well planned, and the retreat was no exception.

Back in the Black Hawk, he told Mike to head back to the chemical depot. "He's gone. Let's return the Colonel's helicopter and see if they've learned anything."

"Roger that. I'm tired of fighting these Gorge winds anyway."

They left to a wave of middle-finger salutes from the crowd gathered below.

"We were a big hit. Kaamil's laughing his ass off. He's been a step ahead today, but now it's our turn," Drake said, staring straight ahead.

Mike flew them back to the chemical depot where they were briefed on the initial investigation of the attack.

Two soldiers had been killed defending the emergency center. Of the five attackers who were dead, only two were recognized at the depot. They were the two killed in the initial explosion at the VX bunker. The bunker bomber was a recent convert to Islam. Twenty years old and an Army reservist, he wore the explosive belt that damaged the bunker and killed the driver in his Humvee parked by the bunker's door. The driver appeared to be an unwilling accomplice. His wife and four children were found shot to death in their home in Hermiston. No connection was found that linked them to the terrorists.

The three gunmen were imposters, with IDs that belonged to security guards at the depot. The real security guards, along with their families, were found murdered in their homes. Three husbands, three wives and eight children. The Army investigators were stunned by the extent of the violence involved in the attack on their facility.

Drake, however, recognized the terrorists' indifference to life. He'd seen it before, in places where Islamic fanaticism flourished. Like the swords they were so fond of raising in their videos, they were created by their madrassas and imams for one thing, killing in the name of Allah.

From what the Army's investigators had also learned, the initial blast in the bunker had not been successful in causing a release of the VX agent. They were investigating a false alarm caused by the Martin Research prototype monitoring system the depot had recently installed.

After debriefing and promising to be available whenever they were needed in the Army's ongoing investigation, they were allowed to return to Portland.

Driving down I-84 along the Columbia in Mike's Yukon, Drake tried to put himself in Kaamil's shoes as he processed the events of the morning.

Kaamil failed to assassinate the Secretary and his father-in-law, which Drake believed was the goal of the attack at the depot. He escaped with a well-planned retreat, but wasn't finished, Drake thought. Whoever had planned an attack like this wasn't going to stop just because a few pawns were sacrificed.

"Mike, I have a feeling this isn't over. It's too big a plan for them to give up now. These guys pray to die for Allah, and there's one too many still alive for my liking. Can you stay on for a day or so?"

"Wouldn't miss it for all the tea in China, as the saying goes, even though India's the leading tea producer in the world," he said, glad to break the silence. "What'd you have in mind?"

"Kaamil will try again. If I were planning this, I'd try sooner rather than later. He lives here, has resources here, and he'll regroup and hit us when we least expect it. Tonight or tomorrow would be my guess. Can you get us some backup?" Drake asked.

"It's two in the afternoon. I'll call in some of my best guys. You'll like them, but it's going to cost you. The best Special Forces guys don't come cheap, and I've got the best, hired for my executive protection division."

"Don't worry about it. Between my father-in-law, and his friend who got me into this, they'll be good for it. I'm more concerned about what these assholes are up to, than who's paying for your services."

Drake called the Senator while Mike was on his cell to his office in Seattle. The Oregon State Police had escorted the Senator back to Portland by car before the DHS had arranged air transportation for the Secretary. Liz Strobel had thrown a fit, of course, but the FBI wouldn't budge. Investigating a terrorist attack on a Cabinet member was their turf. They weren't going to rush things. Besides, a photo op arranged for the Secretary at the Portland airport took a little time to put together.

The Senator wanted to know if Drake was available for dinner. The Secretary had agreed to take him up on his

237

promise of a home-cooked meal and would be there. They both wanted to hear Drake's take on the depot attack. Drake promised he'd be there for dinner.

"Mike," Drake said when he'd ended the call, "I think we need your guys sooner than later. The Senator invited me to dinner at his home, and the Secretary will be a guest, seven o'clock tonight. I have no idea what security has been arranged, but I don't want to take a chance. If your guys can get here before then, we can go over what the State Police have planned and what I know about the Senator's home."

"It's what they live for, a little excitement now and then. They're loading up now, they'll be here by five p.m. at the latest. You want to stop and get something to eat? I'm starved."

Drake had to laugh. Eating had always calmed Mike's nerves after an operation, and it seemed little had changed. He could go for a day without eating, rethinking their actions and what might be required of them the next day. His friend needed to feed himself and sleep away the tension.

"You pick the place. I'll drive the rest of the way home. Got a feeling I'll be talking to myself after you've had a burger or two."

Chapter 48

In the Spring Mountains northwest of Las Vegas, the leader Kaamil called Malik, aka David Barak, waited for a report that his strike against the Secretary of Homeland Security had been a success. As the afternoon wore on, the conviction that his protégé had failed darkened his mood, like a summer thunderstorm sweeping over his mountain retreat.

Maybe it was time to re-evaluate his plan to train inmate Muslim converts as assassins. The by-product of their assassinations could be the spark to start a race war in America, but only if they were successful. So far, they hadn't been. He turned to his window and looked down the valley toward the city of Las Vegas. How could a country so venal, so vile, continue to escape Allah's wrath, he wondered.

Of all his lieutenants, Kaamil had been the most gifted. His rage was malleable, easily forged, with an intense desire to kill. His tendency to act on his own and an inability to lead, alas, was proving worrisome. Barak had known about his drug venture with Roberto Valencia, of course, courtesy of Roberto's father. He'd overlooked it because of his need to work closely with the Mexican mafia. That latitude had probably been a mistake.

His immediate concern was what he was going to do if Kaamil was captured. His mountain retreat was thirty-five miles north of Las Vegas, atop a ridge in the shadow of

Mount Charleston. It was the perfect retreat from the city, with temperatures always twenty degrees cooler—a veritable oasis in the Nevada desert. There was only one way into the property, other than by helicopter, and that was by a private, paved road. It was three miles long and wound up through rocky cliffs from the county road below. If anyone came for him, he would be warned with plenty of time to retreat to his other sanctuaries.

The sixteen thousand square foot main building was designed to look like an alpine lodge. It had an eight-car garage on the lower level and two private floors above the first floor, where guests were entertained. Several outbuildings housed a staff of thirty-five, vehicles, and other necessary equipment. All in all, his retreat was, in fact, a small fortress.

The main floor of the lodge was designed for entertaining rich and influential Americans and Europeans, as well as his rich sponsors. With eight bedroom suites, each as lavish as any found in the casinos, a great room with an adjoining cantilevered deck that featured the distant night lights of Las Vegas, the place was spectacular. When guests weren't being formally entertained, they had the use of a zero horizon pool, a spa, an attended exercise facility, a magnificent library, and a complete video and game room. Guests were always impressed with their accommodations.

His sponsors, however, had always been more impressed with the operations level, housed on the second floor of the lodge. Four main rooms were staffed around the clock by his secret army, all loyal ISIS employees.

One room housed his communication and surveillance equipment and staff. The second room was manned by those in charge of the facility's security. The third room contained his off-the-books financial operation. The fourth room was his personal control room. From it, he could video conference with any of his offices or talk privately to his operatives anywhere around the world.

Safe in his control room, he knew Allah was proud of the power he had organized. He would not be pleased, however, that the infidel he'd targeted wasn't dead.

Barak needed to hear his plan hadn't failed, and he needed to hear it now. He turned on his heel and marched down the hall to the communications room. He ordered the on-duty communications operator to call the ranch in Hood River and tell them to report anything they were hearing about Kaamil's operation.

Just to be safe, he also ordered his Sikorsky S-76D helicopter to be made ready for his immediate return to his office in Las Vegas. If Kaamil had failed or been captured, it wouldn't be long before the government came looking for him.

Chapter 49

When the helicopter flew away from The Hatch, Kaamil left the bed and breakfast and drove himself back to Portland. His transportation was a 1988 Chevy One ton step van with Johnson Farms Fresh Produce stenciled on the sides. It was the van Roberto Valencia used to run drugs down the river into the city. It had never been stopped or searched, partly because Roberto had installed a governor that kept the van from doing more than sixty miles per hour and getting a ticket.

On the way, his first call was to an informant in the Portland Police Department. He learned extra security had been assigned around Senator Hazelton's home, where it was rumored the Secretary of Homeland Security was dining. There was no indication the Secret Service would have command authority for the added security. His next call was to his backup team. He told them they would be working tonight and to meet him at the mosque.

In the quiet time during the slow drive along the Columbia River, he went over the plans he had made in case Malik's plan at the depot failed. Circumstances had intervened to defeat them, but Allah was providing another opportunity, maybe even a better one. He would just have to make sure nothing intervened again. Overwhelming force would always overcome unexpected circumstances, especially if the overwhelming force wasn't afraid of dying. That had always been their advantage, and it would be again.

Four hours after leaving his pursuer walking around the parking lot at The Hatch, Kaamil and four of his men solemnly entered the men only prayer hall of the mosque and prepared to say their afternoon prayers. Each of the four had cleansed himself before meeting Kaamil. Each understood the importance of performing their role with the pure and clean intention of pleasing Allah uppermost in their minds. In fact, it was what they had been training for, and dreaming of, since they had been recruited.

When their last prayers were finished, Kaamil led them out of the mosque to a catering van borrowed for the evening. It belonged to a well-known catering company that had used ISIS to screen its employees for an upcoming socialite's home wedding.

The van had actually been more of a problem to steal than the weapons he had borrowed from the warehouse ISIS maintained in the city. He'd been able to supply each of his men with a HK Mark 23 .45 pistol with six twelve round clips and a M4A1 carbine with collapsible stock. Malik had purchased the weapons abroad for his international security service, and then had scattered some of them around the United States for the day they were needed. Today was such a day. No Secret Service detail would be able to stop them.

In case the Senator's house was more secure than expected, however, Kaamil had two of the M4A1s equipped with M203 grenade launchers. One would carry a special surprise he would use himself.

He wasn't planning a suicide mission. But if the body armor his men would wear didn't get them into the Senator's house to kill everyone there, he would do it himself. If he didn't, he was probably a dead man anyway for failing Malik again.

The first step was securing a base to launch their attack, and he had just the place in mind.

Chapter 50

After Mike dropped him off at the Flightcraft terminal, Drake picked up his 993 and drove to his office. He didn't have time to drive back to his farm, and he needed a shower and change of clothes before he met his father-in-law for dinner. Fortunately, both were available at his office.

He called Margo to make sure she didn't hang around waiting for him.

"What happened?" she asked.

"You're supposed to say Adam Drake law office, how may I help you, remember?"

"Caller ID, you're stalling."

"Save me some money and go home. I don't want you involved until this is over."

"Sorry, been with you too long not to be involved. What do you need?"

"A shower and change of clothes. I'm having dinner with the Senator, nothing you can help me with."

"Paul called, was that you in the helicopter chasing that guy down the Columbia?"

"I went along for the ride, Mike flew the Black Hawk. Look, put a pot of coffee on and go home. I'll tell you all about it tomorrow. Everything is okay, really."

Her silence told him she wasn't convinced.

"Margo, go home, please. I'm just having dinner.

There will be plenty of police protection. Take Paul down to McCormick & Schmick's, have some oysters, and put it on the office account. Just stop worrying," he pleaded and ended the call.

He loved her like a sister, but sometimes she was too protective, too motherly. Not that he minded most of the time. Tonight, though, he needed a quiet moment in his office to clear his mind. Whatever else he thought about the familiar exhilaration he'd experienced when they stopped the terrorists' attack at the depot, he knew more would die if Kaamil wasn't stopped.

With that thought, he called Mike.

"Wondering when you'd call. My guys are on their way with the stuff you mentioned. I checked us into rooms in the Crowne Plaza off Kruse Oaks Drive. I'll be in 301, so join me whenever you're ready."

"Outstanding. I'm in my office. After a shower and some coffee, I'm headed your way. How are we set for transportation?"

"Two commercial vans we use for surveillance and my Yukon. You think we need anything else?"

"That's enough. I'll drive my car to the Senator's house. We can park the others on the street. See you in an hour."

Chapter 51

Kaamil hated the town he was driving through, but he loved the thought of smashing its smug sense of security. He'd grown up in an all-black neighborhood in the virtually all-white city of Portland. Ten miles away from his neighborhood was the suburb of Lake Oswego and its ostentatious displays of wealth. People spent more money here each month taking care of their lawns than his mother had made in a month. Thirty-five thousand people living in a fantasy world, letting their children dress like little whores and drive BMWs to school.

The house he'd chosen as a base of operation was a seven-thousand-square-foot French Country mansion, with a boat dock on the lake. It belonged to a client with an ISIS home security system. Owned by a used-car dealer who had twenty-seven used-car lots spread across the city, it was also just around the point from Senator Hazelton's home, less than five minutes by boat. It was just what he needed for the night.

At precisely six o'clock, Kaamil drove the borrowed catering van up the driveway and stopped in front of the elaborately carved double doors of the Peterson's house. He parked the van so their front door was hidden from view, and jumped out wearing the catering company's uniform. He carried an invoice on a clipboard, and held a silenced HK

Mark 23 pistol underneath it. When Mrs. Peterson opened the front door, Kaamil jammed the pistol in her stomach and invited himself inside.

When the door closed behind him, Kaamil dropped the clipboard, grabbing the blond woman's hair at the back of her head and pulling her close. Her frightened eyes made him smile.

"I don't want you to say a word, or you'll die where you stand. And then I'll kill the rest of your family. Nod your head if you understand me."

Casey Peterson was beautiful but not dumb. She saw the hate-filled eyes and powerful build of the tall black man holding her hair. She nodded quickly to show she understood.

"Signal with your fingers how many others are in the house right now."

Casey raised her right hand and signaled with three fingers.

"Does that include your husband and your two children?" Kaamil asked softly.

Casey nodded yes.

"Are you expecting anyone else tonight?"

Casey shook her head no.

"I hope you're telling me the truth, Mrs. Peterson. Take me to your husband."

Casey led the way down the main hall to the den. Her husband was watching the news and enjoying his first martini of the evening. Thirty years old and thirty pounds overweight, Ron Peterson didn't look as handsome as the billboards around the city made him look. When he looked up and saw a man holding his wife and pointing a gun at his head, he didn't smile as brightly either.

"Stay seated. I asked your wife three questions, and I'm not sure she told me the truth. Too bad for you." Kaamil shot Ron Peterson execution style. When Casey screamed, he grabbed her hair, yanked her head back, put the .45 beneath her chin and said, "If you lied to me, tell me now or I'll kill your children. Nod your head if you told me the truth."

Casey nodded. Kaamil let go of her hair. Then he slapped her with his left hand and gave her his last set of instructions.

"Show me where your children are. I need to borrow your house for a while. If you can keep your children quiet until I leave, I promise they won't be harmed. Will you do that for me?"

A stunned Casey Peterson nodded before she numbly accompanied Kaamil down the hall to the screening room. The two children were watching a Disney movie when she led Kaamil into the room. She stood frozen as she watched him quickly walk behind each of her children and shoot them in the back of their heads. She hadn't moved when he turned, walked back, and raised his gun to her head.

The house was now his, Kaamil acknowledged with a smile, as he shot Casey Peterson.

Chapter 52

After a shower and change of clothes, Drake left his office and drove south on I-5 to meet Mike and his hastily assembled team.

There was no way to know what they would be up against if Kaamil tried to finish what he had started. Drake knew the layout of his father-in-law's house in Lake Oswego, and the likely avenues of attack. But he had to make sure there was little or no collateral damage if Kaamil came.

Senator Hazelton's house was located in the middle of a three-acre parcel on the southern shore of the lake. In addition to its other accommodations, the house also had a recently added safe room. If Kaamil attacked, Drake knew everyone inside would be safe if they reached that sanctuary. His concern was how to keep attackers away from the house so no one had to use the safe room. The grounds around the house were what he had to concentrate on.

Twenty minutes later, Drake turned off I-5 and followed Kruse Way east to Kruse Oaks Drive and the parking lot of the Crowne Plaza Hotel. Drake couldn't fault Mike's choice of accommodations for his men. The hotel was close to the Senator's home, business-travel anonymous and comfortable. He entered the hotel. An atrium with a waterfall cascading from the upper floors did little to deflect his concentration as he made his way to the bank of elevators.

An elevator took him quickly to the third floor, and a short walk down the hall brought him to Room 301. Three knocks on the door and he was greeted by his smiling friend.

"Come in, meet my men," Mike welcomed. "We delayed ordering room service until we knew a little more about what you have planned, and whether your credit card is any good. Hope you don't mind."

Drake gave his old friend a one-arm hug, then made his way around the room, greeting the team.

Mike made the introductions.

"This is Capt. Ricardo Gonzales, formerly of the Green Berets. One of the first guys I hired when I started the company. He's one mean man, except when his wife Linda is around," Mike said, punching the man's shoulder.

"Sounds like a wise man," Drake said. "Glad to meet you, Captain."

Capt. Gonzales got up from his stool at the counter of the kitchen/wet bar and shook Drake's hand. Gonzales stood five foot ten and looked like an Aztec Indian chiseled from obsidian, his features were so sharp. He was mid-thirties but carried his years like a proud eighteen-year-old recruit.

"Mike told me he served with you, and that you're a good operator," Gonzales said. "I look forward to working with you tonight."

"Likewise. Mike said you're good, which tells me you're the best. What was your team specialty, Captain?" Drake asked.

"Weapons, medic secondary," Gonzales said.

"Glad you're here, Ricardo. We wore the uniform, but this is private, sort of. Call me Adam."

Sergeant Billy Montgomery was next to stand and be introduced. Sandy red hair and freckles across his nose, he looked like the prototypical southern white soldier boy.

Drake didn't need to be told he was one gung-ho soldier. His look and confident glare said he'd been there and seen it all.

"Call me Billy. I'm only a Ranger, but then I'm younger than these guys. If you need someone with younger, sharper skills, then I'm your guy."

"Billy, your accent isn't what I expected," Drake said, cutting off the boos from the others. "Where are you from?"

"Manhattan, sir, born and raised. Dad's a Wall Street type, but he knows what's going on in the world. He didn't stand in my way when I chose the Army over an MBA."

After Sgt. Montgomery, Mike introduced Sergeant Lawrence Green, a stocky black man standing six foot four at least, and weighing in, by Drake's guess, at around two fifty. Sgt. Green didn't smile when he stood and shook Drake's hand.

"Larry was with LAPD before he took a bullet in his shoulder last year. With his master's in criminology from USC, he advises me on criminal behavior, and generally keeps me out of trouble," Mike said.

Drake leaned a step closer and said, "Larry, Mike needs someone to keep him out of trouble, thank God it's you and not me. When I worked with him, it was, well, difficult."

"He's said the same of you. You two must have been a hell of a team. His being good with a gun, and you being good with the ladies," Green said amidst a chorus of hoo-ahs.

Drake laughed with them. "When we have time, gentlemen, I'll be glad to set the record straight. For now, all you need to know is it wasn't my good looks that kept saving his butt."

"Last, but not least, I want you to meet William Richard," Mike said. "He's fondly known among us as 'Dicky,' our best long gunner next to me. Two-time one-thousand-yard national champion."

"Dicky, I'm impressed. I don't think Mike ever officially won that championship, but then some of the stuff we did they didn't give medals for. Welcome to the party."

"Thanks for the invite. Been a while since I've had the chance to do some real shooting."

"Let's hope it doesn't come to that," Drake said. "Take a seat, gentlemen, and I'll go over what I need from you tonight. If you're hungry, order something light now, because I think we might be out for quite a while. But when we're finished tonight, I'm buying steaks and cigars, so keep that in mind when you order."

While Mike took orders for a light, pre-op dinner, Drake told them what he knew and what he thought might happen that night. When he left Mike and his men, all dressed in dark jeans, black T-shirts, and dark blue windbreakers, they were checking their weapons one last time before heading out.

Chapter 53

Drake left the hotel confident in Mike and his team. Their plan wasn't foolproof, and it wasn't rehearsed, but it was the best they could do on short notice. A week ago he was busy, albeit morose, in the day-to-day mundane routine of a lawyer's life. Now he was thrown back into a life he once loved.

He had changed into a blue blazer over a cream polo shirt and tan slacks back at his office. The .45 in its small-of-the-back holster, however, was a constant reminder he wasn't on a social call tonight.

The drive from the hotel to the Senator's house took all of ten minutes in the light evening traffic. There, he was greeted by an Oregon State Police trooper who inspected his ID, matched it to his face and his name on the small list of visitors allowed on the property for the night, before allowing him to proceed. No, this clearly wasn't the usual dinner with the in-laws, he thought.

Drake drove up the curving driveway. Lines of fire, natural protection, avenues of ingress and egress, likely deployment of attacking force calculations flooded his mind. It was training he had left behind, but it was still available in his memory bank. He worried about possible civilian collateral damage and was, for once, thankful that the size of the Senator's estate limited that possibility greatly. Unless Kaamil attacked by air with a bomb, the Senator's neighbors were far enough away to be safe.

When he arrived at the residence, Drake stopped his Porsche next to a second Oregon State Police trooper, who waived him to a parking location. Drake walked to the front door and waited for it to be opened by another trooper. Meredith Hazelton was waiting for him and hugged him tightly, kissing him on the cheek.

"Thank you for protecting my husband today. He said if it wasn't for you, he doesn't know if they would have made it," she said, with a glint of tears in the corners of her eyes.

"I didn't do it by myself, Mom. I had the help of an old friend and the Army. We were lucky, that's all."

"Adam, don't waste my time talking like a politician, telling me what I want to hear. Tell me what happened out there. I'm not blind to the extra security outside. Is my husband in danger?"

"It's possible, but I think they were after the Secretary. He's the bigger headline."

"But he's here for dinner. Is he still in danger?"

"Mom, relax. No one's supposed to know Secretary Rallings is here. We have the State Police outside, and I've asked a few friends to hang around for a while. We'll be okay."

"I don't know how the Israelis put up with this stuff all the time," she said, leading him into the house. "I'm finishing up in the kitchen. Go find the men."

Drake smiled and walked to the den. He found the Senator and the Secretary standing in front of the floor-to-ceiling windows looking out over the lake. The lake reflected the light pink of an early sunset off its shimmering surface. Each man had a drink in hand, talking softly, shoulder to shoulder.

Senator Hazelton saw him first and smiled. "Adam, let me get you a drink and we'll toast your heroics today. What would you like?"

Drake glanced at the wet bar and saw a bottle he recognized.

"I see you've introduced Secretary Rallings to our state's secret, ten-year-old Pendleton whiskey. Just one, heavy on the ice."

While the Senator went to pour Drake's whiskey, Secretary Rallings stepped forward and stuck out his hand. His smile was gone, and slightly squinted eyes acknowledged his concern for the day's events.

"I know I thanked you before, but I didn't understand then how much of what happened today was your doing. Do you mind telling me, how were you prepared to defend us like you did?"

"I'll tell you as much as I can, Mr. Secretary. Parts of it, you're better off not knowing. I stumbled onto something at Martin Research that suggested you might be in danger at the depot. I couldn't leave everything to the Army when I knew things I couldn't tell them about. So, I invited a buddy from Seattle to join me, and we tagged along as your unofficial bodyguards."

"Well, I suspect there's a lot more to the story. For now, know we're both indebted to you. If there's any way I can ever help you, just let me know. They keep me busy in Washington, but I'll always make time for you. By any chance, are you looking for a job?"

"No, he's not. I need him here in Oregon. You have the largest staff in the government, don't start poaching out west. Now, here's to you, son," the Senator said, raising his glass in toast. "You learn anything more about the men behind the attack?"

Drake took a sip from his tumbler. "I haven't confirmed what I suspect. The man we followed is the same man I believe was behind the murder of Richard Martin's secretary, and the three men who tried to kill me. He landed the helicopter in Hood River and escaped across the river. I think he returned to Portland. I think he'll try again, before the Secretary leaves tomorrow."

Secretary Rallings and Senator Hazelton exchanged a look that belied their calm manner.

Drake wondered if the possibility of another attack had even been discussed by the Secret Service. Judging from the reaction of the two men, it hadn't.

"Is there a possibility this man will be arrested any time soon?" Secretary Rallings asked.

"Probably not, sir. This is his home. If he made it back here, we're not likely to find him before you leave. You have the State Police outside, and I asked some of my friends to stick around. From what I'm told, he shouldn't know you're here. If anything does happen tonight, I want both of you to get downstairs with Mom to the safe room until I come for you, okay?"

Secretary Rallings looked intently at Drake. "With everything that's happened today, I'd be a fool to ignore your concerns. I'm not used to hearing about threats my own people underestimated. If it turns out you're right about another attempt, I'm going to have to kick some serious ass."

"Mr. Secretary, with all due respect for your office, that may not be fair. I know things they don't. So, if it's okay with you both, I'd like to go out and let the State Police know that I've brought in additional private security."

Both men nodded their agreement. Drake slipped out to talk with the State Police and to signal Mike to deploy his team.

Chapter 54

Around the jutting point of land to the east of the Senator's home, Kaamil ushered his men into the house commandeered for the evening. He let them wander through the house and see the family he had killed. It was essential they realize that what he was asking of them was more lasting than a mansion and a beautiful wife and children. Every man wanted those common things. But he was offering them immortality and lasting fame.

When they were all seated in the great room, overlooking the lake and the boathouse, he gave them their final instructions.

"I know each of you, and the fire that burns within you. There is no God but Allah, and he will never mislead or fail us. It is time to teach this country and its President that they cannot defeat us. They hide their eyes from the television when we execute one of them, because they fear their god is not powerful enough to care for them in death. We embrace death and have a God that welcomes our sacrifice," Kaamil told them. "Tonight you have the chance to do what you've promised me, and Allah, you were willing to do. Bring me the heads of everyone in the house, and we'll show the world no one hides from Allah's justice, not even the chief of America's Homeland Security. Now, prepare yourselves while I get the boat ready. We leave as soon as it's dark."

Each man in the room nodded his understanding and began checking his equipment for the last time. When he returned, Kaamil would give them the meth cocktail Malik had prepared to make them fight like mighty Muslim warriors.

Kaamil left the house and walked down to the boathouse as the setting sun cast long shadows over the lake. The lawn had just been mowed and smelled of freshly cut grass. It reminded him of prison, and the grounds crew he had worked on.

The boathouse housed one of the most expensive boats that cruised the lake, and that was one of the reasons he'd chosen it for the night's mission. The boat was a 1946 Gar Wood Commodore Runabout, worth a quarter of a million dollars or more. With polished dark brown wood and a classic profile, it was one of a kind and, because of that, it was well protected. It was also so well-known by the lakeside residents who might see it, and not take a second look in the dark to see who was driving it.

Kaamil had two keys he had taken from the key rack in the house, labeled "boat" and "boathouse." The first key opened the door of the boathouse. From the gently moving dock, he stepped inside, closed the door and turned on the lights. To his left, the runabout floated securely in the privacy of its temperature-monitored home.

He'd driven boats before, like the one Roberto kept in Hood River, but he'd never driven a boat like this. He wasn't sure how to start such an old boat, although it couldn't be that hard, he told himself.

Kaamil stepped into the front seat of the boat. The red leather seats looked like the seats in an old, expensive sports car and smelled of leather conditioner. He settled behind the small steering wheel and studied the dashboard. There was a series of controls, including a brass button, to the left of the steering wheel, but no obvious place for the second key to start the boat. If the second key didn't start the boat, then what was it for? He willed himself to be calm and studied the problem before him.

There wasn't anything on the dashboard to receive the key in his hand. There had to be some other place for it, some other way to start the boat. He got up and walked to the rear of the boat, looking for a switch or receptacle for the key. Nothing. He stood beside the engine compartment, turned and retraced his steps. Again he saw nothing that he had missed.

But when he turned again to walk to the rear of the boat, he noticed the keyed lock for the engine compartment. With the second key, he unlocked the cover, revealing an old engine that looked as new as any new car engine. He studied the engine for several minutes. Nothing looked like a starter that required a key. The choke on the engine, however, had a blue label that read "forward to prime engine before pushing starter button on dash."

Kaamil moved the choke to ON then slipped back into the seat behind the steering wheel. Taking a deep breath, he pushed the brass button and heard the engine fire to life. It bubbled powerfully behind the stern of the boat. Allah be praised, he thought.

Kaamil turned the engine off, moved the choke back to its original position and stepped out of the boat. They had transportation. Now his men just needed the courage to fulfill the mission he was sending them on.

Chapter 55

After a dinner of Dungeness crab cakes, fettuccine with Alfredo sauce and a dessert of baked pears, Senator Hazelton invited Secretary Rallings and Drake to join him on the terrace for cognac and a moment of conversation.

While they enjoyed their Remy Martin VSOP, Drake excused himself. He stepped aside and called Mike with a small handheld radio from his jacket pocket. Mike and the rest of the team were using headsets and commo packs. He hadn't wanted to upset dinner by showing up wearing the same special ops gear.

"Delta Two, how are things out there?" he asked.

"Quiet summer night. Nice place to live. Three is lakeside near the boathouse, Four and Five are on the perimeters, and Six is out front. I'm to your left in the bushes below the terrace. The State Police aren't exactly happy we're here, but what the hell, it isn't their spread. How was dinner?"

"Okay, if you like crab cakes, fettucini Alfredo and baked pears in chocolate sauce. You'll get yours later. The men are enjoying a cognac. When Secretary Rallings leaves, we're out of here. Keep me posted."

"Roger that, Delta One."

Drake rejoined the men on the terrace and turned to look at the lights from a couple of boats still out on the lake. The first boat he noticed was a large powerboat, forty feet or longer, motoring slowly to minimize its wake and not disturb the party on the aft deck. It was headed east, he saw, with its green starboard lights showing.

The second boat was smaller and closer to shore. Drake could tell by the rumble of its inboard engine that it was either an old classic or one of the newer ski boats with a large V8 engine. Nothing on the water sounded quite as good, at least to his ears. He watched the second boat for another minute and then stepped away to call Mike.

"Two, what's Three say about the boat headed our way showing green and red? Most boats stay out in the middle at night. Looks like this one's headed our way. Can he see who's aboard?"

"Three, can you tell who's aboard the boat headed our way?" Mike asked.

"Two, it just slowed, and it's barely making wake. I make five men in the boat. They don't seem to be talking much. This isn't a party boat. Might be our guys."

"One, you copy? Might want to get the guests inside. I'll coordinate until you return."

"Roger Two, you have control. Be back in a minute," Drake answered. He moved quickly in front of the two men and turned them toward the house.

"I need you to go inside right now. Senator, take Mom with you to the safe room," Drake ordered, motioning to the Senator's bodyguard stationed at the rear door.

"We have a threat headed our way. Please get everyone down to the safe room, and don't leave them until I come for you, understood?"

The former State Trooper looked to the Senator for directions, where he received a nodded agreement, and started to hustle the men inside.

Senator Hazelton pulled away and faced Drake.

"Are they seriously trying again? Here, my home?" he asked with his jaws clenched and lips pulled tight.

"Leave the lights on in the house when you go down. I don't want them to know they've been spotted," Drake said.

Drake walked quickly down the steps from the terrace to the ground below and stepped into the shadows.

"Two, One here. What'd you see?" Drake asked and plugged an earpiece into his handheld radio.

"One, the boat's fifteen yards off the end of the Senator's dock. They've shut off their engine and running lights. Unless they ran out of gas at the wrong place, wrong time, and the battery died as well, they're our guys," Mike answered.

"Two, make sure we're right. We're civilian security, we have to let them declare hostile intent before we respond. When they get out of the boat, I want Three to ID what they're carrying. If they're armed and head our way, we'll use flash bangs when they're off the dock. If they come up firing, defend yourselves. Everyone clear on that?"

"One, Two here. Clear."

"One, Three here. Clear."

"One, Four here. Clear."

"One, Five here. Clear."

"One, Six here. Clear."

"All right, gentlemen, let's see what they have. Three, where are they?"

"One, end of the dock. Guy driving the boat doesn't steer so well without power. He hit it pretty hard. Two guys are out and holding the boat, two more are getting out. Guy in the back looks like he's staying in the boat."

They watched as four men gathered on the dock and then walked towards them.

"One, Three here. We have four armed men headed our way. Night vision shows four M4s, one with a grenade launcher. Everyone has a holstered pistol. Dark T-shirts, body armor and balaclavas. They're not here to borrow gas for their boat."

"Roger that, Three. When they get twenty yards beyond Three's position, Four and Five throw flash bangs on my count," Drake said. He watched the four men walk toward him in a well-rehearsed V formation. In another ten seconds, we'll find out how rehearsed they are, he thought.

"Four and Five, on my count. Five, four, three, two, one."

Drake watched his men on the left and right throw their flash bangs at the feet of the advancing formation. The new fuel-air devices forced particles of aluminum powder out through small holes in the bottom of the plastic canisters when they detonated. An acoustic pulse and blinding flash of light shocked the still night.

The four men, however, did know what they were doing. Somehow, the man in the boat saw what Mike's men were about to do and yelled, "flash bang." The four men dropped to their knees. With their ears covered and eyes closed, they waited until they regained their bearings. Then they started firing wildly to the left and right, where they suspected the flash bangs had come from.

"Three, what happened?" Drake asked as the smoke was clearing.

"The guy in the boat yelled "flash bang" just before the grenades exploded. He's drifting back out into the lake. Want me to take him out?"

"No, but can you identify the boat?"

Drake watched as the men stood and walked forward, firing their weapons on full automatic. They walked four abreast, like it was the gunfight at the OK Corral.

This has gone far enough, Drake decided.

"Four and Five, take the men on the flanks. Mike and I will take the middle."

While Drake was still acquiring his target, the head of the terrorist on the left exploded in a faint red mist. The terrorist on the right dropped at the same time. Neither of the two men left standing slowed or turned. He heard Mike fire a second before he fired, and the last two terrorists fell.

"This is One, report," Drake ordered.

Each man quickly signaled they were all right.

"Three, where's the boat driver?"

"One, he drifted out when the shooting started. He's fifty yards out, just sitting there."

"Could you see any identification on the boat?" Drake asked.

"Only thing I could make out was the name *Pre-Owned* on the stern," Three answered.

"What's he doing now?"

"One, he's raising what looks like an RPG. Holy shit, he's aiming right at you!"

In the second it took to focus on the boat, Drake recognized the flash and the whitish blue-gray smoke of a shoulder-fired grenade launcher. He dove to the ground next to the wall of the terrace, and hoped Mike had done the same.

The grenade warhead exploded through the door the State Trooper had just closed minutes before. It formed an aerosol cloud in the Senator's house that ignited in a powerful fireball. The fuel-air explosive, or thermobaric weapon, consumed all the oxygen inside, and the lack of oxygen, in turn, created an enormous overpressure, or shock wave. The combination acted like a small, tactical nuclear weapon, without the residual radiation.

In microseconds, the pressure of the explosion flattened the first floor of the Senator's home, collapsing the structure above it, traveling outwards to sheer off the trees near the house.

Drake was stunned and covered with debris—the force of the explosion had vectored outward over his head. He twisted to look at the burning structure behind him, and prayed that everyone inside was protected in the basement safe room.

"Mike, you all right?" he shouted.

After a long moment, Drake heard a shaken answer.

"Think so. Hit the deck when I heard RPG. May have a concussion. Don't know about the rest of the guys."

"Mike, I've got to see if they're safe inside. You okay to check on the team?" he asked, knocking pieces of debris from his shoulders and head.

"I think so. Go."

Drake ran to the east side of the burning rubble that had been a home until minutes ago. He tore his way through fallen and burning flooring to the door into the basement, and kicked away blast debris that had fallen against it. The explosion had collapsed most of the flooring above the stairs leading down to the basement, but the reinforced walls and ceiling of the basement itself hadn't buckled.

Drake ran down the stairs to the door of the safe room and pounded on it three times.

"Senator, it's Adam. Are you all right?"

"This is Agent Miller, Secret Service. Tell me something about the Senator tonight that he can verify before I open this door."

"Well, I had a glass of Ken Wright pinot noir with dinner."

The door opened, and the State Trooper asked, "What the hell happened?"

"They hit us with a thermobaric grenade. Is everyone safe?"

Drake could see the Senator and his mother-in-law were pale and shaken. The Secretary was standing beside them with a grim look on his face. The country had been lucky since 9/11, due to a lot of hard work and dedication, but the look on the Secretary's face acknowledged things had just taken a turn for the worse.

"We're fine," the State Trooper said. "Is it safe to come out?"

"What's left of the house is burning above, but you might be able to bring them out through the basement and up those stairs over there to the garage. If it's blocked, keep them here and get someone to come down the way I did to help you."

Drake ran upstairs and outside to find Mike's team gathered around him. State Troopers were on their radios, calling for assistance.

"Mike, put somebody in charge and, if you're okay, come with me. Defer all questions to the Senator until we get back. I know where Kaamil's headed."

Chapter 56

Drake knew the boat. It belonged to Ron Peterson, the used-car dealer who lived around the point on the lake. Peterson liked to take a couple of laps around the lake each year in his classic old runabout when he'd be noticed, like on the Fourth of July and Labor Day.

Peterson's home was a just a couple of minutes around the point by car. If they hurried, they could be there by the time Kaamil arrived.

"You sure you're okay?" Drake asked as they ran to his Porsche and jumped in. "I can take care of Kaamil, but if there are others waiting there, you'll need to deal with them."

"I've flown missions in worse shape. I'm okay," Mike said as they roared away from the Senator's burning home.

The road to the Peterson estate curved around the lake. It was lined with residences, making it hard to drive as fast as Drake wanted while watching for kids playing outside in the early summer night. He still got them there in less than five minutes.

"I'm pretty sure Peterson lives here. I've seen the place from the water," he said, sliding to a stop at the end of Peterson's driveway. "I'll go down to the boathouse. You block his way out up here. If he gets by me, make sure he knows we're buddies when you kill him."

The lights were on in the house, and a catering van was parked near the front door.

"That's the way they got in," Mike offered, "posing as a catering service. I'll make sure the van's not going anywhere and check out the house."

Drake sprinted across the lawn leading down to the Peterson's boathouse. When he got there, he flattened himself against a cedar-shingled wall around the corner from the door. He listened for sounds from inside, and then heard the rumble of an inboard engine approaching on idle.

Edging his head around the corner of the boathouse, he saw red and green running lights headed his way. Kaamil was drifting slowly toward the back of the boathouse. Drake slipped around the corner and inside.

The lights were off, but there was enough light for him to see storage lockers on the opposite side of the slip. The shadows at the far end near the boathouse rear door, however, provided some cover, and his best chance to surprise Kaamil. Drake ran there, just as the automatic opener cranked up the overhead door and the old runabout nosed into its berth.

One man sat on top of the driver's seat and steered the boat, bumping off the cushioned railings. When the boathouse door closed, he was alone with the terrorist.

"You're some leader, Kaamil. Sacrifice your men and run away," Drake said, as the rumble of the boat echoed off the walls of the boathouse then died. "They're cavorting with virgins, you're still here with me. Pity, you must be envious."

He watched as Kaamil straightened at the sound of his voice.

"Envious in a way you'll never understand. They earned their reward, but their lack of skill condemns me to shame and death. Hardly fair, but you get used to that in this country."

"Spare me the sad song, Kaamil. Raise your hands over your head and step out of the boat. Fairness is not at the top of my list right now."

Kaamil stood, stretched his long arms straight out from his shoulders and stepped out of the boat. He turned to face Drake and the .45 pointed at his forehead.

"I am unarmed and unafraid," he said, as he stood tall and seemed to accept whatever fate Allah had in store for him.

"You're American, Kaamil. What the hell happened to you, trying to kill a Cabinet Secretary?"

Kaamil's eyes blazed at the question. His MP5 lay on the seat of the boat, but there was little chance he'd get to it before Drake shot him.

"You think you've won because you've caught me. Cops thought they'd won when they busted me too, but sometimes that's the price you pay to find the truth. You think you won when you bombed the hell out of Afghanistan and occupied Iraq. All you've done is convince us you want to destroy our religion."

"I could care less about your religion," Drake said. "I've fought beside Muslims, Buddhists, Hindus and atheists. I don't care about your religion. You tried to kill me and you're attacking my country."

"Yeah, the country that made slaves of my ancestors, that's still keeping us down. That's my country for sure," Kaamil sneered. "You don't get it, but you will. There's nothing you can do to change the outcome. You've already lost. Your politicians are afraid to challenge us. Voters don't have the stomach for war, and someday we'll be the majority here and in Europe. We're in the government, the military, we're unchallenged in the universities, and the darling of the media. Who's going to stop Islam?"

"I'm not trying to stop Islam. I just want to stop a traitor named Kaamil. That's enough for me."

"I'm not a traitor, Drake. I'm a Muslim. Islam is my country. I just live here. We don't fear death, that's why we'll win. We have a leader so far ahead of you, by the time you recognize the final blow, you'll already be dead."

"If you mean bin Laden," Drake said, "he's no longer relevant."

"Bin Laden is not our leader. My leader was a warrior long before bin Laden joined the cause. He's operated right under your nose, with a worldwide organization you know nothing about. You will, though, when he makes nations tremble and its leaders hide under their pillows."

"Is he the guy who flew into your ranch the other night?" Drake guessed.

Kaamil didn't answer. His eyes searched for a way out of the boathouse.

"There's no way out, Kaamil. These boathouses have security screens that run down to the bottom of the lake. You're not swimming out of here. There's only one door out of here, and I have someone outside. Try running and you die."

Drake watched as Kaamil looked toward the roof of the boathouse and mouthed what could only be a prayer. He knew Kaamil had made his decision.

"Kaamil, you don't have to do this."

Kaamil lowered his eyes, shouted "*Allahu Akbar*" and ran straight at Drake.

Drake shot him in the head, as he'd been trained, and watched the tall, homegrown terrorist fall before him.

Chapter 57

He met Mike as he stepped from the boathouse.

"I heard the shot. Was it Kaamil?" Mike asked, slowing his run to a walk.

"A true believer. He talked about his leader, someone operating right under our noses with a worldwide organization."

"You believe him?"

"Not sure. What did you find in the house?"

"They're all dead. Husband, wife, and two kids," Mike said, shaking his head. "Two kids on a sofa watching television, shot in the back of the head."

"We gotta get back," Drake said, heading toward his car. "There's nothing we can do here. The Secret Service will want to investigate this ahead of the others. I'll have the Secretary bring them in. Feels like old times, cleaning up messes we were too late to prevent."

"You couldn't know this was in the works. Besides, if you hadn't trusted your instinct about Kaamil, your in-laws and the Secretary would probably be dead," Mike said.

By the time they drove back to Senator Hazelton's, his long driveway was filled with cars from the Lake Oswego PD, Oregon State Police and some unidentified federal agencies. All but the federal cars still had their overheads flashing, and they could see two red and white pumpers from the Lake Oswego Fire Department dousing the flames in the rubble.

"This might be a good time for the head of a well-known and widely respected private security firm from Seattle, hired to provide some extra protection for the Senator and his guest, to explain the dead bodies," Drake suggested. "Just in case the Secret Service get some of it wrong and we're the bad guys with the guns."

"How much do you want me to tell them? What we know, or just about what happened tonight?"

"Just about tonight. I'll go ask the Senator what's been said so far." They walked toward a patrolman keeping neighbors and the press from entering the estate.

"Officer, this is my father-in-law's place. Will you call ahead and get us cleared to enter?" he asked as they both handed the patrolman their identification.

Two minutes later, they were waved on and made the long walk up the driveway toward the firemen working to control the flames. Drake spotted the Senator and Secretary Rallings standing in the center of a ring of Secret Service and State Troopers, and walked over.

Senator Hazelton turned, saw Drake and motioned for him to join them.

"One of Mike's men said you went after their leader. Did you get him?" the Senator asked.

"We got him, but not before he killed Ron Peterson and his family. They used his boat to get over here. When the FBI get here, send them my way. I'll explain things."

"You won't have to do that. Secretary Rallings and I will deal with the FBI and with his people. He's told the State Police he wants this investigated as a crime scene. My God, the Secret Service and the FBI have some explaining to do. If I hadn't let you come tonight, as private security, we'd all be dead."

"Is Mom all right?"

"She's okay, but you need to let her know you're back."

Drake saw Meredith Hazelton standing near what was left of the rear deck of her home, and made his way to her. She was standing quietly with her arms wrapped around herself, staring into the fire.

"Mom, you okay?" he asked when he reached her side.

Without saying a word, she grabbed onto him and began crying silently with her head held tight against his chest.

"Promise me you won't do anything like this, ever again," she said between sobs. "I can't stand the thought of losing you too."

"Don't worry, Mom. The rest of my clients don't have anything to do with terrorists. They may not pay as well as Richard Martin, but they're all boring and safe, I promise."

After comforting her a while longer, Drake walked out toward where the police were standing around the bodies of the four terrorists. Mike was talking to his men a little farther on, briefing them before the heavy hitters from the FBI arrived.

"Everyone okay here?" Drake asked.

"Everyone's fine," Mike answered, "just talking about what motivates these fools. They could have stopped after the stun grenades."

"I know. Kaamil tried to make me understand before he decided to martyr himself. I'll tell you about it when we're all enjoying those steaks I promised. Remember, just tell them what you did here tonight and then send them my way if they want to know why I asked you to provide private security tonight."

Drake returned to talk with the Senator and Secretary Rallings. He got there just in time to hear Secretary Rallings lecturing his assistant, Liz Strobel, and the head of Portland's JTTF, Bruce Burton, who had just arrived. Neither of them returned his greeting.

"This is the second example in one day of what we're doing wrong in this war," Secretary Rallings said. "We can't sit around and wait for them to hit us. We've got to be a step ahead, rather than conceding them the initiative. This is not a law enforcement matter. Tonight, however, we're going to treat it that way, to salvage what's left of the public's trust in our ability to protect them. But believe me, I will change the way we're operating. All of you better have some suggestions for me the next time we talk. Now, go out and convince everyone this was just a criminal matter the FBI is handling because I was here tonight. I do not want to read tomorrow there were two terrorist attacks in one day that the government was not prepared to handle."

When Liz Strobel and Bruce Burton were dismissed, Secretary Rallings turned to Drake and smiled slightly.

"Think it did any good?"

"Hard to say, sir. They might want to do what I was able to do. But when they know they'd probably lose their jobs if they did, or go to jail, I don't think much will change. We're not used to fighting a war at home."

Rallings looked at him and nodded.

"No, I expect you're right. It's all we could do to get the Patriot Act passed. We've got to find a way to do a better job. What allowed you to figure out what was going on?"

"Past training and experience mostly. Being in the right place and time to put the pieces together. Instinct told me they weren't going to give up until you were dead. We were lucky this time," Drake said.

"I doubt that luck had much to do with you figuring it out. I may need your help in figuring the rest of it out. When we get this calmed down, I'd like to hear everything you can tell me."

"If you can clear things up for me with the FBI and local law enforcement, I'll make the time. If you can't, they may not let me leave the city," Drake said. "I think I made some new enemies this last week."

"You let me worry about that," Secretary Rallings said. "I think I can make them see it my way. This is an ongoing investigation. I'm not going to let my people screw it up just because they have a little egg on their faces."

Chapter 58

Before Drake left to join Mike and his men for dinner, he made sure his family was okay. Meredith Hazelton was clearly shaken by the attack. She lived life as the wife of a U.S. Senator. She understood there was a war being fought, but realizing she was not safe in her own home was going to take some time to accept.

Senator Hazelton was more stoic. As chairman of the Senate Intelligence Committee, he was keenly aware of the threat from terrorists living in America. Personally, he was incensed that his wife of forty years was nearly killed. But he had known that sooner or later the war was always going to be fought on U.S. soil.

"We knew they were here," he told Drake, as he stared at the embers in the western end of the house, where his den had been located, "but targeting Americans for assassination has crossed the line. Shouldn't have surprised us, really. It's been one of their chief weapons throughout history."

Drake ached for his father-in-law. No one in America wanted to believe the war was headed their way. It was easier to label the Paul Reveres as pro-war alarmists, using the threat of terrorism as an excuse to strip Americans of their civil liberties. He wondered how many would feel that way if their house had just been blown up.

"Someday, people will understand this is a real war that we have to win," Drake said, putting an arm around the Senator's drooped shoulders. "I promised Mike and his men I'd buy them dinner, so I'd better go. Call me tomorrow and let me know where you and Mom are staying. You know you're welcome to stay with me at the farm."

"Thanks, but we'll be at the Heathman Hotel tonight. We'll head back to Washington tomorrow. Thank the men for me, Adam," Senator Hazelton said with a quick bow of his head, and headed to where his wife was standing.

~~~

Ruth's Chris Steakhouse is located in the Pacific Center Building on Southwest Broadway in Portland. That's where Drake found Mike and his men.

He was greeted with a rousing round of hoo-ahs from the men, and a bear hug from Mike. He signaled all of them to bring their drinks and follow him. When they were all gathered in the mahogany-paneled room he'd reserved, Drake spoke with Mike for a brief moment and then tapped a fork against the whiskey glass he'd been handed.

"Tonight we acted privately, at the request of Senator Hazelton. Our actions will be closely scrutinized. Federal agencies are embarrassed, and the media types that have a hard time believing Americans can be terrorists will be skeptical. The Secretary and the Senator told me to thank you, and that they have our backs on this. Still, please coordinate all statements to the authorities through Mike or your company's attorney. So, well done, men. The T-bone is terrific here and the lobster is flown in from Maine daily. Enjoy the gratitude of those you served tonight," Drake concluded to their applause.

While the menus were being studied, Mike joined him.

"Are they going after Kaamil's boss?" Mike asked.

"Secretary Rallings said they're trying to trace the flight of a jet that landed at the ranch the other night. They're also trying to locate the CEO of ISIS. If ISIS is behind this, you know there's apt to be a lot of companies looking for a new security service. You might find your business suddenly has a lot of potential new customers."

"Wasn't thinking that far ahead, but you might be right. Have to expand operations and all. You know a good attorney who's willing to help with something like that?" Mike asked.

"Might, but I have something to close out before I take on a new client."

Mike knew him well. Drake didn't avoid his questioning look.

"Like the guy pulling Kaamil's strings?"

"Possibly."

"Call me."

After enjoying the men's company, and paying a substantial tab for the post-mission hunger of Mike and his team, Drake thanked each of them for their help, and headed home.

It didn't seem possible it had been only a week ago that he agreed to help Richard Martin. So much had happened, so much had changed. While the steady purr of the Porsche's engine reminded him how tired he was, he wondered how he was ever going to get back to normal.

Normal was his office routine, keeping his promise to clean up the pile of postponed matters on his desk. He had to admit, though, the last week had made him feel alive, energized and on the edge again. He had made a difference, not just for a client, but perhaps for the country he once pledged to serve and protect.

Drake downshifted to take the exit from I-5 onto I-206,

when his cell phone chirped. Caller ID told him his father-in-law was calling.

"Hello Senator," he answered. "Decide on a night in the country?"

"No, but thanks for the offer. Just finished talking with Secretary Rallings about what happened today. We'd like you to come to Washington on Friday, to go over your role in all of this. The Secretary has an idea he wants to discuss with you. Is that something you think you could arrange?"

"You know what this idea is?" Drake asked.

"Sort of, but he wants to explain it himself. You can stay with us, and be back in your office Monday. It's important, Adam, something I think you'll be interested in. It's something you can help us with."

"I'm curious, of course, so yes. Tell the Secretary I'll come. I'll take the red eye and call you when I get there."

Chapter 59

Friday morning, Senator Hazelton's driver picked Drake up at Ronald Reagan Washington National Airport. They were meeting in Secretary Rallings's office in the Nebraska Avenue Center, a former U.S. Navy facility in northwest Washington.

When Senator Hazelton's driver dropped him off, the Secretary's aide met him at the reception desk. She provided him a visitor ID and ushered him directly to the Secretary's office, where Liz Strobel stood waiting.

"Thanks for coming on short notice," she said, "I know the Secretary appreciates it."

"And you? Do you appreciate my being here?" Drake asked, watching her eyes.

"Look," she said, lowering her eyes, "I didn't thank you personally for what you did in Portland. I do appreciate what you did to protect the Secretary. I didn't listen to you, I listened to people I trusted and we got it wrong, okay. But you didn't exactly give us a lot to work with. Next time, I'll listen."

She had lost her commanding presence and was almost deferential. He wondered what she meant by listening to him next time, as she opened the door of the Secretary's office for him.

Secretary Rallings stood up from behind a massive, quartersawn oak desk and greeted him warmly. One of two red leather wingback chairs was unoccupied in front of the desk. Senator Hazelton rose, stepped forward, and gave him a hug before he sat back down.

Drake looked around the office. His eyes settled on the painting of the Battle of Fort Sumter hanging on the wall behind the Secretary's desk. What was it, he wondered, about the battle that triggered the Civil War in April of 1861 that was meaningful to the man charged with protecting the United States.

"Would you like coffee or anything? I know you've come directly from the airport," Secretary Rallings said.

"No, thank you, sir," Drake said. "I've had all the coffee I need for a day or so."

Secretary Rallings settled into his chair and met the eyes of his old friend, Senator Hazelton, for a long moment before he spoke.

"When I took this job, after 9/11, I thought it was about protecting the country from all manner of terrorist attacks, from WMDs smuggled in to be exploded in one of our largest cities, from suicide bombings in our subways, shopping malls or even schools. This week has opened my eyes to a much larger threat, a homegrown fifth column willing and able to fight along with our enemies in ways we hadn't anticipated.

"Richard Martin came to your father-in-law asking for help, because he didn't want to go to the FBI with his suspicions. He has shareholders he knew would knee-jerk if they learned the FBI was investigating a security breach. So he decided to approach us through a back door, using his relationship with his state's senior U.S. Senator. And we didn't react as we should have. His research, and the research of hundreds of our other contractors is vital to us and to the security of this country. We need to react to our contractors' concerns, and do so in a way that protects their companies, as well as the country. If they're afraid to come to us, attacks on these companies will someday be successful. The attacks are happening more and more, from attempts to steal weapons and defense secrets to cyber attacks. A lot of them are made by people living here, Americans who don't believe in this country anymore and support our enemies."

The Secretary leaned back in his chair and looked intently at Drake.

"I've concluded that I need someone to investigate situations like this when they're reported. Someone I can send out, who will quietly investigate and know when to call in the cavalry. Like you did when we asked you to help Richard Martin. I'd like you to be my private troubleshooter. These companies will hire you, you'll be their attorney. You can investigate their concerns. If you feel there's a security risk we need to know about, we'll provide whatever assistance you need. Liz will serve as your liaison. She'll make any intelligence you need available, when you ask for it. Interested?" Secretary Rallings asked.

Drake thought about the offer. He knew it was something he wanted to do, but he had unfinished business.

"Mr. Secretary, I'm honored that you feel I can help, I truly am. Before I say yes, there's something I have to do. The man or men who targeted you for assassination also tried to kill me and my family. That makes this personal for me. If you'll help me track them down, I'll agree to be your troubleshooter."

Secretary Rallings and Senator Hazelton exchanged looks. Both were pleased that Drake had volunteered to work with them, and to deal with a problem they didn't want to read about in the papers.

"Agreed. I'll have Liz get you everything we know about ISIS and its missing CEO. Good hunting Drake," the Secretary of Homeland Security said.

Excerpt from OATH TO DEFEND

1

Undercover agents do not like to stand out, especially when they're in a foreign country, they don't speak the language, and they're new. Randy Johnson, rookie DEA agent on his first deployment, was no different. But standing six foot seven, with red hair, freckles, and a baby face that reminded you of your fifteen-year-old younger brother, he had no choice.

While on assignment in Cancun, Mexico, Randy chose to accentuate the obvious by wearing shorts, a pink linen *guayabera* shirt, and a red Boston Red Sox hat. His job was to look like a tourist and observe and report on cartel members spotted in and near the Mayan Riviera. He remembered faces. He'd been taught to compartmentalize them, identify features, and then compare them to photos in the DEA's cartel scrapbook.

Randy was waiting for Juan Garcia Salina to show up at the Presidente InterContinental Resort. An informant had reported that he liked to eat lobster and shrimp curry at the hotel's seaside El Caribeño restaurant. Salina was believed to be responsible for the recent torture and execution of a Mexican army general who had cooperated with the DEA.

The man Randy recognized on this muggy, overcast day sitting at the poolside bar and drinking a cold glass of Superior Beer was not, however, a cartel member. Randy had recognized the face of the bodyguard of a man at the top of the FBI's most wanted list, the man thought to be behind the assassination attempt on the Secretary of Homeland Security a month ago in Portland, Oregon.

Jamal James, a former NFL defensive tackle weighing three hundred and fifty pounds and standing six foot eight inches tall, worked for David Barak. Barak had been the CEO of International Security and Intelligence Services, or ISIS, a top international security firm. After the attempted assassination, the FBI had wanted to question Barak, but he and his bodyguard had vanished. Both his corporate offices in Las Vegas and his residential compound in the mountains near Mt. Charleston, north of the city, had been searched. The FBI found evidence on a restored computer hard drive that linked Barak to the assassination team and made him appear to be its mastermind. But they didn't find anything that revealed where he might be hiding.

Randy saw the big bodyguard walk to a table where three men were having lunch and lean down to speak with one of them, who handed him an envelope. The bodyguard then turned and walked back to the hotel lobby.

Although the men at the table were not on the DEA watch list, Randy took a quick picture of them anyway with his cell phone, left money on the bar for his beer, and hurried after Jamal James. The man was moving like a bus through the traffic in the lobby.

A black Range Rover sat idling at the parking attendant's stand. James tipped the attendant and hoisted his massive body into the passenger's seat. The Range Rover settled an inch or two with the added weight before the air suspension restored the SUV's balance. The vehicle drove off.

For a moment, Randy Johnson hesitated. Stay on post as ordered, or follow? Follow the bodyguard, he decided. If the Range Rover led him to Barak, he'd be able to send a

Flash Priority One alert that every DEA agent would envy. Handing the well paid attendant a five dollar bill, he signaled for a taxi.

"Stay with that Range Rover, Carlos, and I'll double your fare," he said, glancing at the driver's ID and picture as he slid into the back of a green and white Camry.

"Not necessary, señor. With this traffic I cannot lose it. Where do you think it is going?"

"No idea, no idea at all. Here, swipe my Visa card in case I have to leave in a hurry."

"Does this involve your wife, señor?"

"Why would you ask that?"

"Couples come here after weddings. Sometimes men follow wives after they fight."

The young agent had to laugh. Carlos Rodriguez, the middle age taxi driver, had probably seen his share of honeymoons gone bad.

"Not fighting with my wife, Carlos. You and I might go a round or two, though, if you lose the Range Rover."

For the next forty-five minutes, they drove down the coast from Cancun. Highway 307 was a four-lane divided freeway and they maintained a steady seventy miles an hour, slowing only for a couple of traffic lights and reduced-speed zones. The towns they passed through weren't much to see, Puerto Morelos and Tres Rios, but the beauty of the Caribbean Sea on the left and the thickening mangrove jungle on the right served to heighten the young agent's sense of adventure.

"Señor, the Range Rover is turning. It's heading into the Mayakoba resort. Do you want me to follow?"

"Let's make sure this is where he's staying. Drive in. I'll check it out. I might have to stay here myself some day."

"A very expensive place, señor. The Mayakoba is one of the best hotels in the world."

Carlos appeared to be right. The Mayakoba was surrounded by a mangrove jungle and was built around a network of crystal clear waterways and small inland islands next to a white sand beach.

The Range Rover stopped in front of the main lobby. The bodyguard got out, rolled his massive shoulders, and walked in. No luggage was unloaded before the Range Rover drove off.

"Stay here, Carlos. I'll just be a minute."

The rookie agent approached the Mayakoba valet.

"Hi, could you help me? I think that man who just walked by was Jamal Johnson, the best NFL tackle ever. Is he a guest here? I'd pay a small fortune for his autograph."

The valet smiled. "We do not confirm the identity of our guests, señor." He extended an open palm.

Randy Johnson returned to his cab and sent a text message to his DEA supervisor. Flash Priority One.

Liz Strobel, special assistant to the Secretary of Homeland Security, took the call in her office at the Nebraska Avenue complex from her counterpart in the Drug Enforcement Agency.

"Liz, we have a lead on David Barak. Our spotter in Cancun just reported seeing his bodyguard. He's apparently staying at some expensive resort on the Mayan coast."

"It's about time. Thanks, Phil. Scan me a copy of the report."

"On its way. How do you want to handle this? You want us to send a team down?"

"I have someone we'll send, but I'd like your spotter to meet with him. Give me the contact information and we'll handle it."

"Is DHS flying solo on this?"

"They tried to kill the Secretary, Phil. He was the first on a list. The rest are Americans, too. So, yes, we're handling it ourselves."

"Okay. Dinner sometime?"

She smiled into the phone. "Thanks for the heads up, Phil."

She knew she wasn't winning the award for the most social power person in Washington, but that wasn't her game. Phil was a nice guy, but she just didn't have time for casual dating. She needed the occasional escort for official functions, however, and she could always find one. If she were going to date again, the man would have to be someone who intrigued her, someone special, and she only knew one man like that. Unfortunately, he was mourning a wife he had just lost to cancer. For now, she had a job to do. She picked up her phone.

"Drake, it's Liz. You busy?"

"Just pulling out old grapevines," Adam Drake said, "trying to get the vineyard ready to replant."

She remembered his farm in the heart of the Oregon wine country, and the one time she'd been there. Drake had killed three jihadists who'd come after him one night, part of the same group that had tried to assassinate her boss. She'd been sent to help him get rid of the bodies. This was a favor to Drake's father-in-law, the senior senator from Oregon.

"Why aren't you at your office?" she asked.

"I'm taking a little time off. The media are still stirred up about those three young Muslim men who went missing. It's hard to maintain a law practice with reporters three deep outside your office."

"We think we know where Barak is," she said.

He didn't answer immediately, so she waited.

"Will the Secretary honor his promise and let me go after him?" he asked.

"That's why I'm calling."

"Fill me in."

For the next ten minutes, she told him everything they had discovered and arranged for him to meet the DEA spotter on the island of Cozumel. It was a short ferry ride from there to the Mexican mainland and the resort where the bodyguard was staying.

"Do you want me to reserve a room for you?" she asked.

"No," he said. "I'll take care of it."

"When you find him, don't kill him. We have a reservation for him at our little resort in Cuba."

He chuckled. "We'll see. I'll call you from Cozumel."

Strobel hoped they were doing the right thing. As Drake had reminded her, Secretary Robert Rallings had agreed to let him go after Barak in exchange for Drake's agreeing to serve as a private contract trouble shooter for DHS. The Secretary had been impressed by the way the former Delta Force operator had acted on his own initiative to identify the assassination plot, and then chase down and kill the assassins.

It had been a close call. Four terrorists had tried to kill the Secretary at the home of Drake's father-in-law, Senator Hazelton, after failing earlier in the day to kill him at a decommissioning ceremony at Oregon's chemical weapons depot. With help from his former sniper partner, Drake had saved the Secretary, the senator, and his wife from a rifle-launched thermobaric grenade attack that leveled the senator's lakeside home.

The agreement with Adam Drake had been made because the Secretary of Homeland Security was occasionally asked for help by defense contractors who, among other things, suspected terrorist probes and didn't want to read about an investigation in the press. After his experience in Oregon, the Secretary had decided that someone outside DHS, someone with a legitimate reason to be involved, like a snoopy attorney with special talents, could be brought in to handle things discretely. When he'd asked Drake to serve as his private trouble shooter, however, Drake had demanded a quid pro quo: let him go after the man who tried to kill his in-laws, and he would agree to the proposition.

Liz wanted to make sure her boss didn't overlook the potential for disaster for the agency. Not only would the Mexican government be outraged if they found an American had killed a terrorist on their turf, but Barak's ties to the drug cartels could also lead to more cartel violence north of the border.

She left her office and walked across the hall to see Secretary Rallings.

"Is he alone?" she asked Mrs. Cameron, the gatekeeper who had served as Robert Ralling's personal secretary from his early days as Governor of Montana and later as a U.S. Senator.

"He's previewing the video for cyber security awareness month that goes out next week," Mrs. Cameron replied. "Go on in."

Secretary Rallings was sitting at his desk and looking closely at a monitor. His jaw was clinched so tightly the muscles bulged. He waved her over.

"Have you seen this?" he asked. "People will be afraid to trust us with any of their information. This makes it look like China can hack us whenever they want."

"People need to see what we're up against, sir."

"I suppose you're right, but I don't like people knowing we haven't stopped this."

She cleared her throat. "Mr. Secretary, I told Drake about the DEA spotting Barak in Mexico. He's heading down there."

"You still have concerns, Liz?"

"About Drake? No sir. We've seen how he handles things. I'm more concerned about Mexico finding out we sent a private citizen after a terrorist without telling them."

He nodded and said, "That's the only way to keep Drake safe. With the cartel's access to the Mexican government, I don't want some drug lord letting Barak know we're coming for him."

"Is that why you're not informing the White House?"

"That and deniability. By the time the White House tells State what we're doing, Mexico would know it within the hour."

"What will you say if this goes wrong?"

"I'll say that I let Drake know we spotted Barak, as a courtesy. His plans thereafter were all his own. I owe him, Liz. He saved my life twice last month. I agreed he'd have first crack at this guy. Hunting terrorists is something he's good at." He rubbed his hands together as if washing them. "This will be okay."

"I hope so, sir, for both of us," she said. She left the Secretary's office thinking of the intriguing man they were sending in harm's way.

Did you enjoy *The Assassin's List?*

Word-of-Mouth is crucial for any author to succeed. If you enjoyed the book, please consider leaving a review at Amazon, even if it's only a line or two; it would make all the difference and be very much appreciated.

Amazon US: www.amazon.com

Amazon UK: www.amazon.co.uk

If you want to get an automatic email when Scott's next book is released, SIGN UP HERE. Your email address will never be shared and you can unsubscribe anytime.

URL: http://eepurl.com/zzzxP

SAY HELLO! Scott talks about things that interest him and his books on his blog, http://scottmatthewsblog.com. He would love it if you dropped by to say hello.

Alternatively, you can follow him on Twitter, get in touch on Facebook or send him an email: scott@s-matthews.com

Twitter: http://twitter.com/smatthews OR

Facebook: http://facebook.com/Scottmatthewsfans

Made in United States
Orlando, FL
01 November 2021